C0-AAW-639

"I didn't realize the children would get so tangled up in this charade, not so quickly, anyway," David said.

"Do you want to back out of our agreement?" Carrie asked.

He thought for a moment. "No, then I'd be left with the same problems—how to keep my kids. You were right when you said we needed to explain the truth to them as soon as possible. As for me, I just have to accept that we'll be seeing a lot of each other for the next twelve months."

"Well, that's quite a burden, I must say," she said, rolling her eyes dramatically.

It took him a moment to realize she was baiting him. Then he laughed out loud and observed her appreciatively. "It's not as if you're hard on the eyes, lady. Actually, I see your proximity as a challenge."

"We agreed," she reminded him quickly, a shadow of alarm in her eyes. "No sex."

"Yes. Still, it's an awful shame that we'll never be lovers," David mused.

Dear Reader,

I hope you've got a few days to yourself for this month's wonderful books. We start off with Terese Ramin's *An Unexpected Addition*. The "extra" in this Intimate Moments Extra title is the cast of characters—lots and *lots* of kids—and the heroine's point of view once she finds herself pregnant by the irresistible hero. The ending, as always, is a happy one— but the ride takes some unexpected twists and turns I think you'll enjoy.

Paula Detmer Riggs brings her MATERNITY ROW miniseries over from Desire in *Mommy By Surprise*. This reunion romance—featuring a pregnant heroine, of course—is going to warm your heart and leave you with a smile. Cathryn Clare is back with *A Marriage To Remember*. Hero and ex-cop Nick Ryder has amnesia and has forgotten everything—though how he could have forgotten his gorgeous wife is only part of the mystery he has to solve. In *Reckless*, Ruth Wind's THE LAST ROUNDUP trilogy continues. (Book one was a Special Edition.) Trust me, Colorado and the Forrest brothers will beckon you to return for book three. In *The Twelve-Month Marriage*, Kathryn Jensen puts her own emotional spin on that reader favorite, the marriage-of-convenience plot. And finally, welcome new author Bonnie Gardner with *Stranger in Her Bed*. Picture coming home to find out that everyone thinks you're dead—and a gorgeous *male* stranger is living in your house!

Enjoy them all, and don't forget to come back next month for more of the most exciting romantic reading around, right here in Silhouette Intimate Moments.

Yours,

Leslie Wainger
Senior Editor and Editorial Coordinator

Please address questions and book requests to:
Silhouette Reader Service
U.S.: 3010 Walden Ave., P.O. Box 1325, Buffalo, NY 14269
Canadian: P.O. Box 609, Fort Erie, Ont. L2A 5X3

THE TWELVE–MONTH MARRIAGE

KATHRYN JENSEN

Silhouette®
INTIMATE™ MOMENTS®

Published by Silhouette Books

America's Publisher of Contemporary Romance

If you purchased this book without a cover you should be aware that this book is stolen property. It was reported as "unsold and destroyed" to the publisher, and neither the author nor the publisher has received any payment for this "stripped book."

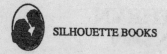

SILHOUETTE BOOKS

ISBN 0-373-07797-1

THE TWELVE-MONTH MARRIAGE

Copyright © 1997 by Kathryn Jensen

All rights reserved. Except for use in any review, the reproduction or utilization of this work in whole or in part in any form by any electronic, mechanical or other means, now known or hereafter invented, including xerography, photocopying and recording, or in any information storage or retrieval system, is forbidden without the written permission of the editorial office, Silhouette Books, 300 East 42nd Street, New York, NY 10017 U.S.A.

All characters in this book have no existence outside the imagination of the author and have no relation whatsoever to anyone bearing the same name or names. They are not even distantly inspired by any individual known or unknown to the author, and all incidents are pure invention.

This edition published by arrangement with Harlequin Books S.A.

® and TM are trademarks of Harlequin Books S.A., used under license. Trademarks indicated with ® are registered in the United States Patent and Trademark Office, the Canadian Trade Marks Office and in other countries.

Printed in U.S.A.

Books by Kathryn Jensen

Silhouette Intimate Moments

Time and Again #685
Angel's Child #758
The Twelve-Month Marriage #797

The Loop

Getting a Grip: Dig
Getting Real: Christopher
Getting a Life: Marissa

KATHRYN JENSEN

has written many novels for young readers as well as for adults. She speed walks, works out with weights and enjoys ballroom dancing for exercise, stress reduction and pleasure. Her children are now grown. She lives in Maryland with her husband, Bill, and her writing companion—Sunny, a lovable terrier-mix adopted from a shelter.

Having worked as a hospital switchboard operator, department store sales associate, bank clerk and elementary school teacher, she now splits her days between writing her own books and teaching fiction writing at two local colleges and through a correspondence course. She enjoys helping new writers get a start, and speaks "at the drop of a hat" at writers' conferences, libraries and schools across the country.

To Bill, my wonderful husband, without whose help
this book would never have been finished.
(I'd have passed out from hunger at the keyboard.)
Thanks for feeding me, and loving me.
—K.

Acknowledgments:

My grateful thanks to Halcott (Beau) Newman,
U.S.M.C.R., pilot; Chip Wright, flight instructor; and
John Pepe III, airport manger at Bay Bridge Airport,
Stevensville, Maryland. All gave generously of their
time and expertise. Any errors in fact are my own.
Thanks, guys!

Also deepest appreciation to Linda Hayes, my
insightful agent at Columbia Literary Associates, Inc.,
whose support and suggestions make every book better
than the last.

Chapter 1

Carrie Monroe frowned up at the wall of black clouds south of the airfield. A typical June thunderstorm was bullying its way across the Chesapeake Bay, heading across the Eastern Shore of Maryland, toward Ocean City. Threatening rumbles occasionally drowned out the chatter of a small plane taking off or landing. Eerie yellow flashes streaked across darkening skies.

Storms didn't usually bother Carrie. This one did, and not just because they'd be flying directly into it if she didn't get the *Bay Lady* off the ground soon. No, she decided, her uneasiness was born of something even more difficult to predict than the weather. The electricity-charged air warned her of change.

Change. A dangerous word.

In Carrie's experience, most alterations in life had meant pain. Excruciating pain. The kind that never completely went away.

Her nerves felt on edge, raw, tingling—a disquieting sensation, strangely arousing, not quite pleasurable. The first spits of rain sizzled on the hot tarmac and cooled her suntanned cheeks. She gave up hoping that anything good could come of this day.

As Carrie climbed the metal steps to the commuter plane's cabin, she speculated on her chances of beating the storm back to BWI. Baltimore–Washington International Airport was her home base. She still might be able to pilot the fifteen-passenger Beechcraft a mile ahead of the first thunderheads if her last two passengers arrived within the next ten minutes. Five would be better.

Had the *Bay Lady* been able to take off on schedule, there wouldn't have been a problem. But an emergency call from the Worcester County police had informed her that an officer transporting a prisoner was on his way. One bank, two credit cards and Baltimore Gas and Electric were already snapping at her heels, wanting to be paid. Adding the law to the list of institutions unhappy with her seemed like a really bad idea.

So, she'd waited.

Stepping through the hatch and into the vintage twin-engine craft her dad had bought thirdhand nearly ten years ago, Carrie manufactured a cheery smile for her human cargo. "Everyone buckled up?"

"Honey, we've been buckled for the past thirty minutes," a man in a business suit commented dryly, closing his laptop computer with an impatient snap.

"Will the pilot be here soon, miss?" a young woman traveling with a toddler asked, looking worried.

Her little boy, who appeared to be about three years old, was fidgeting in his seat, trying to pry open the metal buckle restraining him. The compact structure of the plane allowed for seven seats on either side of a narrow aisle, which sometimes made traveling with children a challenge. Although current FAA regulations allowed parents to hold young children in their laps during flight, Carrie required seat belts for everyone, regardless of age. She'd seen them prevent injuries and save lives. She kept a spare car seat in the cargo bin for infants.

"I have a flight from BWI to Nashville at two-thirty," the woman continued.

"We'll make it," Carrie assured her.

The woman didn't look convinced. The businessman eyed Carrie with blatant skepticism. Her other six passengers stared at her questioningly.

Carrie was about to explain why they were delaying takeoff, when a sorrowful whimper caught her attention.

Glancing down, she noted her youngest passenger's cheeks were puffed out, his forehead scrunched in preparation for an all-out scream of frustration. He wore adorable knit rompers with an embroidered teddy bear stitched on the front in vivid red and blue threads.

Quickly she squatted in front of the child's seat and laid her hands on his plump, bare legs. He immediately stopped his frantic wiggling and sat still, observing her. Carrie made a face at him. He giggled and hid behind his fat, little fists.

"What's the problem, Mr. Worm? Can't you sit still?" She tickled him, loving the spongy feeling of his baby tummy beneath her fingertips.

"But the pilot—" the woman said, fretting. "What's *taking* him so long? That's why we're waiting, isn't it?"

"Actually," Carrie began, "there's—"

A car screeched to a stop on the apron, interrupting her explanation. As heavy footfalls clunked up the metal steps outside the fuselage, everyone on the plane turned toward the open hatch. Carrie lightly rested her hand on the little boy's head as she stood up to face a neatly groomed man attired in a conservative, summer-gray business suit.

Her first impression was that he looked more like a banker or successful attorney than a cop. Close behind him, and linked to him by steel handcuffs was a second man, in far less stylish clothing. Jeans and a navy blue, one-pocket T-shirt, topped by a scuffed black leather jacket.

The second man's eyes immediately focused on her. Blue eyes, pale as frozen water. Ice eyes. Dangerous eyes, she thought. Dangerous man.

Without intending to, she automatically dropped back a step.

"You the pilot?" he asked sharply over the suited man's shoulder.

"I—well, yes," she stammered, doubting she should even be speaking to him. No telling what he'd been arrested for.

He pulled a wallet from the back pocket of his jeans with his free hand and flipped it open with his thumb to reveal a badge. "Detective David Adams, Narcotics Squad, Baltimore City," he introduced himself brusquely.

Carrie stared at him for a moment, reorienting herself to the situation before nodding stiffly. "Find a seat for yourself, Officer…and one for your prisoner. We'll take off as soon as I complete my preflight check."

As he replaced the wallet, his jacket front gaped for an instant. Carrie glimpsed a gun in a shoulder holster. Of the two men, the more questionable-looking one was carrying a loaded firearm. Go figure.

Shaking her head, Carrie moved past them to pull up the hydraulic stairs. She locked the hatch. As she turned back to head for the cockpit, the detective was speaking to the computer man.

"Mind moving up a seat, sir? We need two together." He flashed a grim smile that didn't reach his eyes. "We're on our honeymoon."

The businessman rolled his eyes in irritation, but gathered up his briefcase, laptop and copy of the *Wall Street Journal.* He shuffled forward, taking a seat across the aisle from a college-age girl wearing an oversize T-shirt over a bathing suit, her feet bare. Most of Carrie's passengers this time of year were "heading down the ocean," as the locals put it—to Ocean City, Rehoboth, Bethany Beach or one of the many other resort towns along the DelMarVa shoreline.

During the off-season, she survived by flying the occasional charter for large corporations. It didn't pay to make scheduled runs for just two or three passengers, to the beach or anywhere else, what with the high cost of gas.

She generally liked the variety of passengers her little airline attracted. This was her first cop. She fervently hoped he would be her last.

As Carrie dropped into the pilot's seat and strapped herself in, she shot a quick look up at the small, round mirror to her right. She adjusted it for a clear view of the passenger cabin behind her. The cop sat on the right, his silent, dignified-looking prisoner on the left, their arms extending across the aisle, joined at the wrists by the shiny manacles. He'd taken care to choose seats well to the back of the plane, separated by several empty rows from other passengers.

But she could still see the telltale lump under the detective's jacket. She shuddered.

No pilot would welcome a loaded weapon less than thirty feet behind her back. Carrie liked the idea even less, considering the man who wore the gun. But she doubted she'd be able to talk the cop into leaving the thing with her until the end of the flight. After all, he was on duty.

As she checked off readings on her gauges she listened attentively through her earphones to nearby pilots squawking their intentions to make an approach for landing or takeoff. Like many other small airports, Ocean City had no tower or air traffic controllers. Landing and taking off were cooperative efforts, shared by everyone in the immediate airspace. Squawking over the radio was the way pilots communicated and stayed out of one another's way.

Carrie studied the Baltimore detective's face in the mirror. It was a distinctive face, hard featured with a wide jawline. Sharp cheekbones angled across a two-day growth of beard. A band of muscle outlined a thick, linebacker's neck, which disappeared inside the collar of his worn, leather jacket—a jacket obviously too warm for steamy Maryland summers. A convenient means for concealing his gun? she wondered.

He didn't smile at the little boy who had squirmed around in his seat to peer over the armrest and down the aisle at him. The air around him seemed charged with particles of his barely contained energy, as if he might leap up at a second's notice.

Despite Carrie's instinctive wariness of the man, she felt a mysterious tingle as she spied on him. What attracted her to him, she hadn't a clue. Perhaps it was the James Dean street savvy, the aura of toughness that might…just might…soften at the touch of the right woman.

Carrie shook off the strange thoughts, and stranger sensations teasing her body, to concentrate on her job.

She squawked her heading and altitude, although she'd already filed her standard flight plan with the airport manager's office. Slowly she guided the Beechcraft across the apron and onto the taxiway. There were two light planes ahead of her— one a zippy two-seater Piper Aztec, the other a Cessna 172, almost identical to the one she'd flown to earn her instrument rating, years ago.

The rain was coming down harder now, pinging against the windshield, but they'd be off the ground in five minutes or less. She planned to guide the *Bay Lady* up above ten thousand feet. Hopefully she'd find the clear skies there that the airport's radar had indicated.

Glancing once more in the mirror, she caught the little boy's mother and the businessman watching her skeptically through the opening into the cockpit—as if she were a teenager slipping behind the wheel of Daddy's car for her first driving lesson. Carrie grinned, more amused than annoyed by the reaction she got from a lot of her passengers.

She'd soloed when she was fourteen years old, before she could legally drive a car, and started copiloting Baltimore– Ocean City runs with her dad on her twenty-first birthday. Often she felt more at home in the air than on the ground. If some people still had trouble with a young woman being a pilot, well…that was their problem.

Shaking her head, Carrie reached behind her and tugged the heavy woven curtain across the opening, and concentrated on her takeoff.

Detective David Adams felt uncomfortably warm in his jacket, but there was no way he could remove it now. Not without unlocking the handcuff around his left wrist. And he wasn't about to do anything to jeopardize delivering Andrew Rainey to a jail cell, which was exactly where the scum belonged.

However, the air inside the compact cabin felt as if it were ten degrees hotter than the air he'd left on the outside. That would make it ninety-five degrees in the plane. He looked around him, but none of the other passengers appeared uncomfortable.

He tried drawing slow, deep breaths, but his lungs felt constricted. Just above the bridge of his nose, a spot throbbed naggingly, and he reached up to massage it between the thumb and finger of his unshackled hand. He wasn't actually *afraid* of flying; he just didn't trust planes as a logical means of transportation.

If he'd had his way, he'd have driven one of the tactical squad's cars down to O.C. to fetch Rainey from the local uniforms. They'd done the entire East Coast a favor by picking him up at a nightclub the night before on an anonymous tip. But his shift commander didn't want to risk the three-hour drive home in a tac, which would give the cunning drug lord 180 minutes of glorious opportunity to escape.

David shot a look at the man across the aisle from him. Although Rainey might appear resigned to his fate, even relaxed, David knew he must be desperate. This time the D.A. was as close to having an ironclad case on him as he'd ever been.

So this trip David was flying. Damn it.

A gentle tug on his left wrist snapped his attention to the man across the aisle.

"From the look of those clouds, Detective, this might turn into a killer of a storm."

"Shut up," David snapped.

"Whatever you say, Detective." Looking vaguely offended, Rainey turned back to his window.

David studied Rainey's profile, silhouetted against flashes of brassy sheet lightning, with a growing feeling of disgust. Who would figure the guy for a dope pusher? And not just any street-corner, penny-ante hustler. Rainey was big time—allegedly responsible for dumping in excess of fifteen million dollars' worth of assorted drugs on Baltimore and Washington, D.C., streets in the past six months.

Poisons that sapped the life from a struggling society—that was Rainey's business.

David could think of no worse example of humanity than the man shackled to his wrist. It was Rainey's brand of greed that ignored all the pain, saw only dollar signs at the end of a rainbow paved with wasted lives. Yet to the ordinary, respectable citizen, the man looked just like one of them. That's what scared David most. It was only the man's eyes that gave him away. The pale, pumice-gray orbs were always moving, never at rest. They absorbed everything around him and gave anyone in his presence the uneasy impression that he missed nothing.

They were moving like that now—over to the window, down at his polished cordovan wing tips, up to the back of the seat in front of him, straight down the aisle toward the curtain the female pilot had pulled behind her.

David studied the cuffs encircling Rainey's right wrist and his own left, an arrangement leaving his gun hand free to reach inside his jacket if necessary. He could feel the solid weight of the police-issue Smith & Wesson .38 in its leather holster, snug and reassuring against his ribs. He could smell the oiled metal—warm, ready—loaded as always, according to regulation, whether he was on duty or off.

The rolling jounces altered to an even, rough rumble as the plane gathered speed, throwing itself down the runway. He fought the compulsion to close his eyes as metal fencing, a low stucco terminal with a red-tile roof, refueling vehicles and parked planes rushed past the windows. Sitting bolt upright, he stared straight ahead, counting the threads in the jacquard pattern of the upholstered seat ahead of him.

He thought about his children; that helped some.

"Scared of flying, Detective?" the composed voice across the aisle taunted.

"Shut up, Rainey."

"They say it's safer than car travel."

"So they say." He forced out the words in an even tone.

He wondered how a veteran cop like him, who had broken

through doors to face guys with Uzis on the other side, could get so tied up in knots at the simple thought of flying.

My God! he thought dismally. That little blonde does this every day of her life! His gaze automatically shifted to the curtain, and he wished she'd left it open. Being able to watch any portion of her pert figure would have been a welcome distraction.

"Sometimes looking out the window makes it easier," Rainey suggested helpfully. "I have quite a nice view on this side. Care to trade seats?" His free hand moved toward the seat-belt buckle.

"Leave that alone!" David barked, causing the businessman he'd moved to turn in his seat and look back at them with concern. "You're staying right where you are until we land," he growled.

The corners of Rainey's lips lifted, giving him the misleading appearance of a kindly uncle. "Anything you say, Detective. Just trying to be considerate."

"Yeah, right," David grumbled.

Considerate. His mind took a sudden, unexpected twist in another direction. "Just trying to be helpful, David." That was one of his mother-in-law's favorite phrases. His *ex*-mother-in-law, that is. "We realize how hard the divorce is on you and Sheila. Goodness knows, with you both working, there can't be much time for the children. Why not send Tammy and Jason up to Newport to stay with us?"

The Waymans had tried every practical means of stopping their daughter from marrying a Baltimore cop seven years ago. When that hadn't worked, they'd waited in silence while two children came into the world, and no doubt prayed for a divorce. Apparently they'd known their daughter better than he had. Sheila had grown restless even before Tammy was born. Now the little girl was four years old and her brother, Jason, was six. The divorce had been official for two years.

Sheila and her parents had fought tooth and nail for sole custody of the children, but he hadn't let them take his kids away from him. No, he hadn't backed down. He'd gotten himself a damn good lawyer and insisted on his rights as their father. He never would allow them to take his children away from him, not while he had a single breath left in his body. Never.

But what if they found a way? Clenching his fists, he felt an overpowering sense of loss flow through his veins, chilling him like a dip in the harbor in January. He squeezed his eyes shut for a fraction of a second.

It was one second too long.

In a heartbeat, Rainey released his seat belt, leaped to his feet. He spun and rammed a knee into David's stomach.

David doubled over, gasping, pain shrieking through him, as he felt Rainey's hand dive inside his jacket.

My gun! he thought frantically, helplessly.

The realization of what a man without conscience could do with six bullets to a planeload of civilians forced aside the excruciating pain. Years of training and experience on the streets took over.

David rocked forward and shot to his feet, slamming his right shoulder into Rainey's chin. They crashed to the floor of the cabin, between the two columns of seats—Rainey grunting loudly as the weight of David's body crushed the air out of his lungs.

Rolling up the aisle, the two men wrestled desperately for the gun while the other passengers cringed in their seats. The plane leveled off. They rolled again, becoming entangled in the curtain that separated the cabin from the cockpit. The curtain came down with a loud, ripping sound.

David couldn't pry the gun from Rainey's iron grip, but at least he managed to keep the barrel pointed away from the passengers and pilot, at one curving wall. Still, he wasn't sure what a bullet through the plane's fuselage might do to its ability to stay aloft. He didn't have a clue where the fuel tanks were located. A single shot through one of them would be the end of everyone on the plane.

At last David pinned Rainey's gun hand, then angled a knee into his solar plexus. He looked up and caught the terrified expression of the young woman piloting the plane. She was talking rapidly into the tiny microphone attached to her headset.

For a split second, he was tempted to give her a reassuring wink. *Once I get the gun back, it will be over,* he told himself.

Rainey seemed to give up struggling. David cracked the man's wrist like an eggshell against the metal frame of a seat, but he refused to let go of the weapon.

"You're just making things worse for yourself!" David grunted. "You'll spend the rest of your life in prison if you—"

"Who says I'm going at all?" Rainey sneered, a wild look in his eyes.

With a surge of strength, he broke David's hold and slammed the barrel of the gun into his cheek. The blow stunned David. He felt himself go limp for a moment; the cabin drifted out of focus. When he slowly opened his eyes, he was facing his worst nightmare.

Rainey was on his feet, the .38 braced between two hands. The opening at the end of the gun's deadly black barrel was aimed at the middle of David's face.

Carrie gripped the yoke of the *Bay Lady* as the two men struggled only a few feet behind her. Her knuckles had turned bone white; her pulse ripped through her with a ferocity that rivaled her first solo flight. Back then, barely more than a child, she hadn't fully understood the consequences of an airplane pitching into a cantaloupe field from twelve thousand feet.

Her hand automatically reached for the little black IFF box to her right. The Identification: Friend or Foe mechanism linked her with all air traffic control systems within her range. She quickly entered a 7500 code, the international code for air piracy, then hit the send button on the yoke. She waited, her heart beating triple time, her mouth so dry she couldn't swallow.

It took only a few seconds before a voice crackled over her earphones, sounding obscenely calm.

"This is Baltimore. Beech 123, we understand you've reset your transponder to Seven Five Zero Zero. Please confirm."

The emotionless tone was part of ATC training, to avoid arousing the suspicion of a hijacker or terrorist, should he be listening in on communications.

Carrie spoke into the mike in front of her lips, keeping her voice low and level.

"Roger. This is Beech 123, squawking Seven Five Zero Zero. I have an emergency. Firearm involved."

"Advise landing ASAP. Salisbury is your nearest field."

Carrie gritted her teeth and hoped to God she could set down before any shots were fired. "Roger. I'll try. No promises. Out."

The beauty of the IFF system was that she hadn't needed to say anything over her radio. If a hijacker had been listening in and not known the plane's ID, she could have pretended the air traffic controller was talking to another pilot and maintained radio silence. But her silence automatically would have been interpreted as an affirmative response. Then all hell would break loose in control towers all along her flight route, as ATCs alerted other aircraft in her flight path, trying to clear the air for her. She'd automatically be logged into a sophisticated tracking system, which would notify airport security, crash teams and the police to be waiting wherever she landed.

Carrie's glance dropped to her instruments, then flashed up to the mirror again. The exchange over the radio had taken less than a minute, but the two men were no longer wrestling. Her other passengers were dead silent, still belted into their seats with the exception of the little boy, who had somehow escaped to his mother's lap.

It was the police officer's eyes that connected with hers in the mirror. Their dazed expression clutched at her heart. He was halfway up on one knee, his handcuffed wrist still attached to his prisoner's, but the balance of power had shifted dramatically. The man with the gun lifted his lips in a satisfied snarl, as he aimed the weapon at the detective's forehead.

Carrie knew of only one thing to do.

Taking a deep breath and whispering a hasty prayer, she

turned to look over her shoulder at the detective and sharply dropped her glance twice, signaling, *Down... get down!*

She didn't have time to make sure he understood. Immediately she pulled to the left on the yoke, then pushed forward on it. The *Bay Lady* banked a hard ninety degrees, dropping precipitously through the clouds...then there was only land filling her windscreen.

One of the women passengers screamed. A man's voice cursed as the plane dove.

"Stay in your seats! You'll be fine!" Carrie shouted. She watched the speed gauge tremble closer and closer to the red range, which marked the upper stress limits of the plane's engine.

Behind her, she could hear scrambling and a heavy thud as someone fell. She shot a quick look up at the mirror. The prisoner was down on the floor, shaking his head and looking stunned. The cop jerked roughly on his handcuffed wrist, yanking his disoriented prisoner toward him.

The gun flew out of the man's hand. It rattled across the floor, gravity drawing it toward the nose of the plane. Trapping the weapon under the toe of her athletic shoe, Carrie pulled back gradually on the yoke and brought the plane up to a safe altitude. She picked up the gun and stuck it away, out of sight.

There, she thought, at least the odds are even now! She checked all her instruments, reset her course and slowly began bringing the plane up to altitude.

When she looked over her shoulder again, her heart still thudding so hard in her chest she thought it might just burst through her ribs, the detective had subdued the other man and was dragging him through the cabin, toward the back of the plane.

Passengers began to chatter nervously. The little boy broke out so suddenly in a wail that Carrie suspected his mother had been holding her hand over his mouth to keep him quiet.

Carrie watched in her mirror as the cop worked quickly, drawing a second pair of handcuffs from his pocket. He used them to secure his prisoner to the metal bulkhead of the cargo bin, then released the first pair from his own wrist and reattached them to a tie-down bolt, effectively spread-eagling the man and rendering him harmless.

"If you hadn't made a nuisance of yourself," Adams growled, his breath rasping in and out of his lungs, "we all could have had a real pleasant flight."

The other man's glare might have melted rock. But the detective didn't seem to pay much attention to him. He turned and faced the passengers, who became suddenly silent, as if waiting for a speech. "Sorry for the inconvenience, folks," he said, then put his head down and walked forward through the plane.

"Are you all right?" the young woman in the bathing suit asked as he passed her seat. She held out what looked like a beach towel. "It's clean, and you're…well, you're bleeding, Officer."

He smiled weakly at her and took the towel. "Thanks."

"Anything I can do to help, Officer?" the laptop man asked in an exaggerated baritone. "I was in the army, Special Forces in 'Nam. If this fella gives you *any* more trouble—"

Adams waved him off. "Thank you, no…it's all over, sir."

"*Now* he offers to help?" Carrie muttered, shaking her head in disbelief.

Satisfied she was back on course for her original flight plan, she radioed BWI that the emergency had been resolved. "You'd better have security and an ambulance on hand just the same," she told the ATC. "This cop looks pretty beat-up. He might appreciate some help on landing."

She was thankful no one else had been hurt. Even the detective seemed unconcerned with the wound on the side of his face. He came the rest of the way forward, into the cockpit, blotting his cheek with the girl's sunny-yellow towel. From what Carrie could see, the cut didn't look deep, but it was almost three inches long. The metal barrel had scraped the flesh along his jaw, leaving a raw trail that oozed blood whenever the towel came away.

"You're going to need stitches," she said when she saw his reflection in her mirror, directly behind her seat.

"I doubt it."

She grinned. "Real men don't need stitches?"

"I'm not being macho."

His brilliant blue eyes beckoned hers back to the mirror when she started to look away. At close range his gaze was devastating. Her stomach wobbled like a glider in turbulence.

"I know from experience I heal fast. This is nothing."

This is nothing, she mouthed silently, rolling her eyes. Right. Just a flesh wound, ma'am.

He didn't seem to notice her talking to herself.

"My gun?" he asked.

"Under my flight bag." She pointed to the black canvas bag on the seat beside her. It held the lunch she'd intended to eat on the return flight and a change of clothing. Her appetite was gone. "If your friend no longer requires a baby-sitter and you want to sit up here, toss the bag on the floor."

He nodded, studying her face as he slowly eased himself into the copilot's seat. She imagined every muscle in his body must ache. He slipped his arms out of his jacket, then returned his gun to the shoulder holster.

"Guess there's no point keeping it out of sight now," he remarked dryly.

"Guess not. You put on quite a show for my passengers." She tried to keep the irritation out of her voice, but knew from the way his eyes narrowed that he'd grasped her sarcasm.

"That wasn't something I'd planned," he assured her.

"I didn't say it was. It just seems there might have been some way to ensure your traveling companion wouldn't get hold of your weapon and shoot my plane and passengers full of holes."

He glared at her.

"Sorry," she mumbled when she couldn't stand the heat of his eyes on her any longer. "I guess I'm still a little shaken by—" She shrugged. "I'm sure you're very good at what you do, usually."

His eyes still didn't leave her. A muscle at one corner of his lip twitched, as if he was struggling not to smile.

"You're right," he said at last. He slid down in the seat and held the towel against the side of his face. "There's no excuse for what happened back there. I let my guard down for a second. It could have cost lives."

Carrie felt suddenly sorry she'd sounded so condemning. Running her hands lightly around the yoke, she said, "Don't be too hard on yourself."

"I'm not being any harder than I deserve," he said solemnly.

She looked straight ahead as they burst through a bank of noxious gray clouds into blue sky. The sun was shining brightly; it looked like clear flying the rest of the way to Baltimore.

Adams was still watching her.

"What?" she asked.

"Do you have any idea what you just did?" he asked.

His voice was a vaguely accusing rumble she could feel down to her toes. She turned to him, puzzled, and shook her head.

"You saved my life."

Carrie let out a short laugh. "Oh, I'm sure in another minute you'd have pulled one of your cop tricks the way they do on TV and gotten your man under control again."

"Maybe," he said, reaching over to lay a hand lightly on her arm. "I just want you to know I'm grateful. I'll see my kids tonight thanks to your quick thinking."

Carrie blushed, feeling uneasy that he was placing so much importance on her handling of the situation. It forced her to imagine what might have happened if she hadn't acted instinctively. The man beside her might be lying in a pool of his own blood, dead. God only knows what would have happened to her, to her passengers.

"Kids?" she asked, desperately wanting to change the subject.

"Two."

He slowly removed his hand, and it felt as if he were intentionally drawing his fingers across her skin, leaving a trail of warmth.

"A girl and a boy. They're the best."

The conviction in his voice was taut with emotion.

"Does your wife work, or can she stay home with them?" She wasn't sure why she'd asked the question. It had simply erupted from her mouth, and a moment later she was sorry.

"We're divorced," he said, his tone suddenly as brittle as discarded oyster shells.

Adams checked the towel for blood flow. Finding a clean section, he pressed it against his jaw again. She waited for him to go on, but he didn't. She felt awful for reminding him of a difficult time in his life, especially after what he'd just been through.

She could think of no other way to right the wrong than by baring a little piece of her own soul. "Well, at least you *have* a family," she blurted out. "I don't have anyone, unless you count the people I work with. My parents' marriage was a fiasco. They fought constantly, for as far back as I can remember."

He looked at her. "I'm sorry. Divorce is brutal."

She winced, the agony real even now. "I think I could have dealt with divorce much better. When I was ten years old, my mother announced that she'd had enough. I can still see her, carrying that old suitcase stuffed to bulging out the front door. I stood on the porch and watched her get into a cab."

"Damn," Adams said.

Carrie blew out a long breath. "Well, that was a long time ago. I don't really think about it anymore," she lied.

She recalled the day as clearly as if it were yesterday. She hadn't cried. She hadn't run after her mother, tugging at her arm and begging her to stay. She'd just felt an overwhelming sense of relief that there would be no more shouting.

It wasn't until the cab pulled away, with her mother's blond head in the back window, that the fear seized her. The overwhelming, paralyzing fear that her father would also leave. Then she'd have no one.

But Paul Monroe hadn't left. He'd done what he always had done. He worked long, hard hours at the airport, trying to build up the business he'd started years earlier, a commercial charter company. Monroe Air flew politicians, families, commuters and anyone else who wanted a quick hop between the Baltimore–Washington metropolitan area and the coastal towns of Maryland on the other side of the Chesapeake Bay. He kept his rates low, made as many runs as he could during a week, and even took on extra jobs whenever he could. And he continued to take Carrie up with him in his planes as often as she liked, teaching her all he knew about flying.

When she entered the sixth grade she became a cadet in the Civil Air Patrol and took part in local ground missions; when she turned sixteen, she piloted one of her father's planes to South Carolina as part of a disaster relief team, delivering blankets and food for victims of a hurricane. From then on, she'd regularly flown cargo to the Eastern Shore, including delivering the *Baltimore Sun* to Easton and Cambridge.

"So now I know about your mother," Adams said quietly. "Tell me about your father."

When Carrie looked at him, he was studying her. It was almost as if he understood the question was safe to ask, understood that Paul Monroe had done his duty as a father.

Carrie smiled and told him what she'd just been thinking. "Dad was great. I loved the man more than anything in the world. My girlfriends, when we were teenagers—they always complained about their fathers. How mean they were not to let them date…or about the early curfews their dads set during the week…or the kinds of boys they weren't allowed to go out with. They thought their fathers were dull, old-fashioned and stupid."

"But you didn't?" he asked.

It struck her that he still hadn't smiled, not really, the whole time he'd been on her plane. Yet she thought she noticed less stiffness in the muscles across his face, and a tentative relaxing of his body as he slid lower in the copilot's seat, crossing his long legs at the ankles.

"No," she admitted, an almost happy feeling stealing over her as warmer memories cheered her. "I looked at my father and saw the handsomest, smartest, most interesting man in the world—and I couldn't understand why my mother hadn't seen the same things in him."

"I take it he's no longer—"

"He died last year," Carrie managed before a burning sensation closed off her throat.

"I'm sorry. That must have been hard. You sound as if you were very close to him."

Yes—she shaped the word, but nothing came out. Blinking, she chased the tears away before they could blur her view of the cloudless sky ahead. Below them stretched the marshlands, and beyond that the wide, gray-green expanse of the majestic Chesapeake Bay, twenty miles wide at the point they'd cross. They were almost home. "Yes, it was…*is* hard."

She truly was alone now.

And it looked as if that would be the pattern of her life for the foreseeable future. By the time she turned twenty, Carrie had decided she would never become anyone's wife. By then, several of her girlfriends had married and a few even had babies. She watched and took note of the changes in their lives, hoping the best for them.

But bright, interesting, smart young women like her had quickly lost sight of their dreams, put on weight and become complacent with dull lives. Soon their marriages started to crumble. Bitter divorces followed. Children, houses and cars were fought over. And none of her friends seemed capable of going back to where she'd left off—to pick up a dream and try again.

Her own parents' experience reinforced her decision to stay single and concentrate on doing what she loved—flying. The one thing she missed and wanted more than anything was children. She had some ideas about how she might add them to her life. But first she would have to deal with the financial problems of the business her father had left her….

Carrie peered down and to her left, off the tip of the *Bay Lady*'s wing. "Look," she said, "there's Kent Island."

When she got no response, she turned back to the detective. His eyes were drifting closed, as if it was too much effort to keep them open. She wondered if his head hurt badly, then decided it must. The side of his face that had been cut was beginning to purple. As his chin dropped forward onto his chest, his muscled arms fell limply at his sides. The bloodied towel slid to the floor.

"Sweet dreams, Detective," she whispered. Glancing in her mirror, she could see his prisoner, still securely latched in the rear of the plane, as Adams must have known he would be.

Carrie let him sleep the rest of the way. Concerned that he might have a mild concussion, she kept a close watch on him. He didn't stir until she began her approach for landing, fifteen minutes later.

Straightening in his seat, he twisted around to check on his prisoner. Satisfied, he pointed at her headset. "Can you radio the tower to forward a message to Baltimore City Police, Western Division? I want two squad cars and four men to join my partner, waiting for us at the terminal."

"Sure," she said. "They can join the rest of the assault force waiting for us."

He raised a brow as he followed her pointing finger to the official vehicles with flashing lights, parked on the apron of one of the runways. "You already notified security?"

She nodded.

"Thanks."

It was the last word he said to her. From that moment on, he was all business, totally consumed with the job of getting his prisoner off her plane as quickly as possible. Gone was any sign that he might have a life beyond being a cop.

Chapter 2

The next day, Carrie made two round-trip flights between Baltimore and Ocean City by midafternoon. They were entirely routine—no life-or-death scuffles, no handsome law officers to sit in the copilot's seat and keep her company.

Skies over the Chesapeake Bay were a crystalline blue, rare for typical muggy Maryland summers. The drone of the twin Pratt and Whitney turboprops, which had come to seem as much a part of her existence as feeling her own heart beating in her chest, gradually relaxed the taut muscles in her shoulders. Still, Carrie couldn't stop thinking about the dramatic events of the day before, and how close she'd come to witnessing the murder of a man who'd had an inexplicably disturbing effect on her.

David Adams was unlike any man she'd ever met. In the sixty-four minutes they'd flown together, she'd learned a lot about him. He was brave, dedicated to serving the citizens of his city and state, a loving father and a man who'd been deeply hurt by a rotten marriage. Because of him, she had lain awake most of the night.

Ordinarily when Carrie tossed and turned it was because

she was worrying how she would ever make the next loan payment to the bank on time. Last night, her own problems had seemed minor compared with those of the young detective. And that made no sense at all, because, almost certainly, she'd never see him again.

Later that afternoon, Adams still slipped into her thoughts every few minutes. She welcomed the distraction of a last-minute charter her receptionist, Rose, had arranged. Carrie flew a U.S. senator from a small airfield outside of Washington, D.C., to Virginia Beach. He'd told her he was meeting golfing buddies for a weekend on the links, and she could pick him up that Sunday afternoon. But when she'd loaded the senator's golf bag, it had been so thickly covered with dust she wondered how many decades had passed since he'd last played. Then a pretty brunette wearing white spandex jeans and a sexy crop top that bared her midriff met him at the airport...and Carrie decided golf probably wasn't uppermost on the statesman's distinguished mind.

"Shame on you, Senator," she said with a chuckle as she taxied toward the runway in preparation for takeoff on her return flight. "She's young enough to be your daughter."

Back at BWI, less than an hour later, Carrie turned the *Bay Lady* over to Frank Dixon, her maintenance man. It was nearly 6 p.m., but she knew he'd want to bring the plane into the hangar and run a full safety check before he left for the night. Seated at the desk where Rose usually sat, at the back wall of the hangar, she completed her reports on the day's flights and the unfinished paperwork the FAA and NASB required for in-air incidents. Both the Federal Aviation Administration and National Aeronautics Safety Board had to be notified of any situation that affected passenger safety.

Carrie lost herself in technical jargon for far too long, before she looked up to see Frank, perched on a steel ladder, his head jammed halfway inside the *Bay Lady*'s engine.

"Everything all right?" she called out.

"Yup." Frank wiped his grease-blackened hands on an equally dark rag. "Should be done, less than twenty minutes."

"Good, we have a full schedule again tomorrow."

He straightened to gaze down at her as she stood up from her desk and approached the plane, his heavy gray eyebrows dipping low. "Why do you let Rose book you so many air hours?"

"It's not Rose's decision how many hours I fly. It's mine."

"Wrong," he scolded, pointing a condemning finger at her. "Your daddy made sure you knew FAA regulations from bottom to top, young lady. As chief of operations, it's Rose's responsibility to see you don't exceed your hour limit." He scowled, silencing her when she opened her mouth to speak. "Aside from regulations, you'll burn yourself out, girl. Flying a plane fatigued is asking for pilot error."

Carrie propped her fists on her hips. "I understand the rules. I just don't have a choice, Frank, and you know it. I've got my bases covered with the FAA. You're Monroe Air's chief of maintenance—"

"I'm your *only* maintenance," he corrected.

She waved him off. "Rose is chief of operations, and I'm chief pilot…oh, all right, I'm *the* pilot." She groaned. "And maxing out my hours is the only way I can make a go of this business. You know I can't afford to hire another pilot." She noticed the deep worry lines crisscrossing his aging face and softened. "Listen, I promise I won't fly tired. Promise."

He observed her from the top of the ladder, looking unconvinced.

"Besides," she continued quickly, "the more flights we book during the summer season, the better my chances are of paying off the loans and building up a list of repeat passengers."

"The bank still making noises like they're going to shut you down?"

Carrie blew out a long puff of air in exasperation. "You could say that. Things are beginning to look pretty desperate."

Frank climbed down the ladder and rested a hand on her shoulder. A hand that had been there whenever she'd needed it, for all her twenty-seven years.

"I worry about you, young lady. You got your daddy's stubbornness. He never was one to admit to his limits." He hesitated for a moment, but plunged on. "I was thinkin', if you sold the *Bay Lady* and—"

"I *don't* want to hear this, Frank." Carrie stepped away from him.

"I'm not saying leave the business. Maybe just trade her in for two six-seaters and hire one more pilot, then—"

She held up her hand, silencing him. "I'm not selling Dad's plane. That's final. The *Bay Lady* was his pride and joy. Just finish getting her ready for tomorrow."

He touched his cap, closed his mouth and climbed back up the ladder.

Carrie felt a twinge of regret for having spoken so sternly to her father's old friend, but she couldn't let her employees, as dear as they were to her, start making decisions for her. That would be admitting she couldn't work out her own problems. She turned back to her desk. Rose had returned with sandwiches for the three of them, since it was becoming a late day.

Rose ate while they reviewed the month's financial records. Carrie was too worried to think about food. "I don't see how I can make more than the minimum payment to the bank again this month," Carrie muttered, looking up from the ledger at Rose.

The older woman sighed. "Honey, if that's all you can do…there's no sense worryin' about it."

Carrie slapped the ledger shut, frustration boiling up inside her. "There has to be a way to get ahead. If Dad had just not taken out that loan the last year…"

"He didn't want to leave you no medical bills," Rose said gently. A mix of second-generation Italian dialect and Bal'morese colored her words. "There was no other way after he sold the two smaller planes but to put up the business as collateral."

Carrie felt heartsick. "I know. But it doesn't seem to make much difference now. I mean, at least if I were paying off medical bills instead of loans on our equipment, Monroe Air would be technically operating in the black." She dropped the ledger on the scuffed metal desk and pressed her face into her hands.

"It will be slow going," Rose assured her, "but in five or six years, maybe you can pay down the loan enough to—"

Carrie looked up at her sadly. "That's just it. I don't have five or six years, Rosie. The bank wants four months in back payments, along with this month's. If they don't get their money soon, they have the right to call the whole amount due and foreclose. They'll take away my plane."

The older woman stared at Carrie, her forever cheerful expression fading. "I didn't realize it was that bad." She laid a hand on Carrie's arm.

"It's more than just keeping my business afloat. I don't want to let Dad down." Carrie ached to let the tears gathering behind her eyelids fall. But she refused to let Rose see her crying. "I can't lose the business he worked so hard to build."

"He wouldn't blame you, hon. You know he wouldn't."

"No. But I'd blame myself. Besides, there are other reasons I have to make this work...." She wished she hadn't said it, but now that the words were out she could only shrug and try to avoid Rose's questioning stare.

"What reasons are they?"

Carrie bit down hard enough on the pencil end to taste eraser. "Rosie, if I don't have this little bit of an airline, how am I going to support myself?"

"Like anyone else, I guess."

"You don't understand," Carrie said, a wave of shame washing over her. "There's nothing I'm good at other than flying a plane. *Nothing.*"

Rose gave a knowing laugh, like a mother about to reassure her child that there was no monster in the closet. "Why, you could work in any office in Baltimore—"

"As what? Now, be honest, Rosie. As what?" Carrie dropped her pencil onto the desk.

"Filing...typing...clerical whatnot." Rose shrugged.

"That's what you've done all your life. I've never worked in an office. I don't type. I suppose I could learn to file since I'm fairly well versed in the alphabet, but I haven't got a clue what to do with a computer...unless it's part of an instrument panel."

Rose looked suddenly anxious. "I'm sure you could learn. I could teach you enough to get an entry-level job."

Carrie nodded. She supposed that was true, but it wasn't what she'd been hoping for.

"Didn't your daddy leave the old house in Catonsville paid for?"

"Yes, I have that," she admitted thankfully. "But there are still the property taxes to pay every year, and the utilities, and all my other living expenses. He'd cashed in his life insurance."

"Still, you'll get by," Rose said encouragingly.

"Getting by isn't what I had in mind."

Rose just looked at her. "You mean, you've been thinking about a family of your own."

Carrie stared at her, astounded. The woman seemed to be able to read her mind. "How did you know?"

"The way you go crazy about bambinos? How could anyone not know?"

Carrie laughed sadly and shook her head. "I'm that obvious, huh?"

"Don't worry. You'll have your babies, all in good time."

"I'm not sure I can trust time," Carrie murmured, pushing off of the desk to walk away. She knew she'd left Rose confused, but she didn't feel up to explaining. Not now. She'd only upset Rose.

Carrie strolled toward the huge hangar doors, aware that her receptionist was slowly following her, perhaps hoping to continue the conversation. But it was getting late. The sun had begun to set, tinting the evening sky plum streaked with apricot. Summer colors, she thought. You never see a winter sky like that. She sighed. How glorious.

"Oh, my!" Rose let out a strange, surprised noise behind Carrie.

Carrie looked up, then followed Rose's awestruck gaze, past the silver fuselage of the *Bay Lady*. A tall, wide-shouldered man in blue jeans, wearing an orange-and-black Baltimore

Orioles cap tugged down over his eyes, was moving across the hangar toward her. Carrie squinted at him, at first thinking he might actually be a professional baseball player. His body had the natural grace and strength of an athlete's, although he now moved somewhat stiffly, as if he'd just gotten up off the ground from sliding home.

"Detective Adams!" She grinned, not bothering to hide her delight.

Rose moved in with amazing speed and elbowed her in the ribs. Carrie could feel waves of curiosity emanating from the woman, like ripples set off by a pebble dropped into water.

"Is he the one...you know...from yesterday on the plane?" Rose whispered in her ear as the detective took his time closing in on them, looking around with interest at tools, equipment and the three planes parked under the corrugated tin roof.

"He's the one," Carrie said.

The detective's eyes moved vigilantly from object to object, shadow to shadow. Carrie wondered if he was ever able to override that nervous cop-edge and totally unwind...then remembered he had already let down his guard once in her presence, when he'd fallen asleep from sheer exhaustion in her copilot's seat. He'd looked oddly serene, even boyish, and she smiled at the intriguing contrasts in the man.

Adams stopped directly in front of her and observed her coolly from beneath hooded, darkly lashed lids.

"Yes, Detective? Can I help you?"

"Do you have a minute or two to answer a few questions, Ms. Monroe?" His glance slipped sideways toward Rose.

"I was just leaving," the receptionist announced, flashing Carrie a look of shared female appreciation. "I'll finish the accounts over supper, at home." She dashed for the desk, clutched the ledger to her ample bosom and strode away, humming.

Carrie shook her head in amazement; Rose never gave up. She'd been trying to pair her up with available men forever. But Carrie had already made up her own mind about the men she'd allow in her life, and how far in that would be.

She turned back to the police officer. "What is it you want to know, Detective?"

"'David.' Call me 'David.'"

He didn't quite smile, but his chiseled face arranged itself along less threatening lines. This time he was dressed more in tune with the weather. A short-sleeved, golf-style shirt was tucked into the slim waistband of casual khakis. He wore no jacket. She didn't see a gun, but something told her he carried one, somewhere on his well-muscled body.

She grinned to herself, thinking it might be fun to go hunting for it. Then she met his blue stare and found herself blushing furiously.

His eyes narrowed, taking stock of her. "Is something wrong?" he asked.

"No, of course not, Det...David. I assume these questions have to do with that wrestling match on my plane yesterday?"

"Some, yes. I do have to finalize the IR—the incident report, that is." He turned to study the *Bay Lady*. "How often do you fly to the coast and back?"

"That depends upon the season," she said. "In the summer, I might make the trip twice a day, six days a week. It takes less than an hour one way, so it's easy enough. Winter is our low season. Without the beach crowd we don't get enough business to fly a regular schedule. Monroe Air becomes strictly a charter operation. Some weeks, we might not get even one contract."

"Do you transport cargo as well as people?"

Carrie shifted her feet at the unexpected slant of his questions. "Yes," she said slowly. "We deliver the *Baltimore Sun* and *Washington Post* to Easton and Salisbury on the Eastern Shore. During the holidays, we contract with the post office to fly their overflow of mail to the same areas."

He turned back to face her. "Any out-of-state flights?"

"Sometimes I take a charter to Virginia Beach, Myrtle Beach or the Outer Banks, for fishermen, golfers or groups of vacationers. Used to be we'd sometimes get a call from one of the hospitals for an emergency medical airlift, but these days that's handled by specially equipped helicopters. I've flown as far south as Orlando, taking a family group or travel club down to Disney World, or headed up north to Vermont with a planeload of skiers. But fuel's so expensive these days, most people take one of the large commercial jets, which is actually cheaper.'' She hesitated, drew her tongue across her lips, which seemed to have suddenly dried out. ''Why do you need to know all this?''

David's gaze circumvented the hangar again. ''And do you do all your own flying?''

''Yes.'' She crossed her arms over her chest. A warning tingle crept around, down low in her stomach. She'd always pushed FAA air-time limits to make a go of the business, but a Baltimore City cop shouldn't be concerned with that.

''So you are aware of the contents of all cargo?'' he asked.

''Yes, I am. I personally check everything before it's loaded onto my plane.'' She squinted at him, suddenly thinking she understood. ''Listen, if you're implying that I might be transporting contraband—drugs or guns or something—you're wrong. This is a squeaky-clean operation, *Detective*.''

He acted as if he hadn't heard the resentment in her voice. ''Married? Serious boyfriends?''

Carrie fixed him with a stony glare. ''You'd better tell me what my personal life has to do with your investigation.''

''I'm interested in you,'' he said simply, as if that explained everything.

She pressed her lips together and gave him her best evil-eye stare.

''I'm sorry, I guess I'm just coming across as nosy. A guy on narcotics detail has to be careful about the people he hangs out with.''

''Hangs out with?'' she asked.

He focused on the toe of his shoe. ''Dates.''

''Dates,'' she repeated.

''Yeah, I guess you'd call it that.'' He looked up at Frank as her mechanic climbed down from the ladder propped against the *Bay Lady*'s gleaming fuselage. ''I wanted to find a way to thank you for helping me out on the plane. I don't like thinking what might have happened if you hadn't thrown Rainey off balance with your aerial acrobatics.''

"As I said yesterday, I'm sure you would have gotten him under control without me.'' The words brought to mind the way David Adams had looked wrestling with his prisoner, and an unexpected thrill coursed through her. There was something explicitly sexy about watching a man exert himself to his physical limit. She felt a little ashamed for even thinking something like that, but she couldn't help it.

"Maybe…" he allowed.

"Besides, you don't need to thank me,'' she said. "I was protecting my passengers, plane and myself as much as you. Maybe more. If he'd shot you, one of us might have been next.''

The shocked laugh that burst from his lips made her jump.

"I'm sorry,'' she stammered. "That sounded terribly cold.''

"Not cold, just practical. Anyone in law enforcement can identify with that kind of rationalization,'' he said, nodding as if he were pleased that she hadn't put his survival at the top of her list of priorities. "Listen…'' He took a step closer to her. "I really do want to take you out for dinner, to say thanks the right way. You certainly deserve it.''

She eyed him speculatively. "Are you sure I pass muster?''

"Huh?''

"Your game of twenty questions.''

"Sorry, it's become automatic. Anyone on special squads— narcotics, homicide, vice—has to be careful. There are too many ways for a cop to jeopardize a case.''

"Like the one you're involved in, with your uncooperative prisoner?''

"Exactly.'' He lifted his cap and combed thick, dark hair back from his forehead with his fingers, then tugged the felt brim low over his eyes. "This guy, Andrew Rainey…we've got some evidence against him, through a sting operation we pulled last week. But the cameras that were supposed to record him trading a briefcase of heroin for the briefcase of money I'd brought him malfunctioned. Then he managed to give us the slip. So now I'm the only witness that he offered to sell me enough drugs to supply the whole East Coast for a month. If Rainey's lawyers come up with some way to discredit me, he might get off without ever seeing the inside of a court-room.''

"We wouldn't want that." She grinned to let him know there were no hard feelings.

"No, we wouldn't. Forgive me for butting into your life?"

Carrie pretended to consider her options. "For a five-course dinner in Little Italy, I'd give it serious consideration."

He winked at her. "You've got yourself a deal."

He hadn't been completely honest with her, David admitted to himself. If Carrie Monroe had looked anything like her formidable, elderly bookkeeper, he might have gone as far as telephoning to thank her for being an exemplary citizen.

But Carrie wasn't a thick-waisted Italian matron with a shadow of a feminine mustache across her upper lip. She was an adorable, feisty blonde who coaxed tons of machinery into perilous maneuvers at thousands of feet in the air. She looked like an angel, and flew like the devil himself.

On top of her sweet curves, her long, tanned legs and her talent for flying, she had an intriguingly sharp wit and a mind any cop would envy. On the plane the day before, she'd sized up the situation and her options in the final seconds before Rainey could pull the trigger and blow him away. She chose the one path open to her that had any probability of saving his life, while protecting her property and her passengers' lives. He still felt a little numb, he was so in awe of her, and it was as much because of this, as her physical appeal, that he'd returned to ask her out for dinner.

Besides, he'd learned the hard way that putting too much stock in physical attraction was risky. He'd come close to idolizing Sheila Wayman when they first met. She was sleek, smart, and sexy as all get out. She came from money, and he didn't. She got a kick out of taking him to her society functions and introducing him to her friends. Most figured him for a brief amusement, but he'd wooed Sheila and won her. He felt as if he'd taken a prize at a carnival. He was the kid strolling the arcade, carrying the giant pink teddy bear.

Then the inevitable happened: reality set in. He discovered that carnivals only came to town for a short stay. By the time Sheila had told him she was pregnant, he knew he'd made a mistake. She probably knew it, too, but it seemed to amuse her to have an excuse for snubbing her parents and staying away from Newport. She was flaunting her independence, while he struggled to keep them on a budget.

The marriage went downhill from there. But they'd hung on for little Jason's sake...then because neither of them had anywhere else to go...then because Sheila was pregnant again. Sometimes he wondered if Tammy was his. He knew Sheila's Georgetown crowd; she liked to socialize, meet her friends in the bars in the trendy D.C. neighborhood. He was certain she'd had at least one lover during their rocky marriage, although he'd remained faithful to her.

They fought. They threatened each other with divorce, then made up for a few days or weeks. But it had never been right, and eventually they'd gone through with the separation and divorce. They were given joint custody of the children, with the stipulation that they both continue to reside in Maryland unless the other party agreed to a move.

Life before Sheila had been simple, blue-collar, proud. The Adamses were nothing like the Waymans of Newport. His old man had been a driver for a bakery. He was as simple and honest a man as they came. But to David, he was a hero. He drove the big blue-and-yellow truck stocked with flat, plastic trays of squishy-soft bread that smelled like heaven. David remembered sitting on the floor in the back, looking up at rows and rows of wrapped loaves and hamburger rolls and pies. His dad always "bought" him one of whatever he wanted, and David sat there while the road rumbled beneath him, and let the flaky pastry and juicy filling melt in his mouth.

When he was ten years old, his father didn't come home one afternoon. Instead, a man in a police officer's uniform knocked on the door and told his mother that Al, his father, had been killed in a robbery attempt. Two teenagers had thought he carried cash on the truck; they didn't understand that all he did was deliver. They'd gotten angry when seven bucks was all he could produce from his wallet. They shot him dead.

Idols changed, or deserted you…or died and left you alone. David had stopped searching for them years ago.

But Carrie Monroe was, at the very least, a special woman, and he'd found in the past thirty hours he couldn't stop thinking about her. So he'd told himself it wouldn't hurt to indulge himself and take her out, just once.

"You hungry?" David asked, as he pulled the car alongside a curb on Albemarle Street, in one of the few parking spots available in an ethnic section of Baltimore that had long been known as Little Italy.

He'd left the late-model, unmarked car with his partner, Pete, and drove his own eight-year-old sedan.

"Starved," she admitted. "I haven't eaten since this morning. No time for lunch or dinner with today's schedule."

"Good. The servings at Villegia's are enormous."

She smiled at him, her brown eyes toasty warm and alive with reflections from the nearby streetlights. A small pool down in his gut began to simmer. He thought how interesting it would be to kiss her and watch those eyes darken even more. Or maybe they'd erupt in fiery sparks.

David looked down at the simple blue slip of a dress she'd swapped her flight gear for. He'd followed her to her house outside the city, so she could change clothes. The sky-colored fabric clung and slid in a fascinating way over her slim body. It looked as if it had been designed to come off fast—no visible zipper, buttons or snaps.

He grinned at the thought. Perhaps that was his own wishful thinking.

"What's so funny?" she asked.

"Nothing." He quickly wiped the smile off his face. He took her hand to lead her up the three granite steps to the restaurant's entrance. "Just considering my own appetite."

She gave him a quizzical smile before stepping through the ornately carved oak door he held open for her.

The hostess seated them at a table covered with a brilliant red linen tablecloth. When they'd ordered and were sipping from glasses of bubbling *spumante,* David took time to observe Carrie's figure and delicate features more thoroughly. He could tell she was pretending not to notice his roving eyes, as she glanced casually around the room at the other diners, their faces flickering in the candlelight.

Abruptly, she turned to him. "Tell me about your job, David."

"Pretty dull stuff, most of the time."

"What *is* interesting to you, then," she said.

"You." He could have kicked himself for blurting out the truth like some naive schoolboy. The truth because, at this moment, she was *all* that was on his mind. Talk about subtle. "Your job, flying..." he amended lamely.

She lifted one shoulder in a half shrug and helped herself to a thick, crusty chunk of bread from the basket a busboy had just set on the table. He joined her. The butter was chilled and sweet on the bread as he chewed, reminding him of the old days, at his grandmother's table.

"Flying. It's just something I do," she said softly. "I don't think of it as a job as much as a way of living." She paused to slather more butter on her bread. "Was your father a police officer?"

"No," he said. Ironically, he might have still been alive if he had been. "But your old man flew. *You* followed in *his* footsteps."

"Yes," she mused. "He was trained as a pilot in the air force. He flew an F-4 in Vietnam. After the war, he dreamed of starting his own local air shuttle business. He flew commercially for one of the big airlines until he saved up enough money to get started and buy a couple of thirdhand Cessnas. After a few years, he added the Beechcraft, which was larger and could hold more passengers and cargo."

"So his dream came true—that's wonderful."

Carrie deliberately placed the remainder of her bread on the butter plate to her left. "He got Monroe Air off the ground, so to speak, but it cost him dearly. My mother hated the idea— all our money had to be poured into equipment and upkeep for the planes, when she wanted new furniture. Dad put in a lot of flight time, but she wanted someone to take her out dancing."

"I'm sorry," he said. "I'm really sorry."

Carrie pursed her lips, looking as if she was gently arguing herself out of tears. "It's just something that happened. Like Dad dying. It didn't take long, actually. I'm glad for him, because he wasn't the kind of man who would have wanted to be a burden to me or others." She drew a finger beneath each eye before tears could smear her makeup. "The cancer was too far along for surgery. He elected not to take the chemo treatments. Two months, and he was gone."

"But it was long enough to leave Monroe Air in debt." That was another fact he'd picked up while chatting up pilots and ground crews in neighboring hangars. It seemed general knowledge that Carrie Monroe was putting up a fierce struggle to keep her little shuttle service afloat.

"Yes," she admitted. "I'm still working on that."

"What about your personal goals?" he asked.

"I suppose I'm a lot like most women. I want a family..."

He thought he caught a brief catch in her voice.

"Kids. I want to be a mother, a very loving, always there kind of mother. I want to share my world—the sky—with my children." Her eyes grew dreamy and distant. "I'll take them up into the clouds and show them the planet they live on, from high, high up in the heavens. I'll teach them to be kind and love one another, and to do something special and good with their lives."

Her eyes were alive and shimmering with hope. A part of him ached. Why hadn't the woman he'd married seven years ago been able to get high on kids and life? Why hadn't everything he'd given Sheila been enough?

Then he knew the answers—as quickly as the questions had raced through his mind. Because there was no love. Never had been love. And without it, a relationship hadn't a chance of working in any but the most superficial and selfish ways.

Their dinners arrived, saving him from having to change the subject before conversation drifted into too-deep waters. They ate homemade linguine topped with white clam sauce and a grating of fresh Parmesan cheese, while chatting about lighter topics. Carrie told him stories of exciting and perilous flights—sounding more like an old war veteran spouting battle exploits than a pretty, young woman. He retaliated by making her wince and exclaim in shock at episodes involving some of his drug busts and dramatic chases through the city.

Carrie was an enthusiastic audience, but, he noticed, she didn't forget her food. She ate with relish and drank a third glass of wine while she urged him to tell yet another story. He wasn't sure how much she believed, but, unlike most cops involved in traditional squadroom contests of one-upsmanship, he added nothing to the facts.

She laughed long and hard when he told her about the time they'd dressed Pete in drag and sent him out on North Avenue to make a buy. Unfortunately, when his partner slipped the little plastic pouch of dope into his bra after the transaction was complete, it fell straight through and plopped on the sidewalk. The pusher immediately realized something was wrong. Pete, in black patent-leather pumps, blond wig flying off his head, had run after the guy, chasing him for blocks before he tackled him in the street.

"As if it wasn't bad enough," David added over Carrie's hysterical laughter, "a photographer from the *Baltimore Sun* happened to be doing a ride-along with one of the neighborhood uniforms. Before I could catch up with Pete, the guy snapped a shot of him, still in his dress and makeup, sitting on the pusher while he cuffed him."

"Oh, no!" she cried, her hand over her mouth. "Did the paper run it?"

"Nah. The lieutenant explained to the news editor that printing the photo would jeopardize a cop's life. Any pusher, junkie, gang member who saw the picture would recognize Pete on the street. He'd be a marked man."

Suddenly, all the brightness drained from Carrie's face. "You work undercover, too," she stated solemnly.

"I don't look as good as Pete in a dress."

"I'm serious, David."

He glanced away from her, letting his eyes circle the room as he'd done every few minutes since they'd entered the restaurant. Like Rainey's eyes, his were always moving. A cop had to stay in touch with everything going on around him. Always.

"Sometimes," he admitted.

The coffee and desserts arrived, and he watched with fascination as Carrie forked down her Triple-Chocolate Cake, with its alternating rich layers of white, milk and dark chocolate. He dove into warm apple pie topped with a melting scoop of French vanilla ice cream.

"I used to do a lot of undercover work," he continued after a few bites. "Not as a woman—I'm too tall and wide across the shoulders. They'd spot me a mile away. I'd spend months working my way into an organization, getting on the good side of a couple of pushers by making small buys, becoming a steady customer. I'd dress and talk and act the part. I'd start to think like a junkie, and that was damn scary. Sometimes it would take me hours to mentally shift gears after I went off duty. Sometimes I couldn't find my real self for days."

"But you had to do all that to be effective at your job...right?" she asked.

It sounded so simple, coming from her lips. She had a knack of making sense of complicated feelings. For the rest of the meal he just let her talk while he enjoyed his pie and the sound of her voice.

Later, as he drove her to her home in Catonsville, he thought about their earlier conversation. And he continued to think about it when they stood on the old-fashioned, wraparound porch, close but not touching.

David wanted to kiss her, but a need that wouldn't be ignored urged him to finish explaining his work and what it had done to his family.

"Back at the restaurant," he began, "you said I was just doing my job effectively. It wasn't that easy. One day when I came home, my son, Jason, took a look at me—filthy, grease in my hair to make it look dirty, my jacket torn and jeans shredded from scaling a chain-link fence while we were chasing some guy. The poor little kid ran crying from the room. He was terrified. He honestly didn't know me. That's when I started letting Pete handle most of the contact jobs, while I worked support. He loves that stuff, the crazy bastard." David chuckled affectionately.

"Do you still have trouble relaxing after you're off your shift?" she asked, sounding as if she already knew the answer.

"Always," he answered without hesitation. "That's one reason I had to leave right after we landed yesterday. The other guys could have escorted Rainey through Central Booking. I would have liked to stay and talk to you some more. I just couldn't somehow...."

Carrie looked up at him, her freckles barely visible in the dim porch light. "You need to fly more often, Detective. Nothing in this world matters when the clouds are under your wings." She smiled sunnily at him, and he felt the knot in his chest he hadn't even realized was there loosen a notch.

"Maybe you're right," he said.

"It was a delicious dinner," she whispered, taking a step toward the door.

He wanted to stop her from going inside, but told himself he shouldn't. She wasn't the kind of woman you tried stuff with on a first date. He held out his hand for her key, then opened the door for her and handed it back to her. He wondered if she'd feel as warm as her voice had sounded all evening.

He ached to touch her.

"Good night," she said, and walked into the house, shutting the door behind her.

David stood on her porch, wondering how he'd managed to let her leave without kissing her. A minute later, his pager interrupted his muddled thoughts, and he looked down to see his lawyer's phone number displayed in floating digits.

Chapter 3

Carol Ann Strathmore's office was on Water Street, in the middle of Baltimore's financial district. David had telephoned her late the night before after receiving her page. All she'd say was that Sheila's attorney had contacted her, and they needed to talk, as soon as possible. He arranged to meet her at 9 a.m. sharp, the next day. Given her unwillingness to discuss anything over the phone, he was sure the news wouldn't be good.

Now, as he stepped off the elevator on the seventh floor and strode down the corridor he'd traveled so many times in the past two years, he was surprised he hadn't, personally, worn a track in the plush, wine-colored carpet. He stopped in front of the third door on the right and let himself in.

David thought, for at least the hundredth time, how thankful he was he'd chosen Carol Ann to represent him in his divorce and custody proceedings. She was as sharp as they came, honest on top of that—and it hadn't hurt for the judge to see a woman, respected by her colleagues, standing up for him while his wife tore him to shreds with manufactured lies. The bright young lawyer had earned far more than he'd paid her in fees, and that was something that couldn't be said for many in her profession.

Carol Ann was in her outer office, shaking hands with another client, when David entered the reception area. She wore a trim navy blue suit with a white, shawl-collared blouse under it. Her hair was wound into a no-nonsense twist at the back of her head, which made her look like a woman you wouldn't want to argue with. Those who had tried soon realized they didn't have much of a chance of winning.

She acknowledged his arrival with a flicker of her eyes, then finished her conversation with the man. As soon as the door closed behind him, she accepted a file her receptionist held out to her and tipped her head toward her office. "Let's go, Detective."

David assessed her grim expression and thought, This is going to be worse than I figured.

A lump grew inside his chest and worked its way up into his throat. He followed her, then paced the floor in front of her desk. She didn't sit down, either.

"Tell me," he said.

"Your ex-wife's attorney has requested a hearing to renegotiate custody of the children. It's been scheduled for six weeks from today."

David groaned and shook his head. "Nothing's changed. What grounds do they have?"

Carol Ann plucked a cigarette from the teak box on her desk and lit it. She knew he didn't smoke and didn't offer him one. "You have the kids half of every week, and they stay with you at your apartment—"

"Yeah, so?"

"So, Sheila claims that living downtown is dangerous and traumatic for them."

"Good God, it's not like I put them out on the street to play in traffic!" He couldn't believe Sheila's nerve.

"I know that, but you're not in the best part of town, David. There have been muggings, shootings, rapes. The neighborhood's earning a bad reputation and getting a lot of negative press."

"It's where I grew up…where I've always lived," he objected. "Every city has its violent side these days."

She waved her cigarette hand in the air, leaving a trail of blue-gray smoke. "Doesn't matter. David, she can use this against you. She claims Jason and Tammy are having nightmares. The affidavit her attorney filed states that your children are terrified of staying with you."

"That's a lie…an outright lie!" he sputtered. He stopped pacing. His fists worked themselves into two steel balls at his sides. When he turned back to face Carol Ann, he could tell by her expression that she hadn't finished. "What else?"

"Your job."

"My job? How is that a problem?" he demanded. "I provide a reliable income and pay out a hefty chunk of it in child support. I've got decent health insurance that covers both the kids. Jason attends a private school that's exactly halfway between my place and Sheila's house, and I pay the tuition. When I can't be with the kids and it's my day to have them, I employ a dependable baby-sitter. What more does she want?"

"She and her lawyer will assert that your career, with the violence it entails, is a threat to the children's security and emotional well-being."

David couldn't believe what he was hearing. "She expects me to give up police work?"

Carol Ann took a long pull off her cigarette. She blew a narrow stream of smoke between tight lips. "I'm just telling you what they intend to use against you. Sheila wants to take the children to her parents' home in Rhode Island, where they'll be safe and have a more stable home life, away from the violence of the city. Those are her words, not mine."

David collapsed into the nearest leather armchair. He dropped his face into his palms. "The kids are fine. They love being downtown with me. Jason can't get enough of the science center, and Tammy wants to go to the aquarium every weekend. We have a ball together, and I'd never let anything happen to them. As for my job—"

"As for your job, all the judge has to do is take one look

at the condition of your face and Sheila will have made her point. Did that happen recently?''

She squinted at the left side of his face. Her inspection made him more aware of the pulling sensation of the scarred tissue. Last night, with Carrie, he'd completely forgotten about it.

"Couple of days ago. It'll be healed up before the hearing.''

"I should hope so.'' She manufactured a smoke ring and examined it through narrowed eyes, as if analyzing her own thoughts.

"Okay,'' David snapped impatiently, "you must have some idea how we deal with this.''

She nodded. "First, you make a list of people—neighbors, friends, co-workers—who frequently see you with your children. People who can attest to Jason and Tammy being happy, in a relaxed frame of mind, safely looked after. Get written statements from them. If necessary, we can also ask some of them to come to the hearing and answer any questions the judge might have.''

"Will that work?''

Carol Ann shrugged and puffed twice quickly before grinding out her cigarette in a brass ash tray shaped like a charging elephant—which seemed entirely appropriate to David.

"Sure it will work…unless dear Sheila comes up with statements of her own. She must have something solid as proof of her claims.'' She hesitated, turning to gaze out the window at the street below.

"What is it? There's something else cooking in that clever brain of yours,'' David said, hope swelling in his heart.

"How attached are you to your downtown apartment?''

"Very attached. I told you, that neighborhood is where I grew—''

"More attached to it than to your kids?''

"Of course not!'' He raked a hand through his hair, irritated with her for setting him up. "What are you getting at?''

"The obvious solution is simply to satisfy your wife's concerns, whether they're real or trumped up for her convenience. The way to do that is to move yourself out of the city and somehow alter your work situation to more docile duties than tracking down drug runners.''

"That's giving in to her, letting her run my life!" he roared. "I'm not quitting police work and moving to the suburbs to please that woman.''

"I didn't ask you to. What I'm suggesting is something much simpler.'' She stepped around her desk and sat down in a leather chair, facing David across a gleaming mahogany expanse. "You could apply for a transfer to one of the county forces, couldn't you? Drug detail in the middle of a city like Baltimore is brutal, the worst. You might as well be in homicide. But you could get yourself a job in a quieter county. You'd still be a cop. You'd still be doing a community a lot of good.''

"It wouldn't be the same," David insisted. "The Western District is my neighborhood, where I hung out as a kid.''

"David," Carol Ann said, drawing out the next few words as she reached for a gold-and-crystal Waterford pen, "you have no choice. You can make some changes in your life to anticipate Sheila's line of attack, or you can stand by and let her take your children away from you.''

The bottom fell out of his stomach. David felt suddenly barren, bereft of the love of his children, alone. "There's no other way?" he asked weakly.

"No *better* way, let's say that. There are alternative measures, but you won't like them.''

"Try me.''

"For instance, you might be able to keep your job in the city if you move your residence and change your marital status.''

David stared blankly at her. "My what?''

"Think about this." She pointed the elegant pen at him, as if to be sure he was paying attention. "There are different ways of establishing a stable home for any child. If one parent leads a risky life-style or is unable to spend much time with the child, then it helps to have a second parent with a safer career that keeps him or her close to home. If the worst happens, chances are someone will be around to finish raising the child."

"You're suggesting I marry another woman to foil my first wife's plot to take away my children?" The idea seemed far-fetched, to say the least. He'd be asking for trouble. David glared at her.

"Listen, David, I'm not suggesting you drag the first woman you meet off the street and into a church, or hitch yourself to some bimbo you've been dating whose IQ hovers around fifty on her most lucid days. But if there's anyone serious in your life, someone you have been seeing, and you're both considering marriage—now might be a good time to do something about it."

He still couldn't believe what she was advising him.

She sat back in her chair with a huff. "Cops have no imagination, I swear. Look, move the kids out of the city during the week. You can still drive them downtown to their favorite play spots on your time off. If you can also provide a step-mother, a woman the judge will view as responsible and lov-ing, a woman who can provide the security your job won't—then the court will be hard put to take Sheila's complaints seriously." She pressed her lips closed and regarded him with one of her rare catty expressions. "By the way, how does your sweet ex treat the kids?"

"Sheila's just as bored with motherhood as ever. When they're supposed to be with her, I suspect they're often being looked after by a friend or neighbor. The kids are old enough to talk about where they spend their days—and nights."

"Do you have any proof of overt negligence on her part?"

"No, I don't." He broke off, understanding. "You mean, to use against her in court, to take the kids away from her totally?"

Carol Ann nodded, her lawyer's eyes pinpoint bright with anticipation of victory.

"No. Nothing solid, just unconnected pieces of informa-tion." He thought for a minute. "I don't want to take my children entirely away from their mother. That would hurt them, too. I just want to be able to have my fair share of time with them, and a say in raising them. I'm not out for revenge.''

Carol Ann sighed, looking a little disappointed. ''So we're back to tactics to build you up instead of tearing her down. In a way, that's more difficult, but think about what I've said. We have six weeks before the hearing.'' She lifted a precisely plucked brow and smiled wistfully. ''It certainly would be convenient if you happened to announce your engagement to a schoolteacher, nurse or member of the clergy....''

He was already shaking his head, laughing at the absurdity of it. ''The women I've dated in the past two years I wouldn't trust with my kids. Don't get me wrong—they're not bad people. They're just too much like me—streetwise, risk takers, attracted by danger....''

''I see.''

''I'll think about moving,'' he promised, pushing up out of his chair. ''And maybe a transfer. This morning I'll ask around, see what the chances are.''

''Fine. Just remember, you've got to get your life in order fast or we'll have one hell of a fight on our hands. And don't forget to document situations with Sheila that involve the children. Abuse takes many forms, including passive neglect. Judges can be very receptive to clear evidence of that.'' She reached out and shook his hand. ''They're playing dirty, David. Like it or not, we've got to beat them at their own game, or you might very well lose those kids.''

He swallowed, picturing Jason and Tammy, trying to imagine his life without them. ''I'll do what has to be done,'' he stated.

David drove north along Charles Street, heading through the thriving business district of the city, then hung a left on Franklin Avenue, continuing toward the Western District office. He was barely aware of other vehicles and pedestrians around him, as familiar surroundings altered like kaleidoscopic images, from prosperous steel-and-glass meccas of million-dollar corporations to endless runs of sooty brick row houses, half of them boarded up.

What Carol Ann was suggesting, that he completely alter his life to thwart Sheila, had at first seemed laughable, overkill and certainly asking for more trouble. Yet he knew in his gut that his lawyer was not only unconventionally brilliant, she was right. He had no choice. He had to act and act quickly if he was going to keep his children. Without them, his life would have little meaning. They were the only pure and good things in his world.

He spent an hour in personnel, hovering over a clerk's desk while the man rang through to sister offices in Frederick, Anne Arundel, Montgomery, Harford and Howard counties. "Same story," the clerk said, at last hanging up. "The city's hungry for cops, and the counties are trying to cut bodies any way they can to meet payroll budget cutbacks. You're right where you're most needed, Detective."

David shook his head, straightening. If a transfer was impossible, his options were down to three. Relocate his home, discredit Sheila...find a new wife. The last was a step he'd sworn he'd never again take, but the other two were no easier to contemplate. Muttering, David spun on his heel and marched toward the office door.

"Sorry," the clerk called after him.

"Not your fault," David assured him, without breaking stride.

And not his own fault, either, he told himself as he rushed out of the building, onto the hot pavement in front of headquarters. He clenched his teeth, but that made the still-healing slice along his upper jaw pull uncomfortably. He touched it absently with one finger. Maybe he should have at least had it checked out at the ER. Without stitches, it would probably leave a nasty scar.

Stitches, he mused, and chuckled again at the idea.

The laugh faded, leaving a dry spot in his throat. He stood ramrod straight, his key halfway into the lock of his car door...as he was unexpectedly assaulted by an image of Carrie. She was scowling at him, scolding him for not seeing a doctor. She was absolutely professional when it came to her job. Yet mothering instincts trickled through her veins.

He pictured her as he'd first glimpsed her on boarding her plane. She'd been crouching in front of a little boy, amusing him before takeoff. She'd worn simple jewelry, just a watch and tiny gold circles in her earlobes. Her hair was cut short, in a fresh, carefree style that had nothing to do with the way other women were wearing their hair these days. Meg Ryan playing Donna Reed. That was her. Unpretentious, practical, watching out for others.

She looked like a woman who had never doubted a decision and rarely took anyone's advice over her own common sense. She was civic-minded and a quick thinker. The way she'd handled those critical few seconds after Rainey had overpowered him was, as his son might put it, "awesome." She'd safeguarded her passengers, taken steps to alter the balance of a lethal struggle and brought her plane safely back up to altitude once she was sure the law was in control again. Few men, in the same situation, would have acted as coolly. They sure wouldn't have looked half as good doing it.

As his mind fine-tuned the details of Carrie Monroe, David became aware of a slow burn working its way through his center and out through his limbs. Both times he'd seen her she'd moved as if she were totally unaware of the shapely curves filling out her clothing. His imagination suggested a lovely expanse of flesh beneath the jumpsuit she'd worn while piloting her plane. Ripples of heat shot into all the wrong places in his body.

He too easily imagined her slim shape nestling within the contoured pilot's seat, and he wondered just how gratifying it would be to feel the fullness of her hips and long line of her back pressed into his coiled chest and stomach. In his memory, her long, white fingers gripped the yoke of the *Bay Lady*, firmly controlling the plane's homeward flight. It wasn't difficult to substitute a part of his anatomy for the laminated half circle.

With a pleasurable shudder, David decided he wouldn't mind letting her take control of *him* for a while. Then he'd return the favor, and glory in watching her slowly lose touch with that strong sense of reality he'd seen mirrored in her eyes when he sat beside her in the cockpit. He could imagine her mouth softening, her pretty hazel eyes drifting out of focus, her long legs tightening around his hips…

David blinked, and blinked again, astonished to find himself sitting in his car, staring blindly into the glaring sun through the windshield, sweat trickling down the back of his neck. He had no memory of how he'd gotten from the street into the driver's seat.

How long had he been sitting in the sunbaked vehicle without even turning on the engine to crank up the AC? He swallowed with effort, then swallowed again. Thinking sexy thoughts about women was a man's prerogative. But the strength of the sensual fantasy he'd built around the little, blond pilot had been mind-boggling, disturbingly potent.

"Pull yourself together, Adams," he told himself. "You've got a drug lord to get to court, four other investigations to juggle and two little kids to protect." Enough complications for any man's life.

But as he drove toward his apartment, the car's air-conditioning cooling his outer body while doing little to soothe the sizzle inside, he was unable to banish Carrie from his mind. He toyed with her image, dressing her like a paper doll in various garments—a range of styles from conservative to risqué. He considered the sultry, teasing effect of a wisp of silk draped around her breasts, but that left him squirming uncomfortably in his seat. Trying for something less erotic, he came up with a PTA-perfect skirt and sweater with casual penny loafers.

Chuckling, David steered around a corner. Then it hit him. He quit grinning like a teenager under the spell of a first crush. Suddenly, so clearly it was almost frightening, he could see Carrie standing beside him, in front of a stern-faced judge. "This is my wife, Caroline Adams," he'd say proudly. He supposed the name Carrie was short for Caroline. "She will be taking care of Jason and Tammy whenever I can't be with them."

The judge beamed at him.

"Nah," David breathed, squinting into the bright sunlight

as a van pulled out of a parking space and into his lane. He braked reflexively.

But the image was so clear, so persistently right in his mind, that he couldn't shake it. And because Carrie Monroe was so damn good-looking, in a way that still puzzled as much as fascinated him, that made the fantasy even more appealing. Of course, a woman with her guts and common sense would make a perfect mother. His children couldn't be safer with anyone else. And she'd project the ideal image—centered, mature, capable.

Belatedly, reality gripped him and hauled him back down to earth. Although keeping Jason and Tammy was enough reason for him to marry a woman, if only in name—why would Carrie Monroe marry him? The woman had a business to run, employees to oversee, financial worries. They were virtual strangers, although he sensed she was at least mildly attracted to him.

Still, mild attraction was a long way off from marriage. Not many women would casually wed a cop with two kids.

Unless that woman has as much to gain from the arrangement as you do, a voice whispered from somewhere inside him.

David frowned as he pulled into the parking garage connected to a multistoried brick edifice that was headquarters for the Western Police District of the City of Baltimore. He parked and lifted a hand in a half wave to a pair of uniforms climbing into a squad car. But he was still thinking about Carrie.

Everyone has a weak spot, he reasoned. Give a person enough of a motive to choose one action over another, even if it doesn't seem in his best interest, and he'll do it. He'd seen it happen time and again in police work. People stole, destroyed property, hawked dope and murdered because they believed they had no choice. Even though they knew they'd be punished if they were caught.

What he had to do was find Carrie Monroe's trigger. That sounded cold and calculating; he didn't like himself for thinking that way. But if he offered her the right deal, enticed her with the appropriate bait...if he found something he could give her that she needed badly enough, she'd agree to a temporary marriage. Then, all he'd have to do was go through the motions of a wedding ceremony to convince Sheila, her attorney and a judge that he'd found a new mother for his children.

Carrie released the air lock that dropped the short flight of steps from beneath the *Bay Lady*'s hatch, then climbed down to the tarmac to assist her passengers with their luggage. The weather was warm and clear, and smelled thickly of honeysuckle growing wild over the chain-link fencing that surrounded the private hangars at the south end of BWI Airport.

She thought she heard someone calling her name, and looked up to see Rose puffing toward her, awkwardly bearing a bulky object swathed in green paper.

"If that's someone's idea of cargo for tomorrow's flight, forget it!" Carrie shouted.

People dropped off the most outrageous items for transport. Poorly packed, impossible to secure during flight or to deliver in one piece. Rose was often too generous when local businesses or college students turned up at her desk with items UPS refused to ship. The well-meaning receptionist had once accepted a pair of canaries in a cage. The birds had caught pneumonia on the flight and died, leaving Carrie to stave off a lawsuit from the mourning owner.

Carrie was shaking her head before Rose stopped in front of her. "I don't know what *that* is, but we're not taking it unless it's already dead and packaged properly."

Rose's eyes twinkled. "This isn't a shipment. It's something for you." She thrust the object into Carrie's arms, grinning mysteriously. "Go on and take a peek. I don't think tea roses bite."

Carrie stared at what she could now see were layers of emerald-hued florists' tissue paper. "Flowers? For me?"

"That's what the man said."

"What man?" Carrie couldn't think of anyone who'd be likely to send her flowers, unless it was that U.S. Air pilot who had asked her out a few times. Maybe he was trying to convince her, yet again, that their casual dates should become less casual. But she hadn't heard from him in nearly two months.

"That nice police officer who came to see you the other night. Was it Tuesday?" Rose mused, tapping her cheek with one finger and rolling her eyes skyward. "I don't remember."

"Yes, it was Tuesday." Carrie grinned, carefully unwrapping the bouquet enough to sniff the heavy, cream-colored blossoms. "We went to Little Italy for dinner."

"Oh?" Rose poked a finger thoughtfully at a lush bloom. "You must have really impressed him."

"The dinner was just a thank-you for helping him out," Carrie explained quickly. But why the roses? she asked herself. "I didn't expect to ever hear from him again."

"Seems like you have." Rose beamed at her. "He dropped these off in person, a couple of hours ago."

"You don't have to look so shocked. It's not as if I've never gotten flowers."

"But it's been a pretty long time."

Carrie caught a flash of motion in gray overalls, and looked up to see Frank coming toward them. His expression was a grim contrast to her receptionist's. Rose leaned closer to Carrie. "While your gentleman friend was in the office, Frank grilled him mercilessly. Here, there's a note inside with the flowers."

Carrie pulled a small white square of paper from between the fragrant blooms. It appeared as if it had been torn from a pocket notepad. She read quickly, out loud, while Rose peered over her shoulder at the words.

"'Wanted to see you, but you were in the clouds. Have supper with me tonight? My place, nothing fancy. Call to let me know.'" The note was signed simply, David. His telephone number followed.

Rose whooped exultantly.

"Before this misguided missile of a matchmaker blows your life to smithereens," Frank barked, stopping in front of the two women, "I intend to put in my two cents."

Carrie and Rose exchanged glances that said, "Here he goes again."

"You've never approved of any man who takes me out," Carrie stated, playfully tweaking the grease-stained brim of his cap. "I can save you the trouble of another lecture by reciting it from memory."

"Don't get sassy with me, young lady." Frank glowered at her. "Technically, I work for you. But your daddy was more than my boss. He was my closest friend for more than twenty years. And Paul…he wouldn't want no daughter of his getting serious with no cop."

Carrie smiled affectionately, laying a hand on the older man's arm. "Who said anything about getting serious?"

"Roses are serious," Frank insisted. He turned to their namesake, as if for support, but Rose merely looked amused that he was so upset. *"They are!"* he repeated.

"I don't think so," Carrie said. Nevertheless, she nuzzled the bouquet, breathing in deeply. She couldn't remember greenhouse roses smelling this mind-blowingly sweet. The scent seemed to reach down inside her and loosen up stagnant emotions. "It's just a nice gesture. The man's glad to be alive."

"Listen, when any man spends fifty, sixty bucks on a bunch of flowers that are going to be fertilizer in a week, he *wants* something. Besides which, cops are bad news where women are concerned."

"Now, Frank," Rose began, "leave the girl alone and—"

He shot her a silencing glare. "If you had half a brain in your head, Rose Marie Kelly, you'd be warning her off, too." He swung back to Carrie, before Rose could manage an appropriate reply. "This guy isn't just any cop. He's a narc. They're tough customers, used to violence. They live with the filth and misery of the streets so long it seeps into their veins. Poisons 'em. A man like that becomes what he starts out fighting."

"David Adams isn't going to hurt me," Carrie stated. But even as she said the words, she realized she had no way of being sure they were true. What did she really know of David Adams? Very little, and all of that was only what he'd told her.

Frank groaned and studied the pattern of oil splotches on the backs of his hands. "Girl, what he intends and what comes out of this—" he waved disgustedly at the bouquet in her arms "—they're just two different things. Cops got no staying power. They get bored easy and move on. Or else, when things don't work out their way in their private lives, they deal with them the way they deal with their jobs. They get physical."

No longer amused, Carrie stopped smiling. "You sound as if you're speaking from experience."

He nodded. "My kid sister."

Rose winced and stepped closer to him. "I'm sorry. I'd forgotten about Anna." She touched Frank's shoulder.

The gesture was so natural it seemed as if it might have been from habit. Carrie vaguely recalled a time when they'd seemed closer than they were these days.

"Anna?" Carrie asked.

Frank nodded. "My sister fell in love with a Boston police officer—a beat cop. He seemed like a steady enough fella. But they had a real quick courtship and got married less than three months after they met. Six months later, she was pregnant and they both seemed happy, but before the baby was born, she caught him visiting one of his lady chums on his beat. A prostitute."

"How horrible for her," Carrie breathed.

"Eddie tried to make like he and the woman were only friends, having a drink together, but soon he was staying out late after coming off duty. Between him working close to sixty hours a week and going off with his friends to play cards or prowl bars, Anna hardly ever saw him. The marriage fell apart fast."

"That doesn't mean every police officer is incapable of being a good husband," Rose noted.

Carrie straightened her shoulders and looked down at the roses in her arms, wondering how such a thoughtful gift could cause this much turmoil. Their scent wafted up to her on the summer air. Each petal seemed a perfect, velvety-textured work of art, begging to be touched. She rubbed one between her first finger and thumb, releasing an even more potent, old-

fashioned aroma that reminded her of lace doilies and pot-
pourri.

"I don't know why you're so worried about me and marriage, Frank," she murmured absently. "You know how I feel
about that."

He studied her with concern. "Just because your daddy and
ma didn't make it doesn't mean a good match can't work.
Two people who are *right* for each other *belong* together."
His glance drifted to Rose, but she seemed to be looking else-
where. "Some man will come along and make you realize
that, girl. You just remember—this one ain't the one for you."

Carrie shrugged, taking no offense. "Fine. That doesn't
mean I can't spend some time with him for the fun of it."

Throwing his hands into the air, Frank spun on his heel and
stomped away.

Rose reached out and gently squeezed Carrie's hand.
"Sometimes I don't know what gets into that man." She
sniffed, close to tears. "You just do what you feel like doing,
hon."

Carrie dropped the note back among the full, creamy
blooms and nodded. "That's exactly what I intend to do."

Chapter 4

Carrie had no trouble finding David's apartment building by following the directions he'd given her over the phone. Locating a parking place was something else. She cruised the neighborhood for twenty minutes before giving up on the possibility of a free spot on the street and pulled into the Galleria parking garage, several blocks east of his address.

Since this was across the street from one of her favorite places in the world, the Light Street Pavilion, she didn't mind the walk or the expense. The pavilion held over a hundred quaint shops, one-of-a-kind boutiques, specialty markets, gourmet food stands and every kind of restaurant imaginable, from fiery Szechuan to a sedate steak-and-ale pub. A little more ambitious stroll would have taken her to the Maryland Science Center, with its exciting hands-on displays, planetarium and immense 3-D viewing screen. Following the edge of the harbor in the other direction, she would have run into the National Aquarium, where she'd sometimes hung out on Sundays with her father when they weren't flying. During the summer, concerts on a nearby pier attracted thousands.

Baltimore was the city she'd watched grow and change over

the years, but always from a distance. In some ways, it lived up to its nickname, Charm City. In other ways, it failed miserably to measure up, for the number of violent crimes increased each year.

Carrie was perfectly happy residing in Catonsville, where she'd grown up, in the Victorian house her father had bought for his family when she was a little girl and her mother was still around. Catonsville was a small, homey town with a colorful historic past. During colonial and pre-Civil War days, plantations had flourished and tobacco had been grown in the fertile soil. One of the main thoroughfares was still named Rolling Road because huge hogsheads—as the bales of tobacco were called—had been rolled down the hill from the fields to the Patapsco River. There, they were loaded onto barges for shipment to manufacturers of chewing and pipe tobacco, cigarettes and cigars.

Today, agriculture had all but disappeared from the area. But comfortable towns—like Catonsville, Ellicott City and Laurel—each with its own special character, survived as bedroom communities for people who commuted to Baltimore or Washington, D.C. The towns offered a much lower level of crime and density of population, as well as interesting mixes of architecture.

Carrie thought about all this as she walked briskly along the sidewalk, toward David's building, which seemed to straddle the invisible border between the posh Inner Harbor shopping district and the battle zones of the inner city. It wasn't so much her own safety that she thought of, as David's. For he lived and worked here. If what Frank had said was right, David rubbed shoulders daily with an element of society she'd hopefully never have to deal with—violent criminals. He seemed to think she should be afraid of him.

Rather than being frightened of David, she admired him for what he was trying to do. He was a contemporary lawman, a Wyatt Earp for the nineties.

Carrie pushed the button beside the label Adams. A moment later a familiar voice greeted her.

"That you, Carrie?"

"Yes." She smiled broadly, although she knew he couldn't see her. "Shall I come up?"

"Be right down. I have something...well, it's a surprise."

She let her hand drop away from the buzzer. A surprise, she thought, curious and pleased. Perhaps it had something to do with what they were having for dinner...or it might mean David had decided after all to eat out instead of cooking in. She wondered if he cooked at all. She'd never had much time for elaborate food preparation, but she enjoyed an occasional chance to experiment with friends' recipes.

The heavy metal door to her left, fitted with a formidable-looking security grille, clacked open. She turned to see David walk through. His dark-brown hair was smoothly combed back off of his forehead, and his blue eyes were bright with anticipation at seeing her.

He stepped forward, and before she realized what he intended, he bent and kissed her quickly, lightly, on the cheek.

"I'm glad you could come," he murmured.

He clasped her right hand between his wide palms, and she decided she liked the feeling of his rough-textured hands on hers.

"The roses were lovely," she said.

"They were deserved. Are you hungry?"

"Are you kidding, after flying all day and surviving on a bagel and an apple? I could eat a horse."

"Would you settle for oven-fried chicken?"

"Absolutely."

He held the door open for her, then placed one hand in the curve of her back as he escorted her down the hallway toward an elevator. "We're on the eighth floor," he commented.

It took her four or five seconds to catch his slip, if it was a slip. "We?" She looked up and over her shoulder at him as he followed her onto the elevator.

"Yes, I thought I'd better come down and warn you. We won't be dining alone tonight."

She was surprised to feel vaguely disappointed. With other men, she'd welcomed group dates as a distraction from the possible dangers of romance. "Who are your other guests?"

"They aren't exactly guests," he said sheepishly. "I probably should have told you over the phone—my children will be with us tonight."

"Really?" She grinned at him, genuinely excited. "What are their names again?"

"Jason and Tammy. I wasn't sure they'd be with me tonight. My wife was scheduled to pick them up this afternoon, but she called only an hour ago and asked me to keep them overnight." He hesitated. "I'm afraid they're a little wound up. I don't bring home many dinner guests."

Carrie winked at him. "I feel honored. Actually, I wouldn't be any more pleased if you'd told me Tom Cruise and Keanu Reeves were joining us for dinner."

David threw back his head and laughed. "Now, that's saying something. I know two female police officers who'd turn in their badges for one night with either of those two."

"I'm sure it would be an interesting experience, but I love children." She looked up at him. "If it wasn't for my business, I'd have a busload of my own."

He was watching her intently as she spoke. "Your dad's legacy—Monroe Air."

"Flying is like breathing," she said, and let out a long sigh. "But it doesn't leave much time for raising children."

"I sort of figured you liked kids. I saw you fussing over that little boy when I first stepped on your plane the other day." He pushed the button marked with an eight, and the elevator began to climb. "It was as if the rest of the world had gone away, and there was only you and him, locked in your own private world."

"That's one of the great things about kids," Carrie said. "They can take you away from all your troubles if you let them."

David didn't respond, but he looked thoughtful.

The elevator stopped and the doors screeched open. "Come on and meet them, then," he said. "I just hope they don't scare you off with their enthusiasm. They can be a little overwhelming at times."

As he used his key to let her in, she noted how security

conscious he was. Even though he'd known he wouldn't be leaving the building, he'd locked the apartment behind him.

Swinging open the door, David motioned her inside. There was no foyer or front hall; the front door opened directly into a small living room decorated with a mixed bag of practical, masculine furnishings. The upholstered couch and chairs were shades of beige and brown plaid. The end tables and coffee table appeared to be of a hardwood, impervious to children's spills and gouges.

Carrie stood just inside the door, expecting to be rushed from two sides, but the place was so quiet she could hear David's footsteps coming up behind her on the carpet.

He called out, "Hey! Anyone home?"

There was no answer.

"Jennifer may have taken them upstairs to her place for a few minutes. She's their baby-sitter." He shrugged and moved around an armchair, then looked puzzled as he stepped through an obstacle course of toys.

Carrie followed him. Strewn across the carpet were a half-dozen dolls, a cardboard-covered picture book, two red plastic trucks and a handful of puzzle pieces.

"Jennifer?" David called.

"Sup'wise!" a tiny voice shouted.

Its owner, a roly-poly little girl with long, straight blond hair, who wore a pink gingham sundress, flung herself at David's knees.

"Hey, you weren't supposed to say that until he started getting mad!" A boy, a head taller than the girl, popped up from behind the couch.

In the kitchen doorway, a teenage girl meekly appeared. "I'm sorry about the mess, Mr. Adams. They wanted to surprise you and your..." She blushed, as if embarrassed by the idea that someone as old as her employer might have a girlfriend. "You and your friend."

"Wasn't that a neat trick?" Jason cried, running from behind the couch to tug at his father's arms. "Throwing all the stuff around was *my* idea. You thought we'd finish picking up while you were gone and just sit here waiting for you. But we made more mess and disappeared, instead!''

"The trail of destruction was a decidedly creative touch," David said in a stern voice. "Unfortunately, it isn't a very nice way to impress a guest." Despite his tone, an amused twinkle lit his dark eyes. "Carrie, I'd like you to meet my son, Jason, and daughter, Tammy. Jennifer is their brave and dedicated baby-sitter."

"Hi," Carrie said.

The two children smiled bashfully at her.

Carrie was amazed at the sharp contrasts working within David. He had been polite, sociable to her in the restaurant and on their way up to his apartment, but she always sensed the effort he put into monitoring everything he said, every move he made. Yet around his children, he seemed to mellow, unwind. It struck her that this was a side of Detective David Adams few people ever saw.

She felt privileged.

David bent down and scooped up one child under each arm, then carried them to the couch, where he dropped them from a few feet above the cushions. Squealing with delight, they bounced to their feet and begged for more.

Jennifer cleared her throat and announced in a very grown-up voice that her mother expected her to be home by seven o'clock. "I can help the kids pick up in the living room before I leave," she offered.

David shook his head. "I think these two demons should take care of their toys on their own tonight. I'm sure you had very little to do with the evil plot." He eyed his son as he handed the sitter several bills. "Thanks, as always, Jenny."

Halfway to the door, the teenager turned around. "If you want me again later, like if you two want to go out somewhere, just call."

"I expect we'll be in for the night," he said. "Thanks anyway."

She nodded, then glanced shyly toward Carrie as she twirled a tendril of ginger-colored hair around one finger. "Detective Adams told me you fly planes. I think that's cool."

Carrie opened her mouth to respond, but the girl ducked out the door without waiting for a reply. Carrie laughed, shaking her head. "She's a gem. Where did you ever find her?"

"She lives just upstairs. Her mom has four kids to support, and Jennifer's the oldest. They can use the baby-sitting money, and the girl's absolutely dependable. The kids love her, too. We're very lucky to have her—aren't we, guys?" David reached out and tickled his children until they squirmed in agony and rolled off the couch onto the floor. "Now, pick up your things and wash your hands for supper. It should be ready soon."

"You said we were having *dinner,*" the boy corrected his father, flashing him a smug grin.

"Yes, dinner," David admitted with a sigh, glancing at Carrie. "Jason's a stickler for detail. Come on, you two. Get to it!"

Jason and Tammy swooped across the room, screeching happily as they raced each other to one toy after another. Jason could have beaten his sister to every one of them, Carrie supposed. The little boy was fast and had overcome the babyish clumsiness that caused his little sister to periodically struggle for balance. But he seemed to intentionally stall himself now and then so that his sister could win a few times.

Since the children seemed to be doing fine on their own, Carrie started to follow David into the kitchen, to see if he needed help. She hadn't gone two paces before she felt something dragging at the hem of her skirt.

She looked down, assuming she'd snagged herself on a piece of furniture. A sunny little face surrounded by tendrils of blond hair peered up at her. "What is it, Tammy?" she asked.

"How do you know my name?"

"Your father told me. Remember?" Carrie knelt and tenderly framed the little girl's face with her palms. "Can I call you 'Tammy'?"

"You're a stranger," her brother broke in. "He shouldn't have told you our names."

"Carrie isn't a stranger. She's our guest," David said, hurrying into the dining room with a basket of corn muffins and a platter of steaming, oven-crisped chicken pieces.

"My teacher says strangers can be someone you see a lot, even a next-door neighbor," the boy persisted solemnly.

Carrie couldn't help thinking how much he resembled his father in his on-duty mode.

David looked irritated. "Listen, Jase, Carrie's our guest, not a—"

"No, that's all right," she said quickly, remembering how many Safe Kid public-service ads she'd seen broadcast on TV. She turned back again to Jason. "I don't blame you a bit for being cautious." She propped one hip on the arm of the couch to bring her level down nearer his. "Trusting people is a very serious thing, even for grown-ups."

Especially for grown-ups, she thought. How easy it had been for her friends and her parents to trust in a mate, only to discover that love was fleeting. But the kind of trust Jason was talking about was, admittedly, different. It was the kind that endangered the lives of innocent children daily.

"You shouldn't trust anyone until you know that person very, very well," she said.

Jason gave an emphatic nod. "That's just what my teachers say."

Carrie nodded and patted his shoulder, which he still held stiffly, despite his father's disapproving frown. "I want to be your friend," Carrie said, "but you can tell me when that's okay with you."

"Good," Jason said solemnly.

Tammy stepped between them. "I'll be your friend *now!*" she announced, flinging her arms up and around Carrie's neck.

Carrie laughed, hugging the little girl back. The pair were irresistible. The serious older brother who was just becoming aware of a darker side of life. The little girl, only a blink past babyhood, still wanting affection and afraid her big brother might say something to make their father's friend go away with hurt feelings. Tammy would be the politician of the two, Carrie decided. The one who'd patch up misunderstanding and arguments by using her love. She'd also be the one most easily hurt.

Carrie was deeply touched. But when she smiled up at David, the expression on his face surprised her. He was staring at her, as if both pleased and frightened by what he was seeing. Quickly he turned away and disappeared into the kitchen.

"Finish picking up now," Carrie whispered, releasing herself from Tammy's plump arms. "Go help your brother so we can eat dinner."

"Supper," Jason corrected her, then smiled bashfully at his own joke before diving for a puzzle piece.

Carrie found David in the kitchen. He was scooping mashed potatoes into a serving bowl. He looked as if he knew what he was doing in a kitchen.

"Did you cook this meal yourself?" she asked.

"Would that surprise you?"

"Moderately. You seem more physically oriented. I always think of cooking as a delicate art." She picked a cucumber slice out of the salad bowl and nibbled at it.

"What you mean is, I bust bad guys for a living, so I can't be domestic."

"I didn't say that."

She studied him for several moments. His long, lean legs were covered in denim—the jeans new, she guessed by their indigo hue and crispness. With them, he wore a plaid casual shirt, the cuffs rolled up to reveal muscled forearms, lightly brushed by dark hair. Watching a man like David prepare the food she would soon eat struck her as provocative. Cooking for another person was, she'd always thought, an intimate act, a way of showing you cared about the person.

"I only started cooking at home two years ago," he admitted, sticking a serving spoon into the fluffy, white pile of potatoes, sending a stream of melting butter down its sides. He handed her the bowl. "Table," he said, pointing the way as he picked up the salad and another dish of green peas. "When my wife and I split, I wanted to keep the kids here with me half the time. I refused to do the typical 'single-dad, fast-food' thing. I wanted them to eat right, have home-cooked meals, at least when they were with me. I was pretty sure Sheila wasn't cooking for them."

Carrie looked for signs in his face of the bitterness that tinged his voice. But his expression was unreadable. "I take it the divorce wasn't an amicable one."

"Hardly," he said, setting down the food he'd carried.

"I'm sorry—I shouldn't have asked," she said quickly. "That's the way nearly every marriage I know has ended."

"An uplifting thought."

She seemed to be saying all the wrong things. Carrie set the potatoes on the table and wrapped her fingers around the head rail of an oak chair. "Shut up, Carrie," she told herself under her breath.

David turned and stared at her, apparently having heard. He gave her a puzzled smile. "Do you often scold yourself?"

"No one else left to do it," she said blithely. "Don't you sometimes talk to yourself?"

"I hadn't really noticed," he said slowly. "Although I do carry on conversations with my kids, about things that I'm sure they couldn't possibly understand."

She tilted her head to one side and observed his solemn blue eyes until she felt compelled to look away. "Well, I don't have Jason and Tammy to chat with, so I have to be content with my own company." She gazed at the plastic, flowered tablecloth, set with plain white department-store china and utensils in a simple stainless-steel pattern. The table appeared warm and welcoming and like...like a gathering place for a family.

A tiny spot inside Carrie warmed and hummed.

Suddenly she was aware of David standing close beside her. "But that's not the way you see your future, is it? You said you want a family of your own."

Her spine tensed, causing her shoulders to stiffen and cramp. "Someday I'll have my own children. But I have no desire to marry, so that makes things a little more complicated. Until I work out my financial situation, I can't seriously consider starting a family."

He nodded, studying her face from over her shoulder, feature by feature, as if looking for something behind the hopeful smile that was all she would allow him to see. "We're more alike than I would have thought," he said quietly.

She laughed uneasily. His closeness made it difficult for her to think. He was confusing her, saying only a fraction of what, she was sure, was on his mind.

David stepped around in front of Carrie and took the fingertips of her right hand in his. "Neither of us trusts marriage. Our reasons may differ, but the basic idea is the same. Love doesn't last, does it?"

She shook her head.

"No," he said, his voice clipped, bordering on harsh, even as he turned over her hand and traced light circles in her palm with the side of his thumb. "But there is one kind of love that's impossible to destroy—the love of a child for a parent, or a parent's love for his or her child."

"Maybe that's the only real kind of love that exists," Carrie heard herself whisper.

"Maybe so." David's eyes darkened, as he stepped back from her and let go of her hand.

"There was something more you were going to say," she guessed.

His glance dropped away, and he sighed. "No. Not now. It will have to wait until after dinner."

They sat, the four of them, around the dining room table. A man, a woman and two young children.

The arrangement felt sublimely natural to Carrie. She couldn't imagine why any woman would walk away from a man like David and the children they'd made together. Yet it happened every day...it had happened in her family.

She tried to put the heavy thoughts from her mind and enjoy the meal.

The oven-fried chicken was skinless but juicy and well seasoned. She assumed David was conscious of eating from a low-fat menu, not only for reasons of health but to control his weight. No doubt he had to stay in shape to do his job.

He gave each child a small portion of peas and of lightly

buttered carrots. He seemed to expect them to eat all their vegetables, therefore the scant servings. Tammy played with her peas but dutifully swallowed them, one at a time, while making sure her father noticed.

"Good job there, Tam," he said with a smile, and she beamed at him.

Jason mixed his peas into the fluffy, white pile of mashed potatoes, then forked them down together. His father winked conspiratorially at him.

Carrie ate with relish, helping herself to a third piece of chicken. "This is delicious," she groaned, licking her fingers. "What's your secret?"

"Crushed cornflakes," he told her with a grin. "Makes a great crunchy topping."

She nodded and ate at a leisurely pace, enjoying the playful conversation between David and his children. The innocence, laughter and teasing reminded her of her best friend Patty's family. She drove to West Virginia to visit her high school chum a couple of times each year. The first three years had been pure pleasure; then Patty and Mark had started having trouble, and Carrie began to feel that her presence increased the tension in the household. She hadn't suggested another visit in the past six months, and Patty hadn't invited her. It was still a toss-up whether the couple would make it, but Carrie feared divorce was imminent.

She looked up, torn by dismal thoughts, to find David studying her again.

"A penny?" he murmured, tapping his forehead.

"I was just thinking—" How could she throw a damper on this lovely gathering? "Just thinking what a beautiful family you have."

Jason looked up at her. "Mommy's not here."

Carrie could feel the chill across the table from David. But his voice was steady and emotionless when he spoke.

"She's working tonight. That's why she couldn't be with you."

Jason looked at his sister, who was too involved in nibbling tiny bits of chicken from a wing bone to pay attention to the conversation. "I don't think so," he said, shaking his head.

"Where do you think she is?" David asked him tightly.

Oh, David, don't go there, Carrie thought, not wanting to see him hurt.

Jason shrugged. "Out. She goes out a lot."

David nodded, his jaw tight, his eyes darkening to a stormy blue. He started to open his mouth as if to say something more, but closed his lips with obvious effort. After folding his napkin, he placed it firmly on the table, as if by simply dropping it there, he might run the risk of it scampering away.

"Never mind," he murmured, as much to himself as to anyone in the room. "How about you two run along and get into your pj's so you can have a story before bed."

Carrie sat in silence at the table until the children had left. She was sure the children wouldn't normally be put to bed right after dinner. David must have been terribly upset. She could hear Jason telling his sister that if they asked real, real nice, maybe the lady would read to them. Tammy squealed with delight.

"They're beautiful children," she whispered to David when he didn't get up from the table. "Absolutely charming."

He surprised her by propping his elbows on the table and rubbing his hands over his face. "Yes, they are beautiful, and perfect, and precious. And I love them more than anything in this world...more than life itself."

"That's all that matters, right?" she said gently. "The love."

"I'm afraid it's not enough for some people."

She supposed that he hadn't intended to say anything more about his wife. But David's emotions must have been running so high he couldn't hold in his fears and frustrations any longer.

By the time he finished relating the details of his meeting with his lawyer, Carrie's eyes were prickling with hot moisture, her fingertips twitching with anger at the injustice of what his ex-wife was trying to do.

"Your lawyer is sure Sheila and her family would actually use your job to take Jason and Tammy away from you?" she asked.

"Without batting an eye."

"That's terrible, inhuman, stupid!" She spit out the words, not thinking how they might sound. She didn't know David's ex-wife, but she believed the woman must have a cruel streak as wide as the bay to try to take his children away from him…and Carrie said so.

"Sheila's not intentionally cruel," David said slowly, as if he'd often considered the possibility himself. "She's practical. She married me to spite her parents. I was their worst nightmare—a street cop, a commoner who stole the princess from her golden tower. They'd had such high hopes for their only child. She was to marry Newport money, stay in Rhode Island and raise grandchildren for them, who would grow up to carry on family traditions."

"I thought that kind of class snobbery died long ago," Carrie said.

In the background the squeals of the children provided a music that seemed to ease the tension from David's features. His brow smoothed again; the lines around his expressive mouth softened.

"I would have thought so if I hadn't known the Waymans. They cut off Sheila's allowance when she married me against their wishes. As soon as they realized we were having trouble, they offered to restore her carte blanche expense account and provide a house for her and the children if she'd move back to Newport. Sheila would leave her Georgetown friends in a heartbeat if the court hadn't stipulated that the children must remain in Maryland unless both Sheila and I agree to a change. She knows I'd never give my blessing for her to take them away from me."

"And she won't leave without the children?"

David laughed roughly. "She'd leave all right. I don't think she'd miss them at all. But it would do her no good. Her parents aren't as interested in seeing *her* back home as they are in gaining control of their grandchildren. They wouldn't give her a cent if she ran home without them.''

Carrie shook her head. "That's terrible, forcing people to—''

David stood up abruptly, interrupting her. "A person can't be forced into doing something that runs against his or her grain. They can manipulate Sheila because she lets them. Money talks, as far as she's concerned."

"And it doesn't as far as you're concerned?" Carrie rose and started stacking dinner plates. She felt restless, as she often did before a storm broke. When she was airborne, she raced storms to safe ground. Now she had to move and cover space for the same reason.

"Money means nothing to me," he said. "It's only good for the good it can do. I've seen how greed corrupts. Once you let it control your life, you've lost everything. It's why I have to go out on the street and hunt down junkies—so I can hunt down the people who sell them drugs. Money is a drug, as bad or worse than cocaine or heroin.''

"And Sheila's an addict?"

"Yes," he said grimly, "she is, but I no longer feel sorry for her. She's gone too far this time. Way too far."

He turned with a jerk of his wide shoulders and carried off the half-eaten potatoes and vegetables to the kitchen. Carrie followed with an armload of plates and glasses.

She had no idea what to say to David. There was certainly nothing she herself could do to make his situation any better. Yet she knew that if there had been a way, she'd have willingly offered to help.

David was a good man—a brave, principled, dedicated cop who stood between crime and his city. He defended the innocent on a daily basis. There ought to be someone to defend him when life turned against him.

David Adams didn't deserve to lose his children.

She took the dishes to the sink, squirted liquid detergent over them and automatically began washing them with runaway energy. She wasn't aware of anything in the room. A sense of injustice and powerlessness filled her as she scrubbed viciously at specks of food on the glossy white dishes.

A wide hand reached across her line of vision and turned off the steaming flow of water. "I have a dishwasher."

Carrie looked up slowly, her fingertips dripping with suds, and met David's penetrating gaze.

"Sorry," he said, "I guess I got carried away with my own troubles. This was supposed to be a fun night."

Carrie smiled softly at him. "You needed to talk about what was going on with your children. I'm glad I was here for you."

She could have sworn he never blinked. His eyes felt to her as if they were pulling her into a secret part of him—a place she wasn't sure she dared go. "You're a very compassionate woman. It's easy to talk to you, Carrie."

"Good," she said, trying to lighten her tone but failing.

David took her hands in his, ignoring the slippery suds that dripped on the floor between them. "Carrie, what would you say if I told you there might be a way I could hold on to my children?"

She lifted her eyes to his and smiled. "Why, that's wonderful!"

"There would be a price to pay. A high emotional price."

She sensed that he was weighing each word before his lips formed it. For some reason, this part of their discussion was even more difficult for him.

"There probably isn't a price that's too high when it comes to a parent protecting his right to be with his child."

He nodded. "That's exactly how I feel."

With a sudden blur of bodies and squeals, Jason and Tammy burst into the kitchen, each waving a book.

"It's my turn to pick!" Jason shouted.

"My turn!" Tammy echoed, shoving her brightly colored picture book in front of his, her little face puckered, forecasting tears.

David closed his eyes for just a second, as if to recover his balance.

"We'll finish talking in a little while," Carrie suggested.

"I have a feeling this is a two-book night. I've got a flight tomorrow morning, but I'll hang around until you finish story time."

He smiled at her gratefully. "And you claim you've never been a parent."

Carrie watched the tall police detective being dragged by his big hands from the room by his children, who were chattering excitedly, trying to make a case for which story should be read first. She smiled, thinking she'd never seen a more beautiful sight, not on the ground or from the air. With a sigh, she looked around the kitchen and decided she could easily finish the dishes before two stories were up.

Chapter 5

Carrie grew more and more excited for David as she wiped down the kitchen countertops, listening to the deep, soothing sound of his voice from the children's bedrooms. If there was some way he could hold on to Jason and Tammy, it would be wonderful. Actually, it would only be justice. She couldn't imagine a man being more devoted to his kids.

By the time he'd tucked them into their beds and turned out the lights at the far end of the hallway, she was sitting in the living room, waiting for him. She'd expected him to join her on the couch and pick up where he'd left off with their conversation.

Instead, he crossed the room, plucked the remote control off the top of the television and clicked it on. "There's a romantic old movie from the thirties on cable, starring William Powell and Irene Dunne—one of the Thin Man series. Want to stay and watch it with me?" he asked.

She studied his profile. The lines of his face were strong, unyielding. But Carrie sensed an uneasiness beneath the surface. Something was making him reluctant to return to the topic they'd been discussing earlier.

"Sounds like fun," she said.

Carrie was glad she stayed. She howled with delight as the two dramatic actors outwitted each other and cut up for the camera in their unique, sophisticated style. They were romantic, fun and glamorous—and she couldn't imagine enjoying herself more. By the time the movie was over, David had maneuvered himself across the couch and she cuddled against his shoulder. Her ribs ached from her having laughed so hard.

"I take it you liked that," he said, his voice lightly husky as he gazed down at her.

"They were wonderful. Why doesn't anyone make movies like that anymore?"

"No violence, no nudity, no multimillion-dollar special effects? Who'd watch them?"

"I would," she said firmly.

"Me, too," he agreed. "'Specially if you were here with me."

For a moment, she thought he was going to kiss her, but his ever-vigilant gaze shifted, sweeping the room, and stuck on the clock over the mantel.

"Damn, look at that—it's nearly midnight. And you said you have to fly tomorrow morning."

"Eight o'clock sharp," she said, reluctantly prying herself out of the comfortable curl of David's shoulder and arm. "I really should get some sleep."

She felt him watching her as she paused before twin brass frames, each holding a baby picture. As she stared at the plump, grinning infants—one in blue, the other in pink—she knew she was stalling in the hope he'd open up to her again. Her curiosity had shifted into overdrive. She knew she would never get to sleep if he didn't tell her how he intended to keep his children. What if he was considering something drastic? Like taking the children and leaving Baltimore and his job behind—running away with them.

It would mean a life of hiding. A life of deception with no security for the children or for him.

"Jason and Tammy?" she asked, tracing a finger around the gold-colored frames.

"Yup."

"They're precious. Remarkable."

"Do you go this crazy over every child you run into?"

He was teasing her, but she didn't mind.

She grinned and reached for her purse in the straight-back wooden chair by the front door as he pushed himself up off of the couch and moved toward her. "I'm not usually this bad. Every other teenage girl in America baby-sat for spending money or looked after younger brothers or sisters. If my parents did anything intelligent while they were together, it was to *not* have more children, so there were no siblings. And I was too busy learning to fly an airplane to take baby-sitting jobs. From the time I could walk I was sitting on my dad's lap, holding on to the yoke of a plane."

"He sounds great."

"He was. He was a wonderful, dear man. I miss him more than I can say." Before her throat closed up from the sudden jolt of emotion, she forced herself on. "All I ever cared about was flying, David. I spent every minute of my spare time hanging out at the airport—running errands for other pilots who shared hangar space with Dad, studying flight manuals, preparing for my twin engine instrument rating, doing odd jobs for anyone who'd talk planes with me.

"I answered the phone for Rose, who is still our receptionist, while she took her breaks. I handed Frank, Dad's mechanic, his wrenches, and he taught me their names and uses. Every summer, I flew my father's routes with him, to the Eastern Shore and back to Baltimore. During the school year, after classes, I'd beg rides to the airport from older kids who had their driver's licenses. There was always a chance I might get there in time to fly a late-afternoon or evening charter with my dad. I couldn't get enough of the sky...still can't."

Carrie slung her purse over her shoulder and turned toward the door as memories of those carefree days glowed within her, making the pain of loss sting a little less.

David stepped between her and the door, as if to prevent her from leaving. "It must be amazing to love something that much."

"You love your children."

"That's not the same."

He took her right hand in his and traced the spaces between her fingers with his own index finger. She once again had the impression he was thinking very hard—daring to say out loud only a fraction of what he was thinking.

"Loving people is something you can't help," he said carefully. "You just do it because it happens somewhere inside you. They either love you back or they don't." He sucked in a long breath, then slowly let it out, his eyes fixing on hers. "*Things,* they can't love you back. It's a one-sided relationship from the beginning, and you know it. You don't expect anything more from a thing, like the sky, than it being what it is. No disappointments."

Carrie closed her eyes and leaned back against the wall, letting her mind drift around David's words, concentrating only on the mesmerizing sensation of his touch on her hand and on the effect of his words on her heart. Then she felt his breath on her face, and she knew, without opening her eyes, that he definitely was going to kiss her this time.

She kept her eyes shut. Waited.

At last his warm lips settled gently over hers. She soared, as if guiding the *Bay Lady* into a lazy loop through blue skies. Free. Alive. She felt the heady power of flight lifting her, as their kiss deepened, drawing her higher…higher still.

Flying, she'd always thought, was a little like playing God, although she'd never presume as much. Up in the clouds, she was mistress of her fate. A gentle pull on the yoke, and she zoomed into the heavens, restricted only by gravity and the mechanical limitations of her aircraft. A steady push on the U-shaped steering mechanism, and she would plummet straight to Earth. David's kiss made her feel just as empowered. But in far less control.

When she opened her eyes, David was standing over her, observing her with a curious expression, his arms gently encircling her.

"Maybe the sky can't love me back," Carrie said softly.

"But it's never deserted me." As soon as she'd said the words, she wished them back into her subconscious.

"Are you talking about your mother, your father or a former lover?"

She didn't answer, couldn't answer.

"Or does this have something to do with a relationship that's just getting started?" David whispered.

She tensed. It wasn't fair that he could pick up on her emotions before she was aware of them herself. "I didn't mean my parents. And I've never been left by a man. I've always been the one to break off a relationship, so I can't claim I've experienced that kind of hurt."

His eyes darkened to a midnight blue, intensified with understanding. He was still holding her, as if reluctant to let her go. As though he were afraid that if he allowed her to pass through the door, he would never see her again. "So you always backed out when you feared you were getting in too deep, when the risk was too great and you began to feel threatened."

"Yes," she said, hoping he'd leave it at that.

He drew her closer, laying a hand on the side of her head and gently pressing her cheek to his chest. She allowed him to enfold her, and he started talking again, but his voice was remote, barely audible, as if he'd divided himself into two parts to separate himself from painful memories of his own.

"My parents were..." He moved his shoulders, shifting her slightly against his chest. "Well, I thought my dad was wonderful. My mother...she didn't cope too well after he was killed."

She turned her head to watch his face, but it seemed perfectly composed. "What happened to her?"

"She tried, but maybe I reminded her too much of him. I don't know. I ended up living with my grandparents."

"How sad," she murmured.

"Don't be. They adopted me. She lives in New Jersey, only a few hours' drive from Baltimore, but we hardly ever see each other. I think she's happy now—she has a new husband. I try to stay out of her life.

"But Pap and Moms were the best. They worked hard and made sure I did, too. They raised me to respect people and protect those who can't protect themselves. They got me into the University of Maryland, and we squeaked by with the help of a few loans."

"They sound like wonderful people."

"They were. They even saw to it that there was money put aside in a trust fund for Jason and Tammy when they came along. That was three years ago, just before they died within six months of each other."

Carrie's heart went out to him. Life hadn't been easy for David Adams, as a boy or as a man. "How did they manage a trust fund, when they had so little money of their own?"

"My grandfather had the foresight to put all his property—the house, some stocks and savings bonds he'd accumulated over fifty years—into a revocable trust, naming me as trustee. When he died, the state couldn't touch any of it. Legally, it wasn't part of his estate—it already belonged to me and the kids."

"And you haven't used the money for the children yet?"

"No, I figured Pap worked hard, protecting that nest egg for us. It should be used for something very important. I make enough to support my kids. We're doing fine. I didn't want to touch the trust until they were ready for college—then the money would be there for them, with the accumulated interest from the bank, and they could go to any school their grades deserved." He frowned. "But now I'm wondering if there might be a more important use for at least some of it."

"Which is?" She wondered if this had something to do with their earlier conversation. Maybe the trust money was part of his plan to hold on to his children.

She tried to see through the heavy curtain that seemed to have fallen over his eyes. But he intentionally looked away.

"You've got to be up early," he said abruptly.

He sounded all business suddenly. No emotion. Back to being the cop.

Carrie frowned. Why the sudden change in his mood? What was weighing so heavily on his mind? The tension she sensed in his body as he moved away from her indicated she'd get no answer, even if she asked for an explanation.

So she didn't ask, but she wondered about what he'd almost said all the way home.

The next morning, Carrie lay in her bed, staring up at the white plaster ceiling, remembering David's final, cool goodnight kiss at his door. She'd insisted he not walk her to her car but stay with the children. There were still a lot of tourists returning to the parking garage from the Inner Harbor. She'd be fine.

Their last kiss kept replaying through her mind, gnawing at her. She'd felt David check his passion and purposefully move her away from him. She wished she knew what was going on in his head...why everything about the way he acted around her had changed so quickly from warm and confident to remote and wary. Had she done or said something to offend him? She was sure she hadn't. But if not that, what?

Carrie turned over in bed, imagining what David's next kiss would be like, if it ever came. Perhaps all that was needed was time. Time for them to learn to trust each other enough to become... To become what? Lovers?

The thought sent lovely chills through her body, and she curled up within the smooth sheets, shivering pleasurably at the thought of David's hands on her body, touching her in ways she'd ached to be touched all her adult life.

David took his cup of coffee to his desk and sat down in front of assorted yellow statement forms, incident reports, evidence documentation and mileage logs that formed the case file on Andrew Rainey. He stared blindly at the mountain of paperwork, blocking out the noises of a couple of dozen other men and women in the open squad room. The case was threatening to turn into a red-ball—what they called an investigation that became political, too hot to handle yet too controversial to ignore.

If Greg White, the police reporter from the *Sun*, caught wind of a fraction of what was on David's desk, there would be one whopper of an article the very next day. Then the mayor would be on the phone with the commissioner, and everyone in the department would be running for cover. Because the D.A. had changed his mind and told the commissioner they hadn't given him enough hard evidence for him to bring Rainey to trial.

But, as important as it was for him to concentrate on getting something solid on Rainey, when he looked at the paperwork all he could see was Carrie's sweet face.

The way she'd acted when they'd parted the night before had confused him. He could see his own desire mirrored in her eyes. And he'd known in that instant, with a clarity that surprised him, that they would be good, very good, together in bed. He'd longed to sweep her off her feet and carry her into his bedroom, lie beside her on his bed and make love to her for a long, long time.

Every nerve in his body, every pulse from his libido demanded it. And a voice from somewhere deep within his soul told him he must.

Yet he hadn't made love to her for two reasons.

First, he was certain he would frighten her off if he approached her too quickly. Something in the way she'd responded to his kisses and held herself in his arms made him unusually cautious.

Second, he wasn't absolutely sure in his own mind what role he most wanted her to play in his life. Because one thing had become clear to him last night. Carrie Monroe was *the* perfect woman for the job of stepmother to his children. With her at his side and a home in a better neighborhood he couldn't lose in court. Sheila and her parents would be beaten—no contest.

On the other hand, if he asked Carrie to stand in as his wife, he'd have to do it in a way that left no room for misunderstandings. He wasn't going to marry for real ever again. He didn't trust marriage any more than she did, because it was based on fiction—a romantic brand of love that didn't exist in the real world. An everlasting love. A lie.

So he had to choose between having an affair with Carrie Monroe or proposing a business venture to her that would benefit both of them. That meant there was no middle ground. One or the other, Davey-boy, he told himself. You can't have both.

"Hey, what's cookin', partner?"

He looked up at Pete, who was standing over his desk.

When the younger cop had transferred into the department from a street beat, David had taken an instant disliking to him. He was a know-it-all, a punk with stringy brown hair and bad skin, who smoked and drank and talked too much and looked like a washout waiting to happen.

But after a few weeks of being paired up with Pete on a special detail, he'd learned that most of Detective Pete Turner's public image was show. He was cut out perfectly for narcdom. With his down-and-out, desperate attitude, he blended into the drug subculture. He talked the talk, walked the walk. He was gold to the department, and David had asked to keep him as his partner after the detail wrapped up.

"Nothing's cooking," David answered on a groan. "Just thinking…and getting a headache." He waved a hand at the pile of documents on his desk in disgust.

Someone's phone was ringing nearby, but no one was answering it. A female cop shouted across the room at her partner, and they both ran from the room. The place was a zoo today.

"No sweat. We got a coupla good leads. Check 'em out today." Pete landed a playful punch on David's shoulder. "You have that meeting with your lawyer?"

"Yup. Bad news."

Pete sat on the corner of the desk and picked up two pencils. He rattled out a drumbeat on the few inches of blotter visible between papers. "How so?"

"Sheila's found a way to take the kids away from me."

"What's she doing now?"

David explained to him while he jammed papers into a brown accordion folder and slipped a wide rubber band around it to keep everything inside. "The thing is," he said in conclusion, "I might be able to beat her at her own game by getting married again."

Pete stared at him in disbelief. "Talk about the cure being worse than the disease!"

"No, I mean, I could *pay* a woman to marry me, just for a year. In that time, I'd move out of the city, get the kids set up in some nice suburban school where the judge can see they're safe. I'll be the perfect dad. The only thing I won't give up is police work, and I don't see how he can hold that against me."

"Man, you're asking for trouble." Pete shifted from drumming the blotter to drumming the desktop, which made a harsher, less musical sound.

"Tell me about it. But I'm going to check out all sides of the scenario before I make a final decision."

"I dunno," Pete said, concentrating on his rhythm, syncopating the beats now. "See, you can't just pretend to get married. It's got to be the real thing to convince a judge and Sheila's lawyer. You've got to have the papers to prove it, and witnesses who'll swear it's for real. If dear Sheila's got herself the same lawyer who handled the divorce, well…the guy's sharp. He'll check on stuff."

"Okay, other than a marriage certificate, what else?" David asked. He was getting a sick feeling in his stomach.

"Like, he'll do what we'd do on a case. He'll watch you two, or hire someone to do it for him. He'll check to see if you're spending time together, looking like newlyweds, living in the same house. Hell, the bozo might even try to plant a microphone or surveillance camera in the bedroom. There are private detectives who specialize in that stuff—really get into the high-tech gear."

David laughed at the absurdity of it all.

Pete stopped middrumroll and scrunched up his face, considering. "Maybe that would be overkill. The point is, you've got to produce an honest-to-God marriage certificate. And that means all sorts of legal complications. Like this broad you hire. She could claim it was a real marriage, file for a divorce, then demand half your pension and property."

"We can sign a written agreement at the outset," David said quickly.

"A prenuptial agreement? If Sheila gets hold of a copy, it will blow your whole scheme out of the water. And there are other complications." He pointed one of his pencils at David. "What if this woman, whoever she is, gets it into her head that she's in love with you and wants to *stay* married? Then you got another mess on your hands."

David nodded thoughtfully. "I'd considered that. And there's the other side of it. What if she's ready to go her way, but I've gotten used to having her around? What if I don't *want* her to leave?"

"Sounds like you have someone specific in mind. She's got a killer bod, right?" Pete chuckled. "Well then, my friend, you'll get your heart tromped on—again. I tell you, it's not worth it. Better you just go to bed with the chick and get her out of your system, then handle the kid stuff another way."

David looked up at his friend, his heart feeling like a lead weight in his chest. "That's just it. What about my kids? How do I hold on to them without leaving my job?"

Pete took a deep breath and dropped the pencils into a tomato soup can that had been decorated with crayon-covered construction paper. They clunked when they hit the bottom. "Darned if I know, partner. Come on, the lieutenant wants to see us in his office. Maybe after he talks us into a coma we'll come up with something."

David didn't hear half of what Lieutenant Rogers said to them during the half-hour briefing in the shift commander's office. It was only when he felt a firm hand come down on his arm that he focused on the other man's life-toughened face and chased thoughts of Carrie and his children from his head.

"You're not paying attention," Rogers accused, fixing David with a solemn glare. "This is important."

"Sorry, got a lot on my mind," David mumbled.

"I was just telling you two—" he nodded toward Pete, as well "—that I'm concerned with rumors we've been hearing the past day or so. I know you're out there on the streets, interviewing snitches and contacts, trying to lock down the case against Rainey. But word's out that the guy's kid brother, Carl, is headed back from the West Coast.''

"So?" David asked.

"So the guy sounds like trouble. If the talk on the street is right, Carl worships his big brother, and will probably do whatever he can to screw up the case so Andrew can walk. If he can't do that, he'll find a way to pay back whoever he figures is responsible for his brother being in jail.''

"That's us!" Pete declared, flashing a proud grin.

"Me, more than you," David acknowledged. "I'm the one eyewitness from the sting."

"Right," Rogers said. "He'll come after you, Adams, if he goes after anyone. You're the key to the case. Without your statement, the whole shebang folds. But Pete's with you most of the time, so he's at risk, too. What I'm trying to say is, I want both of you to be careful out there. Do what you have to do to get the evidence we need, but don't take chances. Got that?"

"Got it," David said.

"Yeah, yeah, yeah," muttered Pete.

After spending the rest of the morning chasing down dead-end leads, David and Pete stopped for sandwiches and coffee at Lexington Market. They stood in one of the covered walkways between the stalls of ripe local Silver Queen corn and cantaloupes and tomatoes; spicy, steamed crabs; and Italian sausage with grilled red and green peppers. They watched the colorful crowd move past in waves, while eating at a small stand-up bar loaded with condiments and napkins.

"You know, Captain's right," Pete mumbled around a mouthful of hot pastrami smeared with brown mustard between thick slabs of rye bread. "I had a run-in with Carl Rainey 'bout three years back, before you and me got together. The creep's got only half the brains of his big brother, but he's like three times as mean. He won't even think about it if he gets a chance at a payback."

"Then I expect I'll have the pleasure of meeting him, because I'm going to make damn sure big brother Andy doesn't see a Baltimore street for a long, long time.''

Pete chewed and looked around. "Listen, I don't want to see Rainey out and dealing again, any more than you. But you don't know Carl like I do. He's unpredictable. Crazy. You watch your back."

"I thought that's what you were here for." David grinned at him over his foot-long wiener smothered in sauerkraut.

Pete laughed. "Yeah, well, I am. And you're here to watch mine—don't you forget it. But there're times we split up because we have to." He tore off a mammoth chunk of sandwich with his teeth and somehow chewed while talking. "Just you be careful, man. The creep holds grudges. And I hate breakin' in new partners."

The day was so busy Carrie didn't have time to think about anything but booking flights, loading luggage and passengers and flying. It wasn't until the sun had set and Rose and Frank had left for the day that she found herself alone in the hangar with her thoughts. They darted at her from every direction, like birds blown off course in a storm, fluttering helplessly.

Never had she spoken so openly about her feelings as she'd spoken to David Adams. Not to any of her old girlfriends, whom she rarely saw these days, not to Rose, not to Frank.

But what puzzled her just as much as the way she'd unburdened herself to him was the sense that he'd also revealed a great deal of himself to her. And he didn't seem the sort of man who talked easily about himself to casual acquaintances, or even to second dates. He'd obviously been deeply hurt by his divorce and his ex-wife's attempts to take his children from him. A man who'd gone through that sort of hell wouldn't be likely to confide in other women—who had the power to use their knowledge to hurt him again.

No, she couldn't understand why David had been so forthright with her. His training, his work, his personal history—all seemed opposed to any sort of openness. Hadn't he told her he had to be careful whom he dated, for fear of jeopardizing cases?

Yet he'd confided in her, and that made her feel as if he'd given her a precious gift.

As she walked around the dark hangar, locking up for the night, a warm sensation stole into her veins. It was the kind of feeling she'd fought over and over again when she knew she was getting too close to a man. When she knew she should run like hell or risk falling in love.

But this time, she didn't fight it.

Perhaps David's two children, more than any other factor, pulled her toward him. She'd witnessed how genuinely caring he was with them. She could believe that with the right woman, he would be just as caring, as tender, as freely loving. And the temptation of wanting all that was too intoxicatingly sweet to push away.

Maybe her dream of single motherhood could be improved upon. If the right man wanted to have children with her.

The possibility was no more than a blink-of-the-eye glimmer, more of a sensation than a coherent idea. Nevertheless, it frightened her as much as attracted her. It was as if she were gazing down through wispy layers of clouds from fifteen thousand feet at a mist-enshrouded island that didn't show up on any chart. She wanted to swoop low and investigate this exotic, unknown territory. But she was terrified of what she might find hidden beneath verdant treetops and lush, flowering bushes.

Whatever surprises David Adams might have in store for her, would she be able to handle them and survive? Wouldn't she be better off sticking to the course she'd set for herself? If she continued to focus all her energies on her work, she could save Monroe Air and have a family without risking her heart.

A sharp, short sound made her catch her breath and Carrie snapped around. Her eyes narrowed as she peered into the yawning dark patch that marked the opening in one side of the hangar. Stars shone against an onyx sky. She sensed motion within the space, but saw no one.

Snatching her car keys from the desktop, she approached the door, one step at a time, while fingering the tiny canister of pepper spray attached to her key chain. She listened, thought she heard footsteps heavier than her own. Something connected with an empty can and banged it across the paved surface into a steel drum.

"Ouch! Hey, Carrie, you in here?"

She breathed with relief at the sound of David's voice. "Hold still. I'll put on a light." Her heart in her throat, she ran to the place on the wall where she knew she'd find a switch. Flicking three levers upward, she spun around in time to see the handsome detective shield his eyes from the sudden illumination.

"Wow, when you turn on a light, you mean business."

The hangar glared as brightly as if it were midday.

"Planes sometimes have to be worked on at night," she explained, laughing at the faces he was making as his vision adjusted to the fierce blue-white beams from the overhead lamps. "Would you rather step outside and talk?"

"Yeah." He laughed tightly. "Anyway, it's a really nice night."

They strolled a short distance from the hangar to a grassy area behind a row of shed hangars. Here, private planes—two- or four-seaters, some of them featherlight tail-draggers painted vivid colors—were tied down and sheltered beneath a long, low roof. There were no sides to the structure. It was a cheap way of keeping a plane on a field, but didn't offer enough protection for an aging Beechcraft that had to be shielded from the elements and nursed through annual FAA inspections.

"Did you just get off work?" she asked.

"Yeah, I tried calling your house, but you weren't there."

"So you figured this was where you'd find me. I'm that predictable?"

He shrugged. "Guess so."

She noticed he wasn't smiling.

"David, what's wrong? Are the children all right?"

"They're fine. Jennifer's with them."

"But there *is* something wrong," she said, sure now that she wasn't misreading him.

"I've just got a lot on my mind. You know, what I told you about the kids."

He looked away from her, across the dark field. On the far side, where the jet runways angled away from the strips used by smaller planes, a monstrous 747 with its landing lights on lumbered out of the sky with a high-pitched whine and touched ground. Its engines roared a complaint, as if they objected to being shut down.

"I think I've made a decision about the children," he said, "and it involves you."

"Me?"

"Yes, but I'm not sure how to explain." He took a deep breath, then turned and reached for her hand. "I want you to hear me out before you react to what I'm about to say. This will sound strange to you, but believe me I'm serious about it."

"All right," she whispered.

David's eyes looked almost black in the darkness, and they skittered from point to point, as if he didn't trust what the night hid. His nervousness rubbed off on her, and she found herself gripping his hand. She forced the muscles in her hand to ease up, and let her fingers rest lightly within his.

"I told you how desperate I am to hold on to my children...and about the trust fund my grandfather set up for them."

"Yes."

"Well, I've been doing a lot of thinking about that money and how to best use it. College is a long way off for Jason and Tammy, and if I don't have them with me as they grow up, that money may be useless when college time comes."

"You mean, your wife's parents would refuse to let you pay for their education?"

"Exactly. Besides, by that time, if Sheila's parents have their way, Jason and Tammy won't even recognize me. They'll find ways to alienate them from me, to keep me from seeing them. So I'm sure my grandfather would agree to my using as much of the trust money as necessary to hold on to my children."

"I see." But so far she couldn't determine how any of this involved her.

Nevertheless, she couldn't seem to take her eyes off David's chiseled features. She longed to brush her fingertips over the fading scar along his cheek. It seemed to stand out, white and raised in the dim light seeping into the night from the hangar. His flesh begged her to touch it, to soothe it. She clasped her hands to control them.

"What I didn't tell you last night was that my lawyer has advised me to take certain measures to help my case against Sheila. Transfer to a county police department, move to the suburbs and document instances of Sheila's neglecting the children when they're with her."

"And are you doing those things?"

"I'm working on possibilities. The transfer situation doesn't look very promising, but there's no reason I can't move out of the city and commute up to an hour each way. Proving Sheila's not looking after the kids properly could be complicated and take a long time, unless I play dirty, make up a bunch of lies about her. I'm not willing to do that."

He seemed to hesitate, as if still unsure whether to continue. "There was one other suggestion."

"And that was?"

"I should marry again, to provide a more stable life-style for the children."

Carrie stared at him, taken completely by surprise. "But last night you sounded so set against marriage!"

"I am. I don't believe it works a large enough percentage of the time to risk it again. I'm not convinced I could stay in love with the same woman for the rest of my life, and I'm not convinced any woman could love me even half as long as I'd love her." He shook his head. "No, what I'm thinking of isn't a real marriage. I mean, I'd find a woman who was willing to marry me on paper so that I could present to the court evidence that my children have a safe, stable home life."

"I'm not sure I understand." Carrie withdrew her hand from his and rubbed her forehead, hoping the massaging motion would clear away the day's fatigue so that she could concentrate on his words.

"We'd share a house, of course. And the children would have to believe that I'd married for real, at least until the court date. There's no telling what they'd come out with if a judge questioned them. But there would be no...relationship."

It wasn't until his eyes locked with hers that his total meaning struck home.

Carrie swallowed, then swallowed again, her eyes burning, her breath coming in weak spasms. Suddenly it hit her—what he'd been trying to say for the past two nights.

Both times they'd been together—their first date in Little Italy, their second at his home—she'd thought he was as attracted to her as she was to him. She'd believed he honestly liked her, that they were beginning a warm, mutual friendship she might choose to nourish and build into something more.

The truth was, he'd been checking her out as a prospective employee—a pretend wife!

The realization rocked her, left her speechless for several minutes. But she forced herself, at last, to start talking, if only to hold on to her sanity.

"You'd *marry* a woman you didn't love? Didn't even have feelings for?" she sputtered. "You realize, not many women would consent to an arrangement like that. The whole idea is impractical, irrational, preposterous!"

He regarded her solemnly. "I'm not looking at just *any* woman," he said.

Carrie drew in a sharp breath. "No, David. Oh, no, not me." She held her hands out in front of her like a shield.

"Hear me out," he begged, stepping toward her. "Give me a chance to explain."

His voice sounded strained to the point of breaking, and she reacted as she always had to any creature in pain. She relented. What harm can it do to listen? she asked herself.

"So explain," she said with a sigh.

"Carrie, I watched the way you interacted with Jason and Tammy last night," he said, hurrying on. "You were great with them. I could tell they felt comfortable with you. And after the way I saw you deal with our midflight emergency the other day, I can't imagine worrying about two kids when they're in your care.''

He pressed two fingers over her lips when she tried to object again. Stunned by the direction he was taking, she pushed at his hand. But he simply clasped her fingers and brought them down to her side, then plunged on. "I'm willing to pay you twenty thousand dollars to play the role of my wife for one year. Just one year. That much money will probably bale Monroe Air totally out of debt, or at least come close to paying off your creditors.''

She stared at him in the dark. "Twenty thousand... *dollars?*''

"Too little? Too much?''

He waited for her to answer, but she couldn't remember how to turn thoughts into intelligible sounds.

"I figure that's a fair salary for a year. I wouldn't expect you to clean house or cook any more often than you care to. You could still fly as often as you want. I'd keep the kids with me when I'm off duty. If I'm called in unexpectedly, have to work a double shift or there's an emergency, Jennifer's available. Until I locate a new house—then I'd need to find a new baby-sitter.''

David stared at her lips, which she knew were trembling. She compressed them, hoping they'd look inflexible, pale, unappealing. For a long moment she feared that he was going to pull her into his arms and kiss her. She felt it in the way a woman knows, even before a man makes his move, what he's thinking.

At last, David settled back on his heels and looked away from her. "I don't expect you to give me an answer tonight,'' he said tightly.

A choked laugh exploded from her lips. The words she'd been struggling to form came tumbling out. "Well, that's big of you! What makes you think you deserve an answer at all? Why should I—other than the fact that you've offered me an enormous sum of money—risk my future by involving myself in a confidence game aimed at fooling your ex-wife?''

He shrugged, still avoiding her eyes. "Because I'm a nice guy who doesn't deserve to lose his kids. It's as simple as that."

She stared at him in disbelief. Regardless, she felt herself weakening. "I can't see how this would ever work."

Sensing he had a chance, David swung around to face her. "It *can* work, Carrie. Think of it as strictly business. I'm paying you to do a job for me. You're earning your way out of debt by agreeing to be my roommate—and no one's breaking the law. No one's getting hurt. A year from now, you'll be in decent financial shape, free to pursue your own goals, whatever they are."

He captured her shoulders between his hands and squeezed them encouragingly. But all she could think was, How could I have let him into even a little corner of my heart, when he has absolutely no feelings for me? How could she have been so careless? She had misread him so badly. The man had been using her from day one.

"Carrie?"

She stiffened and stepped out of his reach. "This is insane."

"Maybe," he rasped, "but if there's no other way to keep my kids, I'll risk..." He let the words slip into silence. "I need you, Carrie. *Please* think about it."

Chapter 6

Frank Dixon scratched his head and looked up at the *Bay Lady*'s right engine.

"She's safe to fly, though, right?" Carrie asked over the nervous catch in her throat.

"Oh, sure. But you've got the FAA boys coming 'round next month, remember. You'll need a complete tune-up before then."

Carrie stared at the powerful Pratt and Whitney turboprop, one of two that drove the aging plane. Her dad had bought the Beechcraft because of its reliability and reputation for low-cost maintenance. The sturdy workhorse of the air had been a wise investment. But even the most dependable planes needed routine care. Carrie's stomach tightened at the thought of yet another expense for which she had no money.

"I'd forgotten the annual inspection was coming up so soon," she murmured. Without it, she couldn't fly. The cost usually ran around nine hundred dollars, plus parts and Frank's charge for labor.

"How much for the parts?" she asked.

Frank sucked in his whisker-shadowed cheeks and gave it

some thought. "Between eight hundred and a thousand—that's if we don't run into any surprises. Salvaged parts for these babies are getting scarcer than fleas on a vet's dog."

Carrie blinked, fighting back tears of frustration. She had scrimped mercilessly to save for next month's loan payment. But what good would paying it do if she couldn't renew her certification?

"Fine," she said, drawing her tongue across her bottom teeth, "order the parts. See if the distributor will make a COD delivery."

"What happens when they get here?" Frank asked, his voice gruff as he gently touched the underside of the plane's silver wing.

"I'll figure something out," she murmured.

As Carrie moved away, she returned to the same thoughts that had plagued her for the past two days. She hadn't called David with her answer, but she knew she couldn't put off giving him her decision much longer.

Only one thing was clear to her. Whether she agreed to help him or refused to take part in his scheme, she was setting herself up to be hurt.

He waited outside the police station, taking his time buying a newspaper from the vending machine, then walking up and down the block as he read it. Occasionally, he looked with a degree of urgency into a passing car, as if he were waiting for a ride and trying to recognize the driver. But he never lost sight of the side entrance of the building, where the cops—the dirty, tricky cops—came and went.

I ain't missed old Baltimore, Carl Rainey thought. Ain't missed her at all.

Although the *Sun* and local TV newscasters daily proclaimed Baltimore a crime-torn city, there wasn't much opportunity for profit as far as he was concerned. Andy and a few other homeboys had pretty much cornered the drug scene, and his brother had never been much for sharing. The rest of the stuff going down was gang squabbles—territorial killings that amounted to nothing. A waste of energy.

The West Coast—that was the place to be. Carl had made a tidy start out there, carved out a niche of his own. As long as you stayed out of L.A. and stuck to the smaller towns, a smart dude could operate independently just fine. On the coast-line they were much more open to importing quality stuff. Yep, he was real happy in his new home state. He would have been happy never to come back here.

But family was important, and when they needed you, you had to be there for them. Andy had taught him that. His brother might be a greedy bastard, but he'd stood by him when he'd gotten busted three years ago. He'd bought him a big-time lawyer, who'd sprung him on a technicality. Andy had him on a plane for the West Coast in less than an hour, and he was gone before the cops knew what hit them.

How could he do less for his brother now?

Carl eyed the doorway connecting the city parking garage to the police station. Two cops in uniform came out. He con-sidered crossing the street and strolling past them, just close enough to read their badges. David Adams. That was the name Pammy, Andrew's girlfriend, had given him over the phone. But then he figured a narc wouldn't be in uniform. He'd have to do some nosin' around to find out what this Adams looked like.

Pammy, he thought, and smiled at the image his mind reeled out of her long, sexy legs.

She'd been *his* girlfriend for six months before he left town in a rush. Since then, she'd climbed the family tree, so to speak, moving in with Andy after he left. Carl didn't hold a grudge. The girl had a head on her shoulders. Andy was rollin' in dough these days. Why not go for the pot of gold? He would've!

She'd been the one he contacted for details when he first heard through the grapevine that Andy had been arrested.

"Now, Carl-hon, don't you go doin' nothing crazy. Your brother wanted me to tell you that if you called."

"Hey, I'm cool."

Pammy giggled on the other end. "That's not the way I remember you."

Hmmm, Carl thought, a week in jail and Andy's already got trouble on the home front. But he knew better than to mess with his brother's woman.

"You oughta be thinkin' of Andy now," he said solemnly. "You don't want it to get back to him you've been playin' around while he's been veggin' out in jail. It's bad enough he's got to deal with some filthy cop messing up his life."

Pammy was contrite. "I wouldn't cheat on Andy, and he knows it. You better talk to him when you get into town, before you do anything. You get his permission first, hear?"

"Yeah, yeah, yeah." Like the tramp had any say over what he did.

No. It was up to him to make the decisions now. It wasn't like Andy could do anything for himself, seeing where he was. It was sort of exciting, when he stopped to think about it. Like in them books where the oldest son gets tossed in some castle dungeon, and the young handsome brother rides back into town to rescue him. Yeah, it was just like that. He'd find a way to help Andy. For once in his life, *he* was going to be the one to fix things.

Andy would be so proud of him.

David couldn't wait any longer.

He'd telephoned Carrie's house five times in the two days since he'd last seen her at the airport. But she hadn't been home, or wasn't answering her telephone. He'd hung up without leaving a message on her machine.

David could have kicked himself for being so damn blunt the other night. Carrie had obviously been offended by his proposition, even though he'd thought he was being quite fair. After all, she'd make out quite well by the end of the year. And it didn't seem that he was asking for a great deal in return. A twelve-month acting job was what it amounted to. She'd even get free room and board!

But he'd seen the shadow of disappointment in her eyes. He'd seen it, but had tried to block it out of his mind even as he'd argued his point, telling her she'd do well to accept his offer. The disappointment had surprised him. He'd thought that he was the only one being deprived by his decision not to start an affair. But when the light had drained from those mesmerizing hazel eyes and he'd seen her wince as if he'd actually struck her—he knew that she'd at least considered a romance.

He was sorry for that, because now there seemed nothing he could do about it. There was no going back.

As for his own chaotic emotions, he couldn't explain them to himself, so he had no hope of making another person understand them. They were feelings buried too deep within his psyche to bring out into the light.

He couldn't strip his soul bare and tell her he'd wanted her as much for himself as for his kids. Probably even more for himself, come to think of it. That sounded selfish. Taking her as a lover would be rewarding his carnal desires and tossing away his children's future. Only Carrie, it seemed to him, had the power to help him keep them.

He'd had to choose, and he'd done it. Cops were trained to act on a fraction of a second's notice. He'd given the situation more than enough thought and been as straightforward with her as he could afford to be.

Now it was up to her.

Unfortunately, he didn't have the luxury of time, with a court date breathing down his neck. So, after forty-eight hours, he had to act.

Since the kids were with Sheila that day, he didn't have to rush home after his shift plus two hours of overtime. David left the station and took the old road out of the city, west on Route 40, past miles of redbrick and stucco row houses, toward Catonsville. He remembered where she lived from their first date.

Without any difficulty, he located the white Victorian house on a corner lot on Frederick Road, the only street that could have been called Main Street in the old town, right across the street from the public library.

He was dressed in his favorite stonewashed, lightly frayed denim jeans and black T-shirt. It was his go-anywhere outfit. A suit or uniform made it impossible for him to walk into a bar or 'hood without attracting attention. If he left off shaving for a few days and wore his jeans and a dark, one-pocket T-shirt, he fitted in almost anywhere.

David drove around the corner. Her car wasn't in the driveway, and she'd told him she rarely used the garage. He turned his vehicle around and parked half a block down the side street, facing Frederick so that he could see her the moment she pulled up. He slumped in the driver's seat, prepared for a long wait. It was a little after 6 p.m., but if she had an evening flight, he reasoned, she might not leave the airport for hours.

He preferred not to consider the possibility of her having taken a charter to Florida or some other remote destination that would require an overnight stay. He refused to think about the possibility she wasn't flying and was out on a date.

As the minutes dragged past, his stomach began to twist into knots. Without thinking about what he was doing, he started gnawing at a cuticle. Before he realized it, he'd worried the spot raw.

He needed to hear her answer to his proposal, even if she didn't want to give him one. Even if her answer was no and he'd ticked her off so bad she never wanted to see him again. Then he'd have to try to make her understand that he hadn't intended to hurt or embarrass her; he'd just thought there might be a way they could help each other.

If they'd already slept together, things would have been different, he reasoned. It wasn't as if they were altering a firmly established relationship. He could see a woman getting upset then. Hell, he'd probably find it pretty unsettling himself, having once felt her respond to his touch, having once seen her step out of that pert little blue jumpsuit she used as a pilot's uniform.

He imagined her naked, standing before him…lounging on his bed…playing in the surf at Ocean City.

Damn! He shot up straight in the car seat and took a dozen deep breaths in an attempt to reestablish control over his body. If by some miracle she did agree to move in with him and the children, there would be no more of *that*. Real or imagined. Absolutely none.

Then another thought struck him. Just as certainly, there would be no other women in his bed, either.

His fidelity would have little to do with honoring the feelings of the woman who was pretending to be his wife. No, he'd just have to be careful for the next year. If either Sheila or her lawyer discovered he was dating while ostensibly being married, the result would be disastrous. Sheila could claim he'd been cheating on his new wife, which would be a definite black mark on his character in court.

No matter how he looked at it, if Carrie agreed to his plan, the next year promised to be a long, dry spell. He sighed wistfully.

The sound of a car's engine snagged David's attention. He dropped lower in his seat, then watched as her little red MG, of uncertain vintage, veered into the Victorian's driveway. The top was down and Carrie was wearing sunglasses. Her hair was a tousled mass of curls. She looked deliciously windblown, free, lovely.

David threw himself out of his car, cutting short further thoughts on her appearance, which were doing strange things to his insides again. He had a mission. He must focus on that alone.

Focus. Focus, he muttered as he jogged toward the sports car. "Hey!" he called out. "How have you been? I've been waiting to hear from you."

She slid out from behind the wheel, stood straight and gazed steadily at him, but said nothing.

"Listen," he said, coming to a halt two feet in front of her, "I'm sorry. I'm not known for my tact."

"You can say that again."

He let out a long breath. Although she didn't seem overly thrilled to see him, at least she was talking to him. "I didn't realize you had already formed a mental picture of where we were headed and I—"

"There was no picture," she pronounced coolly. "I had no expectations."

He nodded. Fine, but he knew she was fibbing, just as he had understood he was lying when he'd tried consoling himself the night before by repeating over and over, She wouldn't have been that great in bed anyway. "Good," he said.

"I'm glad you stopped by," she said crisply.

"You are?"

"Yes, it saves me a call." She paused and fastened her gaze on a nearby magnolia tree in full blossom. It looked as old as the house, which couldn't have less than a hundred years. "I intend to accept your offer."

Several erratic heartbeats later, he realized what she had just said. "You're accepting my offer?" he repeated. "You'll marry me?"

"Yes. But I have a few conditions." She held up a finger that promised a list.

"Right." He nodded so enthusiastically his vision started blurring. "That's only fair. I'll promise to abide by them, no matter what they are."

"You'd better hear them first," she advised.

Her expression was grim, her hazel eyes snapping with fire he could see in the dark.

"First, I will have my own bedroom, and *you* will stay out of it."

"I take it that means you aren't planning on visiting mine during the night?"

"That falls under the second condition. No fraternization."

"A civilized way of saying, no sex."

She narrowed her eyes severely. "This isn't a joke, David. Either we do this my way, or I can't see how we can do it at all. You say your children are more important to you than anything else in the world?"

"They are," he insisted, wiping the smile from his face.

"Fine. Separate bedrooms, no sex. But if the kids think there's anything odd about the arrangement, we may have to share a room for a while. I don't want their mother to get suspicious. Continue with your other conditions."

"All right, but this could take a while, so come inside while I get my dinner out of the freezer." She climbed the back stairs to a shady porch overgrown with purple clematis vines.

Following her inside, then through a dark foyer into the

kitchen, he had no sense of the rest of the house. He was too intensely fixed on her and what she might say next.

"I have to be free to fly as many of my usual routes as possible. If I use the money you're paying me to hire another pilot, it will be gone before the loan's paid off."

"No problem, as long as you play the stay-at-home mom whenever you can, for the judge's benefit. Your flying is something I wouldn't tamper with anyway."

"And the last—" she reached into the freezer above the refrigerated compartment and withdrew a low-fat TV dinner "—is probably the most important." She dropped the cardboard package on the countertop with a thud. "As soon as the custody hearing is over, you have to tell the children the truth about me."

He could see that she was serious. "I don't know if that's a good idea. Even after the hearing, the kids could let something slip to their mother, then I'd be right back where I was."

Carrie chewed her lip and looked worried.

"Why is telling them so important to you?" he asked

"I refuse to have their unhappiness on my conscience."

"How will they be unhappy?"

Carrie hesitated for a minute, then another. "This may sound egocentric, but I expect that after I've spent a year with Jason and Tammy, they'll have become pretty attached to me, just as I'll feel very close to them. I can't simply walk out of their lives after going through all the motions of being their mother for a year."

He frowned at her, and she turned away. This was an angle he hadn't thought through. Yes, he could see it happening with a woman as warm and nurturing as Carrie. The children would come to love her.

"Maybe if we tell them you're just their pretend mother until a real one comes along."

"That might help," she said, still sounding unsure. "If we treat my being there as a game, they may feel less dependent upon me."

"All right, we'll do that, but not until after the hearing. Anything else?"

Carrie tore open the carton, pulled the microwaveable tray out and pierced the plastic cover with a knife. She slid the meal into the microwave and pushed a button. "No, I guess not. Just remember—"

She swung around to face him, and the determination in her pretty eyes had him holding his breath.

"You break a rule, the deal's off. I walk. The money's important to me, but not as important as some other things."

"Understood," he said.

It was a shame, he thought ten minutes later as he drove back into the city. A shame that he couldn't have her in all the ways he'd imagined—as a stepmother for his kids, as a companion to watch old movies with, as a lover. He could almost feel what it would be like to make love to her. It was a sensation he'd have given a great deal to experience if circumstances had been different.

The morning air was liquid with light and moisture. Summer dew sprinkled the flowering weeds growing waist-deep beyond the runways. Black-eyed Susans, fiery poppies and delicate blue chicory blossoms flourished with no tending from human hands.

This was the kind of day that Carrie liked best—cool but promising warmth. An early-morning fog would burn off by ten o'clock and reveal a blemish-free azure sky. She knew how it would be because she'd lived through so many like it. She wanted to share mornings like this with someone she loved, with her children.

And now she had a chance of making that dream come true because a Baltimore cop had stepped onto her plane one summer afternoon.

Carrie sighed. So why did she feel so at odds with herself?

Before David had left her house that night, he'd briefly explained how their arrangement would work, and it had sounded logical and fair. She'd be given half the money he promised, up front, as a sign of good faith. She could use it immediately to pay off a good portion of the bank loan and cover some of her current expenses. Next July 15, when their agreement ended, he would give her the remaining ten thousand dollars, and they would go their separate ways. She'd have reestablished her credit, put Monroe Air back in the black and be able to start planning her future and her own family. And David would have his children.

But now, in the honest light of dawn, days later, Carrie questioned her own motives. For the past week, she'd spent every evening at David's apartment, with him when he was off duty, sometimes alone with Jason and Tammy. It had been her decision to spend as much time as possible with them. She'd reasoned that during their short "engagement," they should be seen together by people they knew. Otherwise no one would believe she and David were getting married.

At first, Carrie had felt restless and awkward in the little apartment. She was the intruder, a mercenary brought in to fight in a war of love-gone-wrong. She detested the idea that she was taking money that belonged to Jason and Tammy, which had been intended for their education.

It's not my fault, she reminded herself. If their mother hadn't pursued a heartless legal battle to take them away from their father, David could have kept the money for them. She supposed she could have turned down the money and offered to help David without payment, perhaps for a shorter time, perhaps in a way that would be less intrusive on her own life. But his generous proposition had come at a time when she was desperate for funds.

She felt guilty, but there it was.

Walking along the edge of the runway nearest her hangar, Carrie kicked pebbles with the toes of her shoes and mused over her situation. Eventually she talked herself into feeling better by deciding that as soon as she had her financial feet on the ground, she'd start paying David back in monthly installments. That way the money would be more like a loan.

"You goin' up today or not?" a voice bellowed across the field.

Carrie turned and smiled, recognizing the sandpapery voice. "Frank, if it's half as beautiful up there today as it is down here, you'll never get me down."

"She runs out of fuel after eight hundred miles. You'll come down fast enough then."

Carrie grinned at him and slung an arm around his narrow body. He was closer to her than an uncle. Frank and her father had served in the Marine Corps together. They'd met in Saigon during the Vietnam War. Frank was ten years older than her father, and it had struck him as particularly unfair that they'd both made it through those nightmarish days and nights only for his friend to be stricken with an incurable disease during peacetime.

Frank had suffered along with Paul Monroe in the months it took him to die. After his friend was gone, Frank automatically stepped into the job of looking after his friend's daughter, even though she was twenty-six years old and a grown woman. Sometimes he kept so close an eye on Carrie she felt he was taking his promise to look out for Frank's little girl a mite too seriously. But she adored him and tried to be appreciative when he advised her.

"So, you've been seeing this police officer pretty often," Frank began without segue from their weather discussion.

"Every night," Carrie admitted, swinging her arms like a schoolgirl. She found it remarkably easy to play the role of a woman in love with David Adams.

"That so?"

"Yes."

He mulled this over as they walked and came up on the hangar. "Sounds kinda serious."

"It is, in a way." She wouldn't lie to him. Losing two children was serious, and she was taking her pledge to help David with equal solemnity.

"Don't you think you might be wise to slow down a bit, gal? Take a few nights off? See someone else for a change?"

"Who?"

"I dunno. Lots of fellas on the field would give a clear day in May for a dinner date with you, and you know it."

"I don't have time for dating around."

"So you're biding time with this cop for convenience' sake? That it?"

"No, we just get along well." She paused and faced her mechanic. "He has two little kids, Frank. They're adorable. I think I'm falling in love with them."

He rolled his tongue around inside his cheek. "What about their father?"

She wasn't sure how to get around this one. Of course she wasn't really in love with David, she told herself firmly; couldn't afford to be in love with him. He was her employer; she was the temp. She looked up into Frank's worry-crinkled eyes, then followed them as they veered off to a spot behind her. She turned around.

"How long have you been eavesdropping, Rosie?" she asked.

Her receptionist lifted one shoulder and hand in a characteristic Mediterranean gesture of indifference. "Not so long, but long enough. I want to hear your answer to this one. Are you in love with their father?"

Carrie rolled her eyes. Sooner or later, she'd have to make some kind of statement to her friends. She'd only been putting off mentioning the wedding because she could guess people's startled reactions.

"I suppose there's no sense keeping it a secret any longer," Carrie began, selecting her words carefully.

Frank scowled.

Rose pressed a hand to her ample bosom and shot a questioning look at Frank.

"Go on, gal," he said gruffly.

"David and I are going to be married."

Frank slapped his thigh so loudly several other mechanics nearby swung around and stared at him. "Now, that's the dumbest thing I ever heard. What's the matter with—"

"Frank, shut up!" Rose snapped, rushing to Carrie and wrapping her soft arms around her. "That's great news, hon. Just great!"

"Lordy," Frank grumbled, pacing in a tight circle. "I hope it's a long engagement, 'cause you got some heavy thinking to do, Carrie Ann."

"Now, leave her be, Frank. The girl's been a long time

finding the right man. She knows her own mind. There's no use dawdling around once your heart is set on love.''

He looked away from both women and chewed his bottom lip, rubbing his sandpapery chin with the knuckles of one hand. "When?" he asked.

Carrie slipped out of Rose's embrace. "We haven't set the day yet, but—"

"See? She's more sensible than you give her credit." Rose released her just long enough to trap her shoulders between two viselike hands. "You just take your time making your plans, hon, but don't let that cute detective get cold feet. I could tell from the moment I see'd him he was something special." She beamed. "Are you thinking about a winter wedding? Or maybe next spring?"

"Actually, it will probably be a bit sooner than that."

"Oh?"

"Like in the next week or two."

Frank threw up his hands and stomped away into the hangar,

Rose's troubled gaze trailed after him before she turned back to Carrie. "You shouldn't go teasing the man like that. His heart ain't no teenager's to go taking shocks like that."

"I wasn't teasing," Carrie stated flatly. Even to her own ears the idea of signing a marriage certificate in only a few days sounded preposterous. But they had no choice. Merely announcing their engagement wouldn't be as convincing to a judge. "We *are* getting married very soon. I hope both you and Frank will be there to stand by me."

Rose looked at her thoughtfully, her eyes softening, seeming to melt into the surrounding creases of skin. "You know I'll be wherever you need me, hon. You just tell me the day and time, and there won't be another word said."

"What about Frank? Do you think he'll come?" It was, she realized with a jolt, important to her. Rose and Frank were all she had in the world, and she loved them dearly. What would she do if agreeing to marry David cost her their support and respect?

Rose made a dismissive gesture with her hand. "I'll work on Frank. You just leave him to me."

It wasn't until Carrie had taxied off the asphalt apron and onto the runway in preparation for her takeoff that Rose turned and set off in search of Frank. She didn't know how much influence she still held over the man. At one time they'd been closer. A lot closer. But now she wasn't sure he'd even listen to her plea on Carrie's behalf.

They'd been friends for many years, working at the airport in the charter hangars. It seemed natural for their relationship to grow even stronger after her last husband died. They started having supper together at her place Friday nights. And Frank sometimes called to find out if she wanted to see a movie or make a fourth for duckpin bowling. She liked his company, and it felt good to have someone to spend a few hours with. Then one night, about two years back, while she was slicing tomatoes for their salads, he'd come up behind her and put his arms around her, and kissed her on the back of her neck.

The effect was about as memorable as the day she'd dropped her curling iron into a sink full of water. Sparks everywhere.

She pushed him away, slammed the knife down on the cutting board and glared at him.

"What's wrong?" he asked, looking hurt. "I don't appeal to you, Rosie?"

"You appeal just fine, Frank," she'd said, flustered by his sudden turn toward the amorous. "But I've killed four good men, and I think it's time to stop."

He stared at her, his mouth agape. She didn't explain and it took him a good three minutes of sputtering to recover his ability to speak. "You *killed* your husbands?"

"Might as well have," she said. "I put every one of them in his grave within three years after the ceremony. I'm a jinx or I'm cursed or...I don't know what it is about me. But my men never last long." She tenderly touched his grizzled cheek with the pads of her fingers of both hands. "You deserve to live to be a very old airplane mechanic," she whispered over the sudden burning in her throat. "I can't marry you, Frank. And I'm a good Catholic girl, you know, so I won't...you know, fool around with you."

"That's ridiculous!" he'd roared. "There's no such thing as curses. It was just their time to go."

But she refused to listen to him. She couldn't help wondering about Harold, Manny, Philip and Emmanuel. If she hadn't married them, might they still be alive today?

She'd seen no other course, and Frank never again asked her to cook for him, or to come to his place, or to spend time with him away from the airfield.

Sometimes Rose suspected him of watching her, but whenever she turned around, he had his head stuck in an engine or a repair manual. She knew she'd hurt him and he still bore a grudge, but nothing she said to him made things the way they were.

On cold winter nights, her heart often ached so fiercely she regretted her decision to remain on her own for the rest of her years. She'd had love, happiness, raised three kids by two different husbands, both lovely men. At fifty years of age, she shouldn't expect to start over again. Besides, she'd made her decision with Frank's welfare in mind. How would she ever live with herself, knowing she'd caused the demise of a man as sweet as Frank Dixon?

That day in July, after Carrie took off for Ocean City, Rose found Frank in a neighboring hangar, working on the landing strut of a plane owned by a weekend flier-weekday surgeon at Johns Hopkins. "Frank," she said, pulling her hand back when it automatically reached out to tap his shoulder.

"I'm busy."

"You can listen while you work."

"You can talk, but I don't guarantee I'll hear you." He noisily dug through his toolbox.

Rose prayed for patience. "All right, you stubborn old man. Listening or not, hearing or not, I don't think you're taking all the facts into consideration where Carrie is concerned."

"That so," he mumbled.

"Yes. You know Carrie's a levelheaded young woman

when it comes to most things. She's got a lot of her daddy in her, and Paul didn't jump into situations without giving them long, hard thought."

"Right. But he wasn't a woman."

She fisted her hands at her sides, yearning to belt him. But the last time she'd struck a male, it had been her ten-year-old brother—and he'd hit first.

"Does it occur to you that she might have been seeing this man longer than we know?"

"Couldn't a been much longer."

"No. Probably no more than a month or so," Rose admitted.

"A month still isn't long enough to know a person before agreeing to marry him. Six months isn't long enough. A year is just getting warmed up." Frank fixed her with a scowl that seeped straight into her bones. "And some people hang around each other most of their lives, and it still isn't enough."

Rose grimaced before she could stop herself from reacting. Luckily, Frank had just turned his back to her to fuss with his tools. "You're right," she acknowledged, keeping her voice steady. "Sometimes it takes a long time for a woman to get to know a man. But a month is long enough for a woman to know she's pregnant."

The mechanic froze. Slowly his hand reached for the plane's wheel; he pushed himself to standing, with effort. When he faced Rose, his eyes were damning, as if he blamed her for the news. "She *told* you she's gonna have a baby?"

"No, she hasn't said a word," Rose admitted. "I don't expect she would until she's officially married. Carrie's like that—private, wanting to deal with problems on her own."

Frank narrowed his eyes at her. "Then how do you know, woman?"

"I don't. I'm just saying, it seems pretty obvious to me that there must be some reason Carrie's doing what she's doing. You know how set she's always been against marriage. She drops a man as soon as the breeze blows in that direction. So why would she suddenly change her mind?"

Frank pinched the bridge of his nose with a finger and thumb and squeezed his eyes shut. "I don't know, Rosie."

"We both understand how much she loves kids. She'd never agree to an abortion. She'd do anything but that."

"But marry a cop?" Frank opened his eyes to stare at her bleakly.

Rose blinked away the moisture rimming her eyes. "The point is, she's got a reason for doing what she's doing, and if it has anything to do with a baby... Well, we need to support her. Please, Frank, don't make this any harder on her than it already is."

He drew a long, slow breath, then held it for what seemed an impossibly long time before letting it out in a rush. "I'll try."

"Will you come to the wedding? She says she wants us there."

"I don't know if I can do that," Frank said. "I'll think on it."

Chapter 7

It was a Tuesday night and Carrie took charge of clearing the table after dinner, with the willing assistance of Jason and Tammy. David was usually responsible for cleaning up after meals. But now that she was to become a permanent member of the household, it seemed only fair she take a turn, so she suggested he use the time to finish up some paperwork he'd brought home with him from the station.

"We have a dishwasher, so you don't have to wash the dishes in the sink," Jason informed her, as if she might not have noticed it on her earlier visits. He followed her into the kitchen, carrying his plate and utensils.

"That's wonderful." Carrie smiled him. He was a clever, affectionate child, and she was growing fonder of him every day. "Do you know how to load it?"

The little boy's eyes sparkled. "Sure. Can I do it? Dad thinks I'll break stuff, so he doesn't usually let me."

"Or me," Tammy piped up, teetering into the kitchen with her almost empty milk glass balanced precariously on her dirty plate.

Carrie rescued the dinnerware before it could slip from the little girl's hands.

"He won't let *you*," Jason informed her, "because you're still a baby."

"Am not." Tammy pouted, her tiny fists propped on her hips, her lower lip quivering as she looked up with tears in her eyes at Carrie. "I'm not a baby."

"No, you're not," Carrie said firmly. She cast Jason a mildly chastising look. "Your sister can help out in a lot of ways babies can't. Someday, she'll be able to do everything you can do now. She just needs a little time to catch up with her big brother, and some practice." She rested a hand on the soft crown of his Dutch-boy haircut, which somehow made him look innocent and devilish at the same time. "Why don't you show Tams how the dishes fit into the racks."

Jason considered the merits of being nominated teacher. After a moment, he grinned as if he'd decided he liked the idea. "Okay." He picked up a dinner plate from the countertop and held it up for Tammy to see. "Watch me. First, I rinse it off. Then I put the plate between these little rubber fingers, facing the sprayer thing. That's so all the food gets washed off," he explained.

Tammy's eyes grew wide with admiration for her big brother. "Can I do the next one?"

"Of course," he said magnanimously. "I'll watch to make sure you do it right."

"Pssst."

Carrie turned toward the kitchen door, to see David crooking a finger at her, a smile a mile wide illuminating his handsome face.

She sauntered over to him, feeling smug. "I have everything well in hand."

"I don't know about that. You may have created a monster." He took her arm and led her into the living room.

"How's that?"

"Next thing you know, Jason will be teaching Tammy how to pick up his room for him and bundle the newspapers for recycling. She'll be doing all his chores."

"Now, you can't tell me that sweet little boy is as devious as that," Carrie teased.

"I'm afraid he's already figured out how to get his way with me." David grimaced. "All that aside, guilt goes a long way."

She couldn't let the conversation shift without following up on so strong a lead. David generally came home from his shifts wired, adrenaline still flowing from whatever had transpired during the hours he'd been gone. It sometimes took him an entire evening to unwind.

During that time, she'd learned not to press him for conversation. She went for a walk, played with the children, read a book or worked on her flight reports. Eventually, he came to her and they could talk about the wedding or the children. His cases weren't a topic they often broached. Neither was his past.

"Why guilt?" Carrie asked softly. "What have you got to feel guilty about?"

"No one goes through a divorce without suffering some degree of remorse," he stated bluntly. "I'm not what Sheila wanted. Therefore I fell short. Maybe it's not totally reasonable, but it's the way the mind works."

"What your wife wanted might have nothing to do with being a man of honor and character," Carrie stated dryly.

David looked down at her. His eyes, which had seemed so hard, so grimly clouded by preoccupation with his job when he'd first walked into the apartment, seemed to clear a little more.

She couldn't imagine doing what he did for a living. It must have seemed like going off to war every day. Few people could live two such different lives and remain whole, she thought. Carrie felt deeply moved by his dedication.

"We're done!" Jason cried, streaking through the kitchen door, across the living room. He flung himself into Carrie, knocking her back a step.

She laughed at him, even as his father was pulling him off her. "Hey, watch it, fella. You don't run into ladies like that. You wouldn't want to hurt Carrie."

Jason blinked up at her. "Did I hurt you?"

"No, you didn't hurt me." She smiled at David. "I think it would take a lot more than a full body hug to injure this lady. I'm little but tough."

"See, Dad?" Jason said.

"I still want you to be careful around ladies...*and girls.*"

"Girls, too?" Jason looked taxed to the limits of his patience. "They hit pretty hard sometimes."

David crouched and looked sternly at his son. "Be a gentleman, Jason. You can take a poke from a girl now and then. It just means they like you."

"It does?" He screwed up his face, thinking, then gazed up at Carrie. "Does it?"

She reached down and poked his stomach. "It does."

"Me, too! Me, too! Like me!" Tammy shrieked, running circles around Carrie.

Carrie scooped up the little girl and hugged her hard. "I like you, too. Indeed I do."

"Indeed I do. Indeed I do!" Jason chanted, enjoying the sound of the words.

Carrie set Tammy down, and she chased after her brother as he ran between the furniture, down the hallway and through the other rooms, building his chant to an eardrum-shattering crescendo.

"I wish it were their bedtime," David said quickly. "They regress to pure silliness when they're tired."

Carrie laughed, feeling at one with the joy filling the apartment. She thought, This is how it should be. Two adults, being worn ragged by two parcels of pure energy, who are probably no more rambunctious than their parents were as kids. Generations came and went, but the roles remained the same. Lights-out was always called when the fun became too exhausting for the grown-ups.

"Let's pick out a board game to play for an hour or so, then I'll read them a story," she offered. "I should leave before too late. I'm doing an early-morning run down to North Carolina for a dozen bass-fishing cronies. I have a feeling my fishermen will be more of a handful, with all their gear and tall tales, than your children.''

They had agreed that until the wedding ceremony, there was little reason for her to move her personal belongings into David's apartment. Carrie was reluctant to leave familiar, cherished surroundings. The big, breezy old house in Catonsville was still home to her. She couldn't remember another. From its sheltering veranda, she could walk to every place of importance in town. Catonsville was a cozy town where families stayed put for generations. She felt safe there.

The crime log in the local newspaper noted when a car was stolen—usually by kids out for a joyride—or cigarettes were lifted without payment from an unwisely placed rack near the front door of the convenience store. Occasionally a house was broken into, a stereo or TV taken, but it was a rare occurrence. No one could remember when the last murder had happened, if ever.

David was accustomed to the city, and he evidently felt safe there. Although there were stores within walking distance, Carrie despaired of the crowded, grimy streets immediately surrounding David's apartment. Even during the middle of the day, they sometimes seemed dark, sinisterly threatening. And they smelled not at all like the roses, freesia and lilacs growing in her own yard.

So she usually drove back to Catonsville to a grocery store she was familiar with. David had spoken of looking for a house in the suburbs. She wasn't one to complain, but hoped he'd find one soon.

Carrie read two stories to Jason and Tammy, then tucked them securely into their beds. When she bent low over the little girl's bed to smooth out her sheets, Tammy unexpectedly threw her arms around Carrie's neck

"Will you read to us tomorrow night?" Tammy asked, her eyes bright with mischief that almost overshadowed her fatigue.

"If you like," Carrie agreed, kissing her on her forehead. She smelled of baby shampoo from her bath.

"And the night after that?" Tammy batted her eyes innocently up at her.

"If you like," Carrie teased, seeing a pattern game developing.

"And the night after—"

"And every night that you want me to read, I will," Carrie promised gently, releasing Tammy's arms from around her neck. "But you have to go to sleep tonight if you want tomorrow night to come."

Tammy peered up at her meekly through lashes the color and length of her father's. "All right. I'll go to sleep. Will you be here when I wake up?"

"No. But I'll see you tomorrow night, at supper."

"Why do you have to go?"

Carrie knew much of this was stalling, but she understood the insecurities of being young and needing to trust the adults in your life. That was a luxury she'd had so little of herself. "I have to fly my airplane. But I'll come back, just to be with you."

"With me and Jason," Tammy said loyally.

"Yes." Carrie gently pressed her open hand across Tammy's eyes. "Now, close these and go to sleep. If you're very good, someday I'll take you with me in my plane...if you like."

When she lifted her hand, Tammy's eyes remained shut and the little girl lay motionless, except for her lips. "I'm sleeping so I can fly with you, Carrie."

Carrie smothered a chuckle. "Good girl."

She crossed paths with David in the hallway. "Jason's all yours," he said.

"Tammy's pretending to sleep," Carrie told him, her eyes conveying the message that he should play along. He nodded, grinning. The moodiness that had gripped him for the first few hours he'd been home seemed to have finally and totally lifted. She was glad for him. When he smiled, she could feel her own heart grow lighter.

Carrie stepped into Jason's room, which was already dark

except for the faint orange glow from his night-light. "Are you ready for a good night's sleep?" she asked.

He nodded, but he was still sitting up and his eyes held questions. She waited, suspecting they'd rise to the surface if she gave them time.

"Do you know what my father is?"

It wasn't one she'd anticipated.

"He's your and Tammy's dad," she said softly, "and he's a police officer."

"He's like Batman," Jason said solemnly.

Carrie sat down on the edge of the bed and took Jason's hand in hers. "Do you mean he's sort of like a superhero?"

Jason nodded. "He helps people. And he catches bad guys. But he can get hurt. Batman can't get hurt, not bad enough to…to die." He stared at his lap.

"I see," she said solemnly. "So you understand how your father helps people. He's told you?"

Jason nodded again. Even in the dark, she could see how wide open his eyes were. "I ask him sometimes, and he tells me. He stops bad people from hurting little kids."

"By stopping them from giving drugs to children?" Carrie asked softly. She didn't know how much information David had chosen to give his children, and she didn't want to overstep whatever boundaries he might have set.

"One time, he got beat up. His face was all…" He looked at Carrie, as if he hoped she'd understand without his having to explain in detail.

"Go on, I know," she said, although she wondered how bad it had been, or how often this sort of thing happened to David.

"Uncle Pete came to pick us up at Mom's place, and he said Dad broke down a door to get to a baby that was crying in an apartment. The woman with the baby was sick and wasn't taking care of it. Dad wanted to take the baby to someone who would feed it and change its diaper and do all that baby stuff, but the woman got mad at Dad and she cut his face."

"That's pretty terrible," Carrie admitted. She envisioned

the scene. Even with Jason's sketchy details it was pretty horrible. Perhaps the young mother was an addict or an alcoholic. She'd probably come at David with whatever was at hand—a broken liquor bottle, a kitchen knife. "Your father is very brave," she murmured.

Jason's clear blue eyes slowly rose to meet hers. "I want to be just like him when I grow up," he whispered. "But Dad doesn't like me to say that."

Carrie put an arm around the little boy and pulled him softly to her chest, stroking his head. Suddenly, she understood so much more about this family. David had to be the man he was—trying to make things better for people in his city—he could do no less. That was the measure of his dedication. But he apparently wanted a safer, saner life for his children.

"You have a long time to think about what you want to be when you grow up," Carrie murmured into the soft sheen of brown hair beneath her lips. "By then, I'm sure your dad will want you to do whatever you think is right."

Jason smiled up at her. "I'm going to be just like him."

David waited in the living room while Carrie finished talking to his son. It seemed they were having a rather extended conversation for a final good-night kiss and tuck-in. But David let them alone, content to listen to the soothing rise and fall of Carrie's voice as he had while she'd been reading to his children and he'd been wiping down the kitchen counters, then taking down breakfast dishes from the cupboard to prepare for morning. He caught himself setting four places, as he had for supper, and had to remind himself that Carrie wouldn't be there for breakfast.

All that evening, and the days before when she'd come to the apartment, he'd watched her move through his home as naturally as if she'd always been there. After less than a week, he'd come to expect seeing her when he entered a room. He wondered how he'd feel after a month...after six months...after a year. Then, suddenly, she wouldn't be there.

David looked up as Carrie came into the living room and glanced automatically toward the kitchen.

"Everything cleaned up out there?"

"Spick-and-span," he reported from his seat on the couch, where he'd been pretending to read a magazine while he absorbed the music of her voice.

"I should go, then."

"Do you have fifteen minutes to sit?" he asked, patting the cushion beside him. "We didn't get a chance to talk much tonight."

She walked over toward the couch, but at the last minute elected to sit in the matching armchair to his right. Leaning back, she crossed her long legs. She'd worn a skirt that night, which was unusual for her. Carrie appeared most at home in pleated trousers that reminded him of those a young Katharine Hepburn might have worn. But Carrie had delicious legs that begged for a short skirt, and when she crossed her long limbs he couldn't help letting his eyes drift down to enjoy the view.

"David?" His eyes snapped up. "You wanted to talk about something?"

"Yes," he said, recovering slowly. He could feel his pulse in his throat. How was he going to live in the same house with this woman and keep his hands off her? "I wanted to give you some time to let our agreement sink in. In case you had second thoughts. Have you?"

She pursed her lips and wrinkled her nose in concentration. "No, not the kind of second thoughts you mean."

"What kind, then?"

"I just don't want to do anything to hurt Jason and Tammy, or you. I don't want to screw up my own life, either. Lord knows it isn't in the best shape as it is. It seems inevitable that something will go wrong with this wonderful plan of yours."

He quirked a dark brow at her. "I hadn't pegged you as a pessimist."

She inched around on her chair, drawing her legs up beneath her and leaning forward urgently. "I'm not. I just want to make sure that performing this act for the benefit of your ex-wife won't do more harm than good."

"Believe me, it's going to do *all* of us a lot of good. The children are a part of me. I *need* them. And they would be miserable growing up in their grandparents' house. As for you, how can you not come out in better shape than you're in now?''

"I suppose you're right," she admitted. "It's just that I keep getting these mental twinges that feel like disaster waiting to happen." She smiled weakly at him. "Life hasn't always been smooth flying for me…so to speak."

He nodded, feeling genuinely sympathetic to her situation. He couldn't deny that she'd been through a lot, but if she wanted a way out of her financial dilemma, he was holding out to her a quick fix. "Listen, if you still have serious doubts, I don't know how to argue them away. But if you're ready to go ahead with this, we really shouldn't wait much longer. The closer to the trial date, the less believable the marriage."

"So what's the next step?" she asked stiffly.

"I can apply for the marriage license tomorrow at the courthouse. All I'll need is your social security number and place of birth. There's a two-day waiting period. We could be married at the courthouse on Friday."

Carrie swallowed. That fast. In less than three days she could be a married woman. It didn't matter that her brain told her heart, This is not a real marriage. This is a ruse, a sham, a means to an honorable end. It was the idea of saying *those words:* "Until death do us part." To speak them out loud, even when she knew they were a lie, seemed unconscionable.

Whether David believed her, she knew that the next twelve months held the power to destroy her.

David was talking. She tried to concentrate on his words, to shove aside the panic welling up inside her. His voice sounded like air rushing past her ears, like the time she'd taken her first parachute jump from a plane during flight training. The air rushed up into her face, making it impossible to breathe for the first minute. Needing to break the helpless sensation that gripped her now, she clamped her hands between her knees to keep them from trembling.

"The ceremony takes only five minutes. It should be relatively painless, as informal as we like."

"Five minutes?" she asked, lifting her head to meet his eyes.

"Well, you weren't expecting a big church wedding, were you?" He chuckled.

Without warning, tears filled her eyes and spilled down her cheeks.

Carrie blinked furiously, willing herself to stop crying. "No, of course I don't want a big church wedding!" she choked out. "Don't be ridiculous. What woman in her right mind would want a bunch of friends and relatives hanging around while she took a vow that was supposed to last a lifetime but had a one-year expiration date stamped on it? And those over-priced, atrocious lace-and-pearl gowns? You'd never catch me in one of them!"

So why the hell are you crying? she demanded silently, a weak sob escaping between her lips, despite her best effort to stop it.

David launched himself off the couch and was down on his knees in front of her in the next second. "What's wrong?" He pulled her hands from between her knees and took them in his. His eyes darkened with confusion.

"Don't worry," she said. "I'm not backing out."

"Then why—"

"Because, you idiot man," she shouted, pulling her fingers free of his, "every woman is born with this stupid need inside her that she has to fight all her life. It demands a soprano singing Bach, flowers in a church and a gown with a train so obnoxiously long it requires a limousine. We're *bred* to want weddings, even if we don't believe in them!"

He smiled at her, settling back onto his heels. "Poor Carrie. Life doesn't make much sense sometimes, does it?"

She shook her head. "Every time I think I have it figured out, something happens to change the rules!" Her throat felt as if it were on fire, and her temples throbbed. She pressed one hand to her forehead.

"Tell me," he murmured, deftly catching up her fleeing fingers.

To her amazement, he brought them to his lips in a brief gesture that moved her more than she dared admit to herself.

"Tell me how the rules have changed."

She drew a deep breath, as much to calm her flip-flopping stomach as to help her find the words. "Well, I told you about my parents forever fighting. I suppose I got used to it. As soon as I was convinced that was status quo, my mother left. Just left. I had to figure things out all over again. Then my father—"

She still had trouble saying it.

David supplied the words that always came so hard. "Your father passed away."

Carrie nodded, wanting to pull her hands out of his to blot at her damp eyelashes. But her fingers felt warm and protected in David's steady grip. She thought how good he probably was whenever called upon to comfort a victim at a crime scene. His strength seemed to flow into her body through their touching hands.

"Yes, Dad died. Then I had to get used to living alone, working alone, planning for a future alone...."

"Because you didn't want to marry."

"Not because I didn't *want* to," she said slowly, reanalyzing her feelings. "Because I knew it was useless. It wouldn't work. It never does, you see." She looked at him and could see in his eyes the flip-side version of the pain she felt. She knew he wouldn't argue the validity of marriage, because he felt as she did. "I overheard a woman say the other day that a successful marriage these days was one that lasted ten years. I think...I think that if love can't last a lifetime...it wasn't love to begin with."

"Maybe you're right," he agreed softly. "I believed I loved Sheila when we married and that she loved me. I think there were other attractions, other advantages we saw in each other that had nothing to do with love." He dropped his glance to their linked hands and stared, as if he'd just then become aware they were touching. He looked as sad as she'd ever seen him.

Carrie felt terrible for destroying his cheerful mood.

"Maybe," she whispered, "your marriage to Sheila was meant to be for reasons other than the love of a man and woman…and those two reasons are asleep in their bedrooms, back there." She glanced toward the hallway.

He followed her eyes, then looked up at her gratefully. "If life made that much sense, it would be great. I don't know that it does, but it's a nice thought."

She didn't realize what he was doing until it was too late. The grief in his eyes had been slowly warming as he spoke, like liquid in a saucepan coming to a gentle simmer. He pulled downward on her hands, bringing her face closer to his, until their lips were mere inches apart. Focusing on her mouth as it parted in protest, he quickly pressed his lips over hers.

For some reason, she didn't push away, didn't ask him to release her. Then he was holding her, just holding her as he would a troubled or hurt child, stroking her hair, rubbing the back of her neck soothingly, rocking slightly. "We'll both be all right," he said. "We'll get through this. Just don't back out on me now, Carrie. I *need* you. You can't know how it pains me to say those words to anyone."

She knew he was being absolutely honest with her. David Adams was a proud man and wouldn't ask for help unless desperate.

"I'm not backing out," she said, resting her head against his chest. "I just don't want any more talk about damned wedding gowns and churches."

"Fair enough." To his credit, he didn't laugh at her again.

She stood up, moving out of his arms. "Walk me to my car?"

"Are you feeling all right?"

"I'll be fine…I *am* fine. But if we're going to do this, we'd better do it right. Your neighbors won't believe you're getting married if they don't see some proof of a serious lady in your life. You're a cop. You should understand how evidence works." She managed a dim smile for him.

Some of the sadness left his eyes, but the mood that replaced it worried her. He looked too much like Jason just before he played one of his tricks. His eyes seemed almost too bright.

"You're right," he said, seizing her hand and pulling her along after him toward the door. Carrie had just enough time to grab her purse on the way out.

They stopped just long enough to send Jennifer to watch the kids, before they continued down the stairs.

It wasn't quite dark yet, at eight-thirty on a July night. The day's heat lingered in the granite stoops in front of the brick row houses that ranged down the street from the high-rise where David lived. The stone steps seemed to have been designed for sitting and gossiping on, during hot summer nights. Many of the older Baltimore homes weren't air-conditioned. Neighbors spent sultry evenings chatting, as the sun left the sidewalks to cool and night closed in.

"Evenin', Detective." An elderly man walking a dog flicked his cigar in acknowledgment as they passed him. Two younger men who'd come out for a smoke and to talk about the Orioles' winning streak looked Carrie over thoroughly.

David put his arm around her waist and pulled her snugly against his hip. "Think they get the picture yet?" he whispered in her ear.

She was game. "We'd better make sure." Smiling, she rested her head against his shoulder, adding to the romantic effect.

They passed a cluster of children drawing on the sidewalk with brightly colored chalk. One little boy with mocha skin and eager black eyes raced toward David, who slapped him a high five in passing.

"Hey, that your lady?" the boy asked.

"You watch out for her, Nathan," David called out to him, loudly enough for the whole block to hear. "She's going to be Mrs. Adams soon."

"Whoooeee!" the boy screeched, running over to a group of women sitting at the curb in rainbow-striped, canvas beach chairs. "The detective is gettin' married!"

Faces turned and beamed at the couple.

When they reached her car, Carrie said, "I think word will get around just fine now, Detective Adams."

"Don't want to take any chances," he said.

She fished her key from her purse as David let his arm slacken around her waist, without actually releasing her. She was aware of him watching her, felt the heat of his eyes on her, sensed that he wasn't going to let her just drive away.

"David."

"Yes?" As she turned toward him he slid his hands down to her hips and angled her body closer to his.

"I think that's enough of a show for one night," she cautioned, placing a restraining hand in the middle of his chest.

"I don't."

He leaned down, at the same time stepping forward to back her up against the car. Their bodies pressed together, from chests to hips. Carrie was instantly aware of the level of his arousal, which was considerable. Before she could react to the shock she felt, his lips were on hers. This time there was a hunger, a demand that she respond.

Carrie didn't need encouragement. She shared David's desire.

The kiss lengthened, deepened, muddied her mind. She lost track of the faces around them, lost sight of the buildings and growing shadows and dying light of day, as David coaxed open her mouth and tasted her for a long, sweet eternity. The world seemed to have gone silent. All she heard was the erotic hum of her own body.

When he at last moved slightly away, a dozen sounds burst through, as if someone had turned up the volume knob on life. Hoots, hollers and congratulations echoed up and down the street, melting into the traffic sounds of the city.

Carrie felt her cheeks flame.

"You look beautiful when you blush at dusk," he whispered hoarsely, still holding her. "I'll bet you look just as beautiful blushing at dawn."

Carrie gazed up at him, feeling awash in emotions. All she could think to do was make light of the moment.

She giggled and gave him a playful shove. "Enough, David. Everyone's watching us."

"Ask me if I care."

"I wouldn't dare."

He laughed and turned his body to let her slip away, then leaned lazily against the car, not bothering to hide his interest in continuing their performance. His eyes were smoky with desire. "Guess we put on a pretty good performance."

"Yup." She unlocked her car door and hastily dove for shelter. "I guess we're both decent actors."

He closed the car door for her. She didn't dare look at him again as she rolled down the window to let air into the stuffy interior, then started the engine. "I'll see you tomorrow night," she said.

She felt shaken, but also a little smug. David might pretend to himself that he wasn't attracted to her. He might swear that their time spent under one roof would be only business to him. But she didn't believe it...any more than she believed that the warm ache she felt down low in her body was indigestion.

The stranger stepped from behind the corner of the building, where he'd been chain-smoking to pass time. As he'd watched residents drift home from their jobs, smelled their cheap food cooking, heard them call to their brats playing in the street to come inside long enough to eat, he was barely aware of the cooler night air stealing over the city in the fading purplish light.

It was in another Baltimore blue-collar ghetto not far from here that he'd grown up. He never wanted to live like this again—all crowded together; smelling one another's greasy leftovers; old ladies dumping buckets of wash water on stoops, then sweeping the water into the gutters. He despised these people, who settled for being poor just because they had no imagination. He thought about the meals he could afford to buy in fancy restaurants now, even without the money his brother sent out to California, and he chuckled, feeling superior.

Carl had intended to wait around only long enough to see

the woman again, make sure she was with the cop, figure out their connection. When they stepped out of the front door and started toward her car, he was less than fifty feet away.

He observed them coolly, catching electric vibes in the air, watching them kiss, really get into it. He watched the woman with a special interest and appreciation. She was classy looking for this part of Baltimore. He'd had a woman like her out in Fresno, but she'd gotten spooked when she found out about his business. Funny, she hadn't given back the diamond bracelet. Where'd she think a guy got that kind of money if he wasn't dealing?

As soon as the woman drove off, the cop walked back toward his apartment building, waving to some of his neighbors, exchanging a few words. Adams didn't seem as alert as the other times he'd spotted him. The woman had obviously taken his mind off routine things.

She was a looker, all right. A tight little blonde like that could sexually distract him and steal a man's will to live. Adams. Adam and Eve. Maybe she was his Eve. Maybe she'd offer the apple that would be his downfall.

Carl snickered, dropped his cig on the pavement, ground it out beneath the heel of his shoe. He'd find out her name, too.

Everything was beginning to look easier, he thought as he walked down the sidewalk, ignoring the curious looks from the cop's neighbors. If an ordinary businessman fell in love, he'd have trouble concentrating on his work, might miss a meeting, forget a deadline. But a cop in love got careless, took chances, could get himself killed real easy.

Carl turned toward the open doorway of the high-rise. Damn. It would be so smooth. Just stroll on up there, knock on the door and blast away when Adams opened it. But that's not what Andy wanted. Andy had told him to leave the guy alone until he thought of some way to keep the cop out of court that wouldn't get him in more trouble than he was in already.

So he'd wait. He'd wait, for a while.

Chapter 8

There ought to be organ music playing, Carrie thought. And flowers. Mountains of beautiful white flowers.

She looked around the pragmatic eight-by-ten-foot room in the basement of the courthouse that was reserved for marriage ceremonies. The walls were antiseptic white. A lectern stood in the middle of an almost square remnant of red indoor-outdoor carpet. Six folding chairs that reminded her of high school assemblies were provided for guests. On one sat her purse and the marriage license, for which David had already paid thirty dollars—the entire cost of their wedding.

Because the room was without windows, it lacked the sunny warmth of a church or chapel. No stained-glass windows, no scent of lemon oil on oak pews, no ethereal music surrounded the small wedding party with reassuring traditions.

"You sure you want to do this?" Rose whispered in her ear.

"I'm sure." Carrie forced out the two words, along with a wobbly smile, then looked away.

A green bottle fly had landed on one corner of the lectern and was cleaning its wings. Carrie stared at it, needing something, anything, to think about until the ceremony was over. She wondered, absurdly, how many weddings the insect had sat in on. How many it might have outlived. She seemed to remember hearing a story from one of her passengers, of a friend who had married in Vegas, then six months later flew to Reno for a divorce. Certainly flies lived that long…longer?

Carrie sighed at the weird paths her thoughts were taking. But anything was better than dwelling on what was really happening, right this moment, in this odd little room that wasn't much larger than a closet.

She was only vaguely aware of the five other people present, aside from the city clerk who would marry them. David's partner, Detective Peter Turner, had accompanied him as his witness. Jason and Tammy stood quietly on either side of their father's friend. David had insisted the children come; he felt it might appear suspicious if they weren't at his wedding. Then there was Rose and, of course, David himself. Frank had resisted all Rose's attempts to bring him along. He'd stayed at the airport.

David and Carrie had agreed to keep their arrangement a secret—although David admitted to having an earlier conversation with Pete about the advantages of his remarrying. Still, his partner wasn't aware of any of the details.

Carrie glanced back at Rose, feeling a lump of panic rise like a bubble in a lava lamp, in her throat. She swallowed a couple of times, hoping it would go away.

"You really all right, hon?" Rose asked. She wrapped her plump fingers around Carrie's wrist. "If you're having second thoughts—"

"I'm fine. No."

"I know I've sometimes pushed you to get married," she whispered. "But even if it looks as if you should… I mean, even if it seems there's no alternative, there are…alternatives, I mean…"

She stammered to silence, at a loss for words—an unusual situation for a woman who had something to say on every subject. Carrie had no idea what she was talking about.

"I want to do this," she said, glaring straight ahead, concentrating on the tiny muscles at the corners of her lips that would keep them turned stiffly upward. "David's a fine man. It will be okay."

Rose nodded, but didn't look convinced. She clasped Carrie's hand and squeezed it. "Just come to me any time you need anything, hear? Any time." She glanced at Jason and Tammy and leaned still closer to Carrie's ear. "My, but those are beautiful children. Are you sure you aren't just marrying him so you can play mamma to them?"

Her laugh almost sounded real to Carrie. She loved Rose for trying to understand, although she couldn't possibly know half of what was going on in her head or her heart.

The clerk was speaking to David. It was almost as if Carrie was watching a scene in a play about other people's lives. Lives in which she had no part. The words that would soon be recited would have no impact on her, she told herself. They were just words. They were just sounds that burbled out when she moved her lips.

Nothing. They meant nothing.

She desperately sifted through her mind for something else to think about, to spirit her away from the room that felt as if it were getting impossibly stuffy. Was anyone else having trouble breathing? She thought about David's apartment, her new home.

The night before, she'd moved in some of her personal items—clothing, toiletries, a few favorite books and videos. She'd left all her furniture and most of her nonessential belongings at the Catonsville house. She intended to continue spending what time she could there—when she wasn't flying or caring for David's kids.

The children, she thought again, feeling instantly torn.

There Jason stood, his chest all puffed up inside his sized-down suit jacket. David had told him he was best man and could hold Carrie's ring, a gold band so slender she wondered if it might bend out of shape when she gripped the yoke of the *Bay Lady*. So fragile and weightless, she might easily forget it was on her finger. But she supposed it looked official enough, and that was all that mattered.

And Tammy, sweet little Tammy…she was all fitted out in a pink-and-white sundress with white patent-leather shoes and lace-trimmed socks. Her eyes were enormous, dancing with excitement as she played with the strap of her matching purse and looked around the room at the grown-ups, who were talking in whispers.

Carrie felt a surge of protectiveness for both of them. What sort of cruel trick were they playing on these unsuspecting children? They hadn't told the kids yet that the marriage was "pretend." David still felt it would be too risky, until after the hearing.

Then she did a quick reality check and reminded herself that in the long run, by posing as David's new wife she would be making it possible for them to remain with their father—a man who loved them to the depths of his soul. She, Carrie Monroe, was a means to an end. As long as they had their father, her twelve months would fade in their memories, would become insignificant.

Carrie drew a jagged breath, wishing they could get the whole thing over with. She felt vaguely dizzy, too hot one minute, overcome by chills the next. She shot a frantic look at the only door in the room, but before she could bolt for it, the clerk cleared his throat, smiled at her and asked David to take his bride's hand.

Then he was saying words Carrie had heard repeated, in numerous variations, for as long as she could remember—on television, in movies and in real life.…

David had taken both her hands in his and looked into her eyes as the man read from a slim paper-covered manual about the seriousness of marriage, about their dedication to each other as man and wife. He spoke slowly, distinctly, weighing his words. Not rushing as she'd expected a public official might, who knew that six or seven other couples waited outside the door for their turn at matrimony.

Beyond David's shoulder, she could see Pete, his mouth angling harshly downward. He'd combed his long hair back into a ponytail and shaved for the occasion. When David had introduced them, he'd been polite but unenthusiastic. Now he shot her a look as cold as frost on a wingtip, and she knew in that instant that he didn't like or trust her.

Carrie looked hopefully up into David's eyes, trying to borrow from him a little of his strength. But his blue eyes seemed bland, compared with the way they'd appeared the day he'd walked her to her car. If he felt any emotions at all during the intervening days, he'd been careful to hide them. They hadn't kissed again. They hadn't touched, even as they'd passed in the kitchen or hallway.

David repeated the vows as the clerk prompted him:

"I, David Adams, take thee, Carrie Monroe, for my lawfully wedded wife, to have and to hold, to cherish..."

Carrie listened in astonishment as David pronounced what she'd believed would be meaningless syllables. But the words seemed so very sincere, coming from his mouth. She frowned up at him, trying to understand how he could sound so convincing, as if he actually believed what he was saying. But his steady gaze passed through her, and she realized he must be a very good actor. Wasn't that part of his job? To trick hardened criminals into trusting him so that he could then arrest them?

She should have known he'd be able to handle this moment far more easily than she. Tears crested behind her pale lashes as Jason handed his father the tiny gold band. David slipped it onto the third finger of her left hand and eased it over her knuckle.

Carrie realized from the silence that it was her turn. She cleared her throat and recited the words with the help of the clerk, making her own promises before the small gathering. And God:

"I, Carrie Ann Monroe, take thee, David Adams..." She felt David watching her lips as they moved clumsily over the words. "...in sickness and in health...until death do us part...." Then he was brushing a wayward fringe of hair out of her eyes, as if he were lifting aside a gossamer veil, and he bent and kissed her softly, eloquently, on her upturned mouth.

His kiss felt disturbingly right.

Carrie braced herself by gripping the arm of his suit, taking two full breaths after he straightened, before she trusted herself to stand unassisted.

"Congratulations, Mr. and Mrs. Adams," the clerk said, beaming at them from behind his tidy mustache.

Everyone shook hands and kissed all around, but the room was a blur to Carrie. A minute later, David was offering her his arm. She let him walk her outside the room, to the elevator, then down a high-ceilinged marble corridor and into the summer sunshine.

And all she could think was, *What have I done?*

Rose stormed across the hangar and tossed her hat onto the desk.

Frank looked up from the newspaper he'd been reading. "What's up now, Rosie? You're in a lather, girl."

"That Carrie, she's got something up her sleeve!" Rose fumed, heaving herself into her chair.

Frank turned a page but didn't look up. He seemed comfortable perched on the corner of her desk, even though he was sitting on a stack of bills and at least one pen. "Thought you were more concerned about her middle than her sleeve," he commented dryly.

She shook a fist at him. "Men. They complicate everything."

"Like women don't?" he grumbled into the sports section.

Rose heard well enough but chose to ignore him. "I wish you had been there to see them."

"Glad I wasn't. Two people hitching up because one of them got pregnant. Fool reason for marryin'. Guarantees trouble."

"Frank, you sound so cold. You know you care about her."

He grunted and reluctantly folded his newspaper, placing it on the desk between them. "Tell me what's bothering you this time."

Rose thought for a minute, trying to separate her observations from hunches. "It wasn't like they *had* to get married."

"She's not pregnant?"

"I don't know," she said slowly. "There was something

about the way they looked. Not at each other, though. Most of the time they were avoiding each other's eyes. But they still looked to me like people in love.''

"Fine," he said.

"Maybe," she murmured, although she suspected his "fine" hadn't necessarily meant *good*. "I just can't help thinking that girl's got herself into some kind of trouble, maybe even worse than having a baby. If that's true, I don't know what it could be or why she's hiding it from us. I'm scared for her, Frank."

"What scares me is that detective she's gone and married." He stood abruptly, no longer trying to hide his concern. "The man's gonna ruin her life, sure as anything. You just wait and see. If she's in trouble, you can bet it's because of him."

"Frank, that's a terrible thing to say on Carrie's wedding day!" She shot him an accusatory glare. "Especially since you didn't even show up for the ceremony."

He wouldn't look at her.

She continued, still desperate to convince him. "I only mean, if you'd been there, you would have seen how it was. I've never known Carrie to lie or pretend she felt any different than she really did. During the ceremony and afterward at the restaurant, she looked at David as if she were heart and soul in love with the man, but she was trying not to let it show. You'd think on her wedding day..."

In fact, Rose herself had been the one to insist that the wedding party walk to a nearby restaurant to at least share a celebratory glass of wine. She'd managed to talk them into ordering a light meal, too. But there was no wedding cake, and only one halfhearted toast was made to the couple by David's partner. It was inconceivable to her that neither David nor Carrie had planned a reception of any kind to follow the ceremony.

"Frank, we need to talk to her. We need to—"

"Rose, leave it be," Frank advised, lifting a gnarled hand and letting it fall wearily. "I warned her and she wouldn't listen. Now she's got a husband and two kids. Let her work it out.''

If she can, Rose added silently.

Back at the apartment, Carrie unpinned the single orchid she'd worn on the front of her dress and stood before the mirror in the closet-size bedroom that had been designated as hers. She looked around at the frilly, little-girl curtains. Tammy had been moved in with her brother—much to his annoyance—so that this bedroom could be Carrie's. She stood in the middle of the room, feeling like a visitor on another planet.

No, more like an impostor.

That terrifying question echoed repeatedly through her mind. *What have I done? What have I done?*

She'd vowed before God and witnesses that she would love one man for the rest of her days. Despite all her efforts to shelter her heart from those words, *they had meant something to her!* They had reverberated through her heart and sung a message to her soul no matter how she tried to harden herself against them.

After the impromptu reception that Rose forced upon them, as they drove back to the apartment through rush-hour traffic, she'd dwelled on David's rich baritone promising to cherish her forever. Her brain was willing to reason with her. It accepted that they had merely been parroting phrases.

But her heart believed every word of their vows, as if it alone knew the truth. "I feel married to you, David Adams," she whispered to the reflection in her mirror. She was bound to him in ways she couldn't explain, even to herself.

Carrie looked up, startled by a knock on her door.

David stepped through, then shut it behind him, leaning against the wooden panel. He was wearing jeans that hugged his muscled legs and a dark T-shirt. His shoulder holster looped in front of his upper arms. The gun nestled against the left side of his chest. Over his arm, he carried a lightweight jacket.

"Are you all right?" he asked.

She shrugged, not trusting her voice.

"You looked pretty shaky when we left the courthouse. You didn't say two words all the way home in the car."

"I didn't find lying as easy as I thought I might."

She lifted her eyes, expecting to find him studying her, trying to figure out why she'd been unable to act like the joyful new bride she was supposed to be. Instead, he was looking out her bedroom window. The exotic view of a brick wall and a cluttered alley seemed to fascinate him.

"You appeared to be doing a lot more thinking than talking yourself, at the restaurant and on the trip home," she ventured. "Why was that?"

He brought his eyes back to meet hers. There was no warmth in them. They were blue ice again, the way they'd appeared on her plane the day they'd met.

"I don't know. I guess I was just nervous, like you," he said. "Well, now it's over. We can get back to some sort of routine."

Carrie worried her bottom lip as she watched him pull on his jacket. She felt hollow inside. Or worse, dead. Whatever sincerity she'd believed she was hearing in his vows must have been in her imagination.

"I've got to go out. I sent the kids off to undress for bed," he told her, backing toward the door. "It's only seven o'clock, but they're pretty beat. It's been a long day."

"I thought you had tonight off."

"I do, but I figured as long as you said you'd be here tonight, I might as well head out and get some work done. As long as you don't mind," he added awkwardly. "I know it's supposed to be our wedding night, but—"

"Don't worry," she hastily assured him. "I'm not thinking about it like that."

"Good." He zipped up the jacket. "I shouldn't be too late. I just have some—"

"Go ahead," she broke in. "It doesn't matter." She turned her back on him. Facing the mirror, she watched him observe her from behind. For the briefest instant, she thought she saw a flash of tenderness, perhaps even a distant yearning, pass across his troubled eyes. But whatever it was, it was gone in the next second. He let himself out of the room.

Carrie sat down heavily on the twin bed and lowered her forehead onto the pillow, letting the tears finally come. How could she feel so attached to a man who couldn't bear to stay in the same apartment with her? It was clear David was looking for an excuse to duck out.

She wept softly, her pain made worse by battling emotions. "What do I really want?" she asked herself between sobs. My family—me and my children, with no man to complicate things. That was the automatic answer that always came to her.

And yet...and yet...she ached for the touch of the wide, strong hands that had held hers in the courthouse...for the arms that had comforted her just a few nights before when she'd reacted so emotionally to images of wedding gowns and church music. It made no sense whatsoever, but there it was. She wanted David here with her, for whatever reason.

Carrie became aware of a sound beyond her own muffled sobs. She lifted her head, listening. Had it come from somewhere inside the apartment? Or from outside in the hall?

The sound came again. She pushed herself up off the bed, walked to her bedroom door and opened it. Hiccuping whimpers came to her from the middle bedroom. Evidently, she wasn't alone in being upset by the day's events.

Carrie drew a finger beneath each of her eyes, taking away most of the moisture. She walked hesitantly toward the room the children now shared and peeked inside.

Clad in pink pajamas, Tammy lay on her bed, curled up in a tight ball, her face mashed into her pillow. Jason was sitting on the edge of the mattress, rubbing her back and whispering to her.

The tender scene before her—the older child comforting the younger—wrenched at Carrie's heart. As bewildered as she felt by her own emotions, she could only imagine how much more confusing life must seem to these two.

Carrie crossed the room and Jason immediately straightened

to face her, his expression solemn. "What's wrong, Jase?" she asked.

"Nothin'," he mumbled, dropping his glance to bedspread level.

"Things are happening pretty fast, aren't they?"

He nodded, tucked his lower lip between his teeth.

Tammy sniffled twice more, then rolled over. Her eyes were red rimmed and swimming in tears. Impulsively, Carrie enfolded the little girl in her arms and rocked her against her chest. She touched her lips to the top of her soft head.

"Tell me why you're crying, Tams. I'll make you feel better."

The little girl cuddled even closer. "Daddy went away mad," she whimpered.

Carrie looked at Jason; his bottom lip started to tremble. Now that he was relieved of the task of being the strong one, he was crumbling. "Is that what you think?" she asked him.

Jason nodded. "Before Mommy moved to her condo, she went out at night, mad...a lot. Now Dad's going away mad."

"He won't come back!" Tammy cried.

Carrie's insides curdled. All the years of trying to block out memories of the day her own mother had walked out, never to return, rushed back at her with the force of a monsoon. Yes, grown-ups fought and argued. David and Sheila must have had some terrible fights. Then they'd split up and Sheila had left for good. Carrie understood only too well the horrible fear of desertion. David's children did see their mother a few days a week, but it wasn't like having a full-time mom.

"Your father will be back. He's just left for a little while to do some work. He goes out all the time to do his police work. Right? He's always come back before."

"You're sure he's not mad?" Jason asked.

"He's not angry with either of you or with me. He's just—" She faltered. How could she explain to a child that his father was probably feeling as awkward and unsure of their new living arrangement as she was? David had done what he'd seen as his duty—married to keep his children. Now he had a stranger living in his house and, she supposed, he must be wondering, just as she was, if he'd done the right thing.

The difference was, David Adams wasn't falling in love with her as she was falling in love...if not with him, then at least with his children.

"Your father just needs some time to himself. He loves you. He'll never leave you. Never," she stated firmly, knowing she was right, knowing that the love David had for his children exceeded all else in his life. She put an arm around each child and looked down into one upturned, trusting face, then the other. "He'll be home long before you wake up in the morning. And when he gets here, he'll come straight into this room and give you both a great big kiss."

Tammy slid her a lopsided smile. "Really?"

"Really."

"Maybe we should wait up for him," Jason suggested hopefully.

Carrie ruffled his hair. "No way, José. It could be very late before he gets back. I'll probably be asleep, too." She performed a stage yawn. "Goodness, I'm exhausted."

"Do you have to go flying tomorrow?" Jason asked as Carrie walked him to his own bed and lifted the covers for him to slip down inside. "When Mom comes tomorrow, we could tell her we're staying here with you instead of going to Mrs. Jeffer's house."

"Is that your sitter when your mother's working?" Carrie asked.

"I guess," Jason replied, looking uneasy with the discussion.

She studied his expression, but was unable to figure out what was on his mind. "Your mother has probably missed you terribly. She'll want to spend time with you."

Jason shrugged and scooted deeper down between the sheets. Tammy was lying in her bed, listening to them, holding her eyes half-open, but only with effort.

"I wish I could fly." Jason whispered so low she almost didn't hear him. "Like Batman."

Carrie stroked the shining bangs away from his forehead. "I have an idea, Jase."

He looked up at her expectantly.

"Now that you're out of school for the summer, there's no reason you have to stay in Baltimore all the time."

"Where would we go?" he asked, his skeptical expression a mirror image of his father's.

"Well...." She pretended to mull over his question. "What about the beach?"

He laughed. "The beach is way far away, like almost to China. Dad drove us last summer. It takes a long, *long* time to get there."

"By car it takes almost three hours. But—" Carrie dropped her voice to a conspiratorial whisper "—in my airplane it takes less than *one* hour. Just a hop, skip and a jump and we're there!"

Tammy sat up in bed, her eyes suddenly wide. "We could fly in your airplane to the beach?"

"Sure," Carrie said. She switched beds to tuck in Tammy. "We could start making plans, with your father's permission. When I have a couple of extra seats on the plane, I'll squeeze you two in."

"Could I bring my raft or snorkel?" Jason asked.

"You can bring both."

"Can I bring my pail and shovel, and wear my bathing suit, and eat cotton candy on the boardwalk, and buy a cute little hermit crab on a leash to bring home for a pet and—"

"Whoa!" Carrie laughed, hugging the little girl. "Let's start with a simple swimming trip, then we'll see what else happens." She turned to face Jason. "What do you say? We'll ask your father if it's okay."

"If you're our new mother, why do you have to ask him?"

Carrie sensed a subtle test. "Because parents work together to decide what is best for their children."

Jason looked at her thoughtfully, before a tentative smile started in the center of his lips and spread to their corners. "I think what's best for us is a trip to the beach."

* * *

The children were asleep. David sensed it as soon as he let himself into the apartment. The place was too quiet to contain a fully conscious Jason and Tammy.

Everything seemed in its place, he noted as he crossed the dark living room. Toys in their boxes, TV silent, the kitchen countertops wiped down and uncluttered. He could almost forget that a woman he hardly knew slept in the tiny third bedroom. A woman he'd legally married that day.

Suddenly, his stomach was churning again. His palms began to sweat.

Walking the streets for three hours had done little to soothe his raw nerves. His mind obstinately replayed the events of the day. He had stood in the courthouse and gazed into Carrie Monroe's soft hazel eyes and sweet face, and he'd promised to love and keep her forever. Forever. The terrifying thing was, as the words passed through his lips he'd felt as if he really meant them. God help him!

David knew he had to somehow overcome the helpless sensation that had gripped him during the marriage ceremony. He couldn't afford to let Carrie affect him that way. She had agreed to live with him for a year, then she'd take her money and be gone. There was nothing more he could offer her. There was no way he could bind her to him.

He just wouldn't allow himself to fall in love with her.

Besides, he reminded himself, he wasn't about to let himself in for the heartbreak of a failed marriage, a *real* marriage, ever again. So it was simply a matter of keeping his head—and, he added as Carrie stepped through the doorway at the end of the hall, keeping his hands off her.

"Hi," he whispered, not wanting to wake the children, "how is everything?"

She floated toward him, wearing a simple but very feminine cotton nightgown topped by a thin summer robe. She carried with her the scent of lilacs. Old-fashioned, seductive in their innocence, like nothing he had ever smelled on the streets.

"The kids were a little upset."

He tuned out her fragrance and concentrated on what he

was being told, sensing it was important. "Because I went out?"

"They were worried you might not come back."

He squeezed his eyes closed. "Where did they get that idea?"

Taking his hand, she led him over to the couch in the living room. "Sit down, David. I'll tell you. Just remember it's not your fault."

"I'll decide if it's my fault or not," he retorted stiffly.

She blew a puff of air through her bangs and eyed him narrowly. He got the message.

"Sorry," he apologized. "I'm still a little keyed up."

"Fair enough. So am I." She took one more breath, like a weight lifter before going for a record heft. "Listen, this might not sound entirely rational, but your children are afraid that you're going to desert them—" she held up a hand when he started to object "—because you and I have been avoiding each other and not talking since the ceremony today."

"Oh."

"I think they interpret our silence as fighting. When you and Sheila argued, did one of you give the other the silent treatment, then clear out for a while?"

He nodded. "Usually Sheila. Sometimes I got the feeling she picked fights to give herself an excuse to go out and be with her friends. Other nights, I suppose I used investigations as a reason for leaving the apartment." Like tonight, he thought sadly. He hadn't been able to stay in the apartment without feeling like a fraud.

"I don't think they're worried about my leaving," Carrie said. "They don't know me that well yet. If I disappeared tomorrow, it wouldn't change their lives much, if at all. But if you left—"

"I see," David broke in. He rubbed his palms over his face—hard enough to feel the scrape of his whiskers. "I've been thinking only about myself. I didn't realize they'd get so tangled up in this charade—not so quickly anyway."

"Do you want to back out of our agreement?" she asked. Her voice was tight with a strange emotion he couldn't read.

He thought for a moment. "No, then I'd be left with the same problem—how to keep my kids. You were right when you said we needed to explain the truth to them as soon as possible. As for me, I just have to accept that we'll be seeing a lot of each other for the next twelve months."

"Well, that's quite a burden, I must say," she said, rolling her eyes dramatically.

It took him a moment to realize she was baiting him. Then he laughed out loud and dropped back against the beige cushions to observe her appreciatively. Layers of tension sluiced away, leaving him more relaxed than he'd felt in days. "It's not as if you're hard on the eyes, lady. Actually, I see your proximity as a challenge."

"We agreed," she reminded him quickly, a shadow of alarm in her eyes, "no sex."

"Yes." Leaning forward, he propped his elbows on his knees and took one of her featherlight hands in his. His eyes gravitated to the place where pink-and-white eyelet trim crossed her breasts, demurely outlining their shape. "Still, it's an awful shame that we'll never be lovers." His voice sounded thick and raspy to his own ears.

He was nearly sure he could see the enticingly dark circles of her nipples through the fabric. Or it might have been an illusion created by his imagination shifting into overdrive. He felt himself being pulled toward her, as if by some invisible force field. He made himself straighten up and look away. Yet he couldn't check the sweep of his eyes as they wandered back toward Carrie's breasts.

"It would be dangerous," she said.

"In what way?" Danger meant different things to him. Guns, knives, a guy so high on 'ludes he didn't know what he was doing.

"If we made love," she explained hesitantly, "I'm not sure I—"

"Me, too," he interrupted, thinking he knew where she was headed. "It would be an awkward situation for both of us, living in the same house. Harder for you, I guess. You'd always be afraid I'd come charging through your bedroom door with lust in my heart.'' He swept a hand through his dark hair, combing it off his forehead. ''Don't worry, I'm not *that* out of control. I'd never hurt you or take advantage of you.''

''I didn't mean that,'' she said, her cheeks suffusing with a rich pink hue. ''What I'm trying to say is that I'm a...well, I've never...'' She struggled for the right words.

He loved how easily she blushed. The women he dated never blushed. Probably hadn't since they hit thirteen.

Something drew his hand to the burning patch on her left cheek. He touched it, knowing before his fingertips met flesh that it would be velvety soft. Almost as soft as Tammy's cheek. The thought of his daughter sleeping peacefully in the other room made him pull back his hand, but Carrie caught it and held on lightly.

''I—'' she began, looking puzzled and shocked at the same time, as if she herself didn't understand why she was telling him what she was about to say. ''I liked the way you held my hands today at the ceremony. I was frightened and you made me feel calmer.''

His voice cracked over an uneasy laugh. ''*You* were frightened? I was scared out of my mind.'' He looked down at their entwined fingers, then back up into her eyes. They were a misty gray-green, like fog on a summer night, drifting over the marshlands where his grandfather used to take him goose hunting. ''You feel good, Carrie.''

The words lingered in the air, neither of them daring to interrupt their vibrations by speaking over them.

At last David could no longer deprive himself of another few inches of her skin. He told himself that by touching the undersides of her wrists, he'd soothe her now, as he had during the ceremony. His thumb circled her pulse, once, twice, three times, then moved higher, beneath the sleeve of her robe.

''David,'' Carrie whispered.

The sound of his name on her lips tortured at the same time as it pleased him.

''I've never wanted a woman the way I want you at this moment,'' he heard himself say. ''Never.''

She audibly swallowed. ''I don't know what's right or

wrong any longer. We shouldn't...can't..." Carrie melted forward into his arms, all soft woman, pure emotion.

He held her, just held her, feeling her heart thud against his chest and echo within him. He didn't know how many men she'd been with, but from the little she'd told him and the rest that he'd sensed about her, he expected it wasn't many. He, on the other hand, was experienced enough to know when a woman needed to be loved. Carrie might be hoping, subconsciously, that their coming together could last forever, or it might be that she didn't care if it was only for one night. But the scent and pulse and pent-up energy from her body sent a desperate message to him: she needed him tonight.

The knowledge was too powerful for him to ignore. No man could be that strong, he told himself.

David listened instinctively for any motion or sound from the middle bedroom.

There was none, and he sensed that the children wouldn't stir until at least seven o'clock.

His fingers carefully loosened the bow at the neckline of Carrie's robe. He lifted the ruffled neckline down over her creamy shoulders. Even the sleeveless gown beneath was modest, intended less to seduce than to provide a decent covering for the body while its wearer lounged about the house during an evening. She could have answered the door in the outfit without embarrassment.

He had, he saw, been imagining the shadow of her nipples through the robe. But without the extra layer of translucent cotton, they now appeared—round, perfect and enticing.

David flattened his hands over the fullness of her breasts and gently pressed. Her flesh yielded warmly to his touch. Curling his fingers inward, he found her nipples with thumb and forefinger and coaxed them to peaks through her gown.

Carrie let her head drop back with a soft moan. "David, I must tell you some—"

"Tell me to stop and I promise I will. But until you say the word, I—" I'm absolutely, utterly, beyond hope, he thought. To cease touching her now would be unthinkable, although he knew he must if she demanded it.

Her hands lit like trembling butterflies on his chest, fluttering in wide circles across his T-shirt. He understood that she was experimenting with the contours of his body, feeling the hard ridges, muscular mounds, tight hollows—her touch growing bolder. Her hand came up behind his neck, fingers softly caressing the short hairs until they stood on end. She invited him forward until their lips touched.

He was lost.

With one swift motion, he slipped his hands into her gown's neckline and pushed it down over her shoulders, revealing the ivory mounds of her breasts as he laid her back against a cushion. He moved over her. His mouth played across hers, sampling the flavor of her kiss, before skimming the long line of her throat. Seeking the taut points of her breasts framed by his palms, he sketched light circles around each erect nipple with his tongue, before drawing one breast fully into his mouth.

The taste of her, the warmth of her body beneath his, overwhelmed him. He was only remotely aware of her reactions until she groaned and pressed her hips upward, meeting his arousal. He knew she couldn't possibly question how desperately he wanted her. He was hard. He was ready. All he had to do was make a short trip into the bathroom for protection, and he'd satisfy both their needs.

But before he could ease away from Carrie, her hands burrowed between their bodies, pressing almost timidly beneath the waistband of his jeans. Then the coolness of her fingers wrapped around him, crowding out all rational thought but one.

Get up and go find a damn condom! Now! Before it's too late!

His body had other ideas. He couldn't stop his hands, his mouth from seeking out each succulent and sensitive inch of her, although he was still fully clothed. Lifting the hem of her gown, he reached beneath it and smoothed his hand up the outside of her thigh, expecting to find cotton panties as demure and sensible as her gown, but he found none at all. He rounded the swell of her hip and gently slid his hand beneath her to investigate the lovely bottom he'd admired in her jumpsuit. Slowly he brought his hand around to her velvety center.

Carrie arched up to meet him as he stroked her. A whimper of pleasure escaped from her lips as he touched his fingers to the outer lips of her moist femininity. The whimper grew deeper, coming from low within her throat in husky gasps.

He lowered his head and kissed the soft, pale triangle, wanting to taste her, wanting that and so much more. All the time, the voice demanding he leave her just long enough to protect them both. Then another voice cut in from a part of him he hadn't known existed.

Do this to her now and you'll ruin her dreams forever. She wants a family of her own. She said so, and she means it. Don't screw up her life the way you've screwed up your own. She's too good a woman....

David closed his eyes, exerting the last ounce of willpower left to him. Withdrawing his hand from between her thighs, he pushed himself up off the couch and stepped away from it. Unable to remain close to her and do what he had to do for both their sakes, he took two huge steps backward.

"Sorry," he blurted out. "Lord help me, I'm sorry, Carrie. I can't do this to you."

He caught a dazed, drugged look in her eyes that turned to shock as he continued to back from the room, hurrying for the bathroom. Not for the protection he'd thought of moments earlier. He urgently needed a hundred gallons or so of cold water in his face and most everywhere else on his body.

Chapter 9

Carrie stumbled toward her room, aware only of the throbbing heat clutching her insides, and a hunger more fierce and demanding than any she'd ever experienced. David had left her clinging to the couch, no better off than the survivor of a sunken ship on a leaking life raft. The need he'd aroused in her had to remain unsatisfied, she realized, dashing away tears as she ran.

What she was feeling was an automatic physical response, primitive, animal-like. She understood all of that and tried to fight the sensations, ignore them, block them from her mind—but she failed.

She wanted David, longed to feel his hands on her again, ached for the return of his touch to flesh that still prickled with agonizing pleasure. His sudden desertion drove her, blindly, to her bedroom. She shut the door behind her, leaned against it, breathing in great gulps of air.

She heard David leave the bathroom, hesitate outside her door, then pass by and begin to pace the living room floor. His heavy steps were charged with frustrated passion. He slammed something—his fist against the wall, she thought—and swore out loud.

"I'm glad you stopped us," she whispered, hoping that by saying the words she'd believe them. Her throat ached, protesting against speech, but she had to anchor the moment in reality, had to force herself to accept the necessity of not becoming David's lover. "It has to be this way. It has to...."

Tears rimmed her eyes, burning before trickling in steamy trails down her cheeks. Damn logic. Why did everything have to make sense? Why, for once, couldn't she ignore the wind shears, the thunderheads, the icing conditions? Fly straight through the storm. Dare to cheat the odds!

In fact, she admitted to herself, that's what she'd been doing. If David hadn't put a stop to things, she would have slept with him.

Thinking about the way they'd touched, kissed, fondled each other, she wondered why she hadn't felt embarrassed. Loving David seemed so right, so natural. Knowing that, feeling it deep within her soul, made it all the more difficult to deny herself the pleasure. But she must, she knew. If they'd consummated their wedding vows, they would have established new rules for the coming year. Ones neither of them could live by...because, in the end, the pain of parting would be so much more difficult to bear.

If she once surrendered herself totally to him, their physical needs would be satisfied for the time being, but the novelty of their lovemaking would certainly burn itself out. All that would be left would be bitterness. They'd learn to despise each other. She'd seen it happen to so many other couples.

Carrie couldn't bear watching cool disinterest and boredom replace the rapture she'd seen in his eyes that night.

Falling away from the door, she stumbled to her bed, collapsed onto it, curling into a fetal position as tears washed down her face.

What had David been thinking as he looked at her naked breasts, as he'd stroked her, excited her, woven dreams in her heart she had no right to hold?

Lust, there was certainly that. He'd wanted to have sex with her—but had he wanted to *make love to her?*

She rolled onto her back and stared desperately at the ceiling, unable to answer her own question. She missed the comfort of her own bedroom, with its familiar plaster swirls above her bed. Did intentions really matter? Did any of it matter? Sex…love…physical need or a passionate love so strong it might overcome both of their resolutions to end their arrangement after one year? What defined what she felt for David and what he felt for her?

She felt utterly confused, empty, exhausted. All she could do was release herself to despair. Let the dark little room enclose her and, eventually, carry her off to a place of calm, if not of love…which was, after all, the best she could hope for that night.

David awoke the next morning to hear Carrie in the kitchen—running water, opening and closing the refrigerator, walking softly so as not to disturb the children. Nevertheless, he could easily trace her path through the apartment—from kitchen, to bathroom, to her bedroom, then down the hall and back to the kitchen again.

He could tell she was barefoot. He could tell she wasn't happy.

Her normally springy steps sounded as if they were dragging listlessly through a necessary but hated routine. He wedged his hands under his head and stared at the ceiling above his bed, purposefully tensing every muscle of his body to a rigid line. Harder, harder still, he worked the muscles, until at last he released them all and lay still…waiting for the sense of peace he could expect to follow the stress-relieving isometric exercise.

He felt no better.

Hours after he'd left Carrie's side, he still wanted her, still longed to touch the silky parts of her that had responded so beautifully to him. Still wanted to hold and comfort her, even as he fed his own dark hungers.

David groaned and made himself get up off the bed. The

night before, after Carrie had shut herself in her room, he'd blown off some steam by slamming things around for a few minutes, then retreated to his own room, where he shucked off his clothing—tossing jeans, shirt, underwear on the floor. He literally threw himself down on the bed. He'd done nothing beyond take a cold shower to mollify his lust, because he wanted to punish himself. So he lay there, still wanting Carrie, and eventually the hunger subsided enough for him to lapse into a fitful sleep.

Now he chucked his dirty clothing into the hamper in his closet and found a bathrobe he rarely wore. It was made of thick, navy blue terry cloth. It was long, bulky and service-able—not at all sexy. He plodded into the bathroom, washed his face, ran the brush through his hair and decided he didn't have the energy to shave.

David tried to form a blank of his mind, but immediately realized that was the worst way to go. An empty mind invited thoughts of Carrie—half-undressed, wriggling invitingly in his arms, letting out tiny feminine moans at his touch.

Keep body and mind busy, he told himself. Very, very busy. That would be his only chance of surviving the next 364 days.

David strode into the kitchen, to find Carrie seated at the table, sipping a cup of coffee. She wore no makeup and her hair was casually brushed in loose waves off her face. Gray circles undershadowed her pretty eyes. He could have kicked himself. She looked as if she'd gotten as little sleep as he had.

He poured himself a mug of strong coffee from the carafe beside the toaster and stood at the sink, drinking it black and so hot it scalded all the way down—his form of self-flagellation.

"I take it the kids are still asleep," he muttered. His voice sounded sandpapery rough.

She nodded, focusing on the cup cradled between her fin-gertips.

"I'm sorry about what happened last night." He got it out quickly. "It was my fault. I should never have—"

"Yes," she said before he could finish.

"I promised you I wouldn't take advantage of our business

arrangement, and then I nearly forced you to have sex with me. I don't know what came over me." He knew. Of course he knew. She'd looked so beautiful, so soft, so natural, sitting in his living room in her nightclothes. How easily she might become a part of his world—sharing his children, his food, his space—if he let her. Why shouldn't he reach for her when he felt the need for a woman?

"It was as much my fault as yours," she said stiffly. "I let things get out of hand."

He drank more slowly now, swirling the still-steaming liquid in the mug between swallows. "All right. We don't need to argue over who's to blame. Are we agreed that we can't let it happen again?"

"Absolutely," she whispered, her eyes still evading his.

He took a deep breath, let it out in a forceful gust. "Fine. Then we have to find ways to make this easier on both of us."

"Now that the wedding is over, I can get back to my normal flying schedule. I won't be here much of any day."

He nodded, thinking of his own workload, which was spilling over with investigations. The lieutenant had assigned him and Pete another new case the day before. As to Rainey's case, the most crucial of the lot, dozens of statements had already been taken, but many were useless, conflicting or required time-consuming follow-up. Whether any of them would result in hard evidence the D.A. could use to back up the sting, no one yet knew.

"I have a lot to keep me busy, too," he admitted. "But we'll still cross paths, like last night."

"*Not* like last night," Carrie shot back, her eyes flashing up to meet his. "It won't happen again."

He shuddered at the icy edge to her voice. Clearly she regretted their intimacy. She seemed to find it easy to switch from hot to cold. He swallowed, hurting inside. A man could have lascivious feelings without being in love with a woman. Why should he be shocked that it had been that way for her?

They'd both been carried away by the moment. Simple as that.

He set down his coffee mug with a sharp whack, then faced her from across the kitchen. "Carrie, look at me."

She was back to staring into her cup.

"I said, 'Look at me!'" His voice crackled with unpredictable, barely contained menace, and he didn't try to mask it.

Her eyes snapped up, fearful, wary. "Yes?"

"Let's make this as easy as we can on each other." He had to clear his throat before he could go on. An idea had occurred to him. He wasn't sure how much it would help, but anything was better than the torment of another scene like the night before. "We need more space so we're not on top of each other when we're both at home. I really think it will help if I can give you more privacy."

"What did you have in mind?"

David crossed the kitchen in two long strides and pulled out the chair on the opposite side of the table from her. He spun it on one leg and straddled it, supporting his arms and chin on the high back, as he studied her dubious expression.

"Remember I told you that my lawyer suggested I move to the 'burbs? Find some place outside the inner city, where the kids would be in a lower crime area?"

"I remember."

"There's no reason I can't start looking for a place now, even if a job transfer doesn't work out. No law says a Baltimore city cop has to live in the city. I'll look for a house, something with more rooms, larger rooms. Maybe even a house with an in-law apartment. We could call it your 'office' so it won't sound as if we are sleeping in separate rooms. Hell, I don't care if you lock yourself off from me, if it will make this easier on you...on both of us."

Carrie drummed her fingernails on the tabletop, as if the repetitive motion made it easier for her to think. "Fine," she murmured at last. "I guess that makes sense." She hesitated, chewed her bottom lip. "Won't that be risky, though?"

"Risky?"

"What if someone discovers I live in what amounts to a

separate apartment in the house? What if it gets back to your wife?''

My wife, he thought. The term felt so wrong when applied to Sheila. How could he have ever believed she could be that important to him?

"We'll make sure the master bedroom looks shared. You can leave some of your off-season clothing in my bureau, some dresses in the closet. Keeping toiletries in a separate bathroom is an arrangement made by a lot of couples these days. Makes getting ready for work or a night out easier. We can find a house with the right floor plan, something comfortable and private for both of us."

"It will at least help us stay out of each other's way," she admitted. Then she nodded as if she'd made an important decision. Looking directly at him, her eyes brittle and determined, just as they'd been in the second before she'd plunged the *Bay Lady* into the dive that had saved his life, she asked, "When will you start looking?"

"Tomorrow afternoon, if I can reach a willing real estate agent today," he said. "I have to work tonight after Sheila picks up the kids. If you like and you can spare the time, you can come with me. I think it would be a good idea. After all, you'll be living in the place for a whole year."

Carrie closed her fingers around her cup and took a quick swallow of coffee that looked stone cold. "I'll cancel my afternoon flight."

Carrie had never been a brooder. She didn't sulk, didn't hold grudges and refused to dwell on negatives. What was done was done. She'd even learned to cope with the haunting rejection that sometimes returned when she thought of her mother. She probably wouldn't recognize the woman if they passed on the street. She hoped she wouldn't.

But this time was different. Although she felt sure David's motive for wanting to sleep with her was purely male libido, her own motives were less clear to her. She couldn't shake the sense that she was treading on perilous ground when it came to her feelings about David...and his children.

Whenever she spent time with Jason and Tammy and their father, even if it was for just a few minutes, her life seemed to start leaning in a new direction. If a single day passed without her seeing the children, she found herself wondering if they were sleeping well. Had they been getting enough attention from their mother? What about their meals? Were they nourishing? Timely? David had told her the woman was sometimes lax in finding suitable baby-sitters for them. Carrie worried about them. So many terrible things could happen to children in this modern, fast-paced, dangerous world.

Then there was David. They might miss seeing each other for an entire day and night, when he was working an extended night shift and catching a few hours' sleep while she was flying. But when Carrie did run into David at the apartment, if only for a few minutes, she felt a strong instinctual tug somewhere deep inside her. Her heart? Or was it her soul?

She feared it might be both.

That Saturday she returned to BWI Airport after a morning of shuttling vacationers to the beach and found David and the children waiting for her at the hangar. Rose had taken Jason and Tammy back to her cubbyhole of an office and was feeding them chocolate chip cookies from a jar she kept on her desk, while David looked on in mild disapproval.

"Hi-ya, gang!" she called cheerfully as she strode toward the little group. "Rose, I swear, you'll spoil their appetites."

Her receptionist rolled her eyes. "A few cookies never hurt any child."

David gave her a tentative smile, as if unsure how she'd greet him. "Rose tells me this was your last flight until Monday."

"Yes," she said. "I'm logged up on my hours for the week. I can't fly tomorrow, so I'm not losing any time by canceling that afternoon flight today. I'm taking tomorrow off, too, and letting Rose and Frank do the same."

"Good, that will leave us plenty of house-hunting time." He nodded at the children. "Sheila begged off again. Says she can't take the kids until she finishes a special job on a diplomat's house. Still want to go along? This could be a pretty lively afternoon, with Jason and Tammy along for the ride.''

She considered the situation. Spending time with David as long as the kids were with them was safer anyway. And, as he'd suggested, it would be in her interest to have some say in where she lived for the next year. "Just give me twenty minutes to file my flight report and change.''

Before long, they were on their way. The real estate office was located in Columbia, Maryland, less than thirty minutes' drive southwest of Baltimore. The community had risen out of hundreds of acres of farmland starting in the early seventies, and was divided into tidy neighborhoods with whimsical names like Long Reach, Oakland Mills and Steven's Forest; elegant single-family homes often blended into a section of practical, midpriced town houses. Now and then a modern, brick-and-glass apartment complex rose beside a man-made lake that was circled by dreamy willow trees.

Most of the houses the real estate agent had selected for them to see would be in that area.

"Can you remember a time before this town was here?" Carrie murmured as they drove.

"Yes," David said. "It was a shame when the last orchard fell to the bulldozer blade.''

She sighed, gazing out the car window as they sped along Route 175, which split the town into north and south halves. From the road, only the roofs of a few houses were visible. All commercial buildings and most of the homes were screened by strategically placed landscaping, which gave the town a countrified, open appearance. It was a drastic change from the concrete-and-brick facades of Baltimore.

"By the time I was old enough to take an interest in anything outside my own house in Catonsville," Carrie explained, "my dad was flying me over this place, pointing out the clusters of new houses springing up everywhere. They looked like little, square mushrooms to me. I couldn't have been more than three or four years old.''

"You must have grown up with an entirely different perspective from that of most children," he mused, his blue eyes thoughtful. "The world must have seemed so much larger from the air. Until I was twelve years old, my entire world was an area of about ten blocks, starting at the harbor and running north along Charles Street toward old Oriole Park. I was anchored to the ground. Pavement, granite stoops, family-owned shops run by Germans, Jews, Koreans and African-Americans.

"In the summer when the weather got unbearably hot, we played in water gushing from fire hydrants. In the winter, we slid on sheets of cardboard down steep alleys clogged with gray snow. The only time I looked up at the sky was to see if it was going to rain." He let out a wry chuckle. "Even then, there never seemed to be much of it—sky, that is."

"I sometimes feel as if I've spent more of my time in the sky than on the ground." Carrie laughed to herself, surprised that the memory was such a happy one. Maybe it seemed so because she was sharing it. Contrasting her childhood to David's gritty years growing up in the streets, she realized her good fortune. "I wasn't a very good student," she admitted. "It was more fun to study flight manuals than memorize spelling lists and chemical equations." That was one reason she felt so ill prepared to earn a living by doing anything other than fly.

"I'll bet you were ten times smarter than the other kids." David shot her a sideways smile that lit his eyes.

She laughed. "I doubt it. But thanks for the compliment." Looking out the window, she felt herself begin to relax in a way she hadn't in weeks. Maybe house shopping would be therapeutic, or even fun. She was determined to loosen up and enjoy David's company. Sex didn't have to be part of every relationship between a man and a woman. He was an interesting man with a lot of good qualities. She told herself she should focus on these and simply enjoy being around him while she could. Why dwell on the future?

Besides, David was probably right. Once they were in a larger house, there would be more ways for each of them to protect his or her own privacy. There would be safe ground to retreat to if the situation threatened to turn steamy again.

David steered into a large parking lot landscaped with brilliant red geraniums and spikes of a vibrant blue flower whose name Carrie couldn't remember.

"Are we here?" Jason cried. "Where's our new house?"

"We have to meet with Mrs. Morgan, the real estate agent," David explained, reaching over the back of his seat to tousle Jason's hair. "She'll show us a lot of houses. We get a choice."

"I want a pink one," Tammy whispered in Carrie's ear.

"Pink—yuck!" Jason groaned loudly.

"Don't worry, Son," David said. "Whatever we decide to get, it won't be pink."

"Aw, gee!" Carrie groaned in mock disappointment. This *was* going to be fun.

She was right. At the end of the day Carrie felt as if they'd been window-shopping for dollhouses. The best part was, the financial arrangements were of no concern to her, because David was the one buying. Her only obligation was to occupy whatever home he purchased, for a year. No more of a commitment than moving into a college dorm.

So she'd relaxed and enjoyed soaking up new decorating ideas—wallpaper treatments, innovative painting techniques from faux marble to stenciling, creative fixtures in the bathrooms and kitchens, unusual floor plans. She felt as if she were walking onto a series of movie sets, except the sets were homes of real people.

David, however, seemed a lot less enthusiastic and a great deal more stressed by the grand tour. "I don't think any of the places we've seen today are right for us," he said when they retreated to his car after thanking the hopeful female agent. "If there's enough space for all of us inside, there's no yard for the kids, or the house is more than I can afford. If it's affordable, there are too many renovations to be done. I don't have time to put a lot of work into a house."

"That ranch style with the brick fireplace in the family room was nice," Carrie suggested, peering over the seat into the back to check on the children. Exhausted by the great adventure, they were already starting to fall asleep as David pulled out of the parking lot and into traffic. "It seemed in good condition, and the real estate agent said the owners were anxious to sell quickly. They might take a low offer."

He shook his head. "I didn't like the way that one backed onto a heavily wooded lot."

"I thought it was lovely."

"The entire rear of the house was sheltered from the road and other houses. Anyone could break in through that sliding patio door, take their time doing it, and no one would see them."

"Oh, well..." Remembering similar reactions from David to several of the properties, Carrie realized that security was an important issue with him. That made sense, given his job. His apartment had been carefully protected with dead bolts and double locks on the windows. "We can look some more tomorrow, or maybe next weekend."

He raked a hand through his hair. "I've got a gut feeling this is going to take a lot longer than I expected. I need to move the kids out of Baltimore fast. From what Mrs. Morgan said, even after I make an offer on a place, it could be six weeks or more before final approval on the loan and closing."

"That's past your court date," Carrie observed. Time was a definite problem. "Maybe just starting the process of buying a house will be enough for the judge."

"I wouldn't count on it."

Carrie thought about each of the houses they'd seen. Many of them had practical floor plans that would suit their needs, and sleek, modern kitchens. Two had in-law apartments; she suspected David had mentioned this option to the real estate agent when he'd set up the appointment with her. But not one of the houses felt like home. Not like her own comfy Victorian cottage.

Carrie twisted around in the passenger seat and looked at David. "What would you say to a temporary home for you and the kids? One that would look like a permanent move to the court and would be perfect for what we need?"

"What do you have in mind?"

"I was thinking about…about *my* house," she suggested tentatively, watching David's eyes for a reaction.

He glanced quickly at her, then turned his attention back to the road again. "I don't think that's a very good idea. It's your family's home—we'd be intruding. Imagine having houseguests stay for a whole year."

Carrie supposed she might end up feeling that way, but somehow she doubted it.

"No, Jason and Tammy would fit right in there. It's a great place for children, and there are enough bedrooms for each of them to have a room." A seed of enthusiasm grew to excitement as details fleshed themselves out in her mind. "You can take the master bedroom, upstairs, near theirs. I can use my parents' digs on the first floor. The bedroom suite has its own bath and sitting room. My father remodeled the sunroom when he first bought the house, thinking they were going to have more children after me."

It was sad when she thought of his lost dreams now. But somehow, the hope of moving David's children into her own home made her feel better. If houses had emotions, she was confident the aging Victorian would be thrilled with its new tenants.

The muscle along David's jaw worked rhythmically. He scowled through the windshield, as though he were the captain of a ship, trying to see through a pea-soup fog to treacherous shoals. "What about the yard?"

"It's big enough for the children to play in, protected from the main street, but another large house backs on the lot. Our kitchens overlook one another. They're good neighbors, and alert. We've always watched over each other's property when one family or the other was away on vacation."

She paused to give David a chance to respond. When he still appeared skeptical, she continued.

"Since it's a corner lot, the sidewalk passes down one side and across the front, along a low hedge. Dad put in three motion-detector lights a few years ago. They light up the place like a landing strip." Carrie's heart warmed at David's endearing timidity. He looked more like a little boy trying to decide if he dared trespass on his neighbor's yard to avoid the town bully than a hardened narcotics cop.

"At least bring the children over tomorrow, let them check it out," she suggested.

David dreaded the trip the next day.

Although Carrie's suggestion seemed a sensible one, he wondered if she had an ulterior motive in trying to move them all into her father's house. He knew she missed familiar surroundings. She often stopped off at the old house to pick up a favorite sweater, item of jewelry or a particular pan for preparing dinner. The errands were more excuses for a visit than a necessity, he guessed. But he still didn't feel it was right for him and his children to encroach on her turf.

Yes, he was paying her for the interruption in her life, to pretend to be mother to his children and wife to him. But he knew their deal was still a lot to ask of a busy woman like Carrie, with a business to run and responsibilities of her own. Wouldn't he and his kids become even more of a burden in her parents' house? Children were hard on furniture, woodwork and plumbing. Little shoes scuffed up polished oak floors and peanut-butter fingers smudged plaster walls and draperies. She almost certainly would regret having made the offer after a month or two.

He was also concerned that the children would become attached to a house, neighborhood and routines they found comforting. By the end of a year they'd have fully adjusted to their new surroundings...and he'd be moving them out.

But as soon as Carrie led Jason and Tammy up the front walk that Sunday morning, his misgivings evaporated into the sunshine-warmed summer air. He knew the quaint old house was perfect. It had the look, even the smell, of respectability. He could show photos of this place to a judge, who would immediately understand that this was a loving haven for children. Between Carrie herself and this house, he felt at last assured he would be able to hold on to his children.

As to the other two factors that affected the ongoing custody battle with Sheila—there probably was no way he could use either to reinforce his case. He still had no proof of Sheila's negligence toward Jason and Tammy. She'd dumped the kids on him with little or no notice a few times, but that could be explained away by a heavy work schedule. No judge would hold working against a single mother. And he still had only snatches of information he'd picked up from the children, about nights spent at locations other than Sheila's condo. He relied on baby-sitters, too. The most he could do was write down dates and summaries of conversations, hoping a pattern of sorts would emerge that might add one more point in his favor.

But now, as he stood in the foyer of Carrie's house, soaking up its reassuring warmth and listening to his children ricochet from room to room as they joyfully investigated the second floor, he knew the place was perfect.

He turned to Carrie. She stood facing him, her expression determined, watching him as if he were a storm cloud blocking her flight route. "Are you sure?" he asked.

"Absolutely. This house needs to get used to children again. It's far too quiet here."

He thought about the way she'd phrased her answer. Get used to children again. She was thinking about her dream family, the one she'd start after he removed himself from her life. The thought needled him, hurt.

"Fine," he said quickly. "I'll rent a van for next weekend and notify Pete we need a hand."

As it turned out, half the Baltimore City Narcotics Squad turned out to help. They emptied David's entire apartment in one long, exhausting afternoon. Personal items and the few inexpensive-but-usable pieces of furniture were moved to the Catonsville house. They were either absorbed into existing room arrangements or stored in the basement. Overflow and unwanted items were delivered to the Goodwill Thrift Store.

It seemed to David as if his entire life had been absorbed into Carrie's world, which was a strange sensation. He compared it to making love to a woman. Entering her, feeling her envelop him, reaching deeper into her and then losing himself in a rush of sensations.

Here he was, in her house—a home that far exceeded the quality of any other place he'd lived—and he was amazed at how right it felt. He hadn't fully appreciated the contrast until they'd finished moving the furniture and he took the time to roam about on his own. There were four spacious floors—the partially finished basement, two main living floors and a fully inhabitable attic with dormers for light.

His grandparents would have thought the house a mansion. He watched in delight as his children raced up and down flights of stairs, searching out favorite toys that were still packed in boxes, hiding from each other in stairwells and built-in cupboards, as enchanted with the place as he was.

At 10 p.m. on the night of the move, after Jason and Tammy were in bed and asleep, David found Carrie in the little sitting room that was part of her first-floor bedroom suite. She was sitting in the middle of a braided rug, surrounded by neat piles of clean laundry. She wore men's-style, striped cotton pajamas several sizes too large for her petite frame. She looked lost in the fabric, and utterly adorable.

"You don't have to do that," he said quietly. "I've always done the children's wash with my own."

She didn't look up, but he caught the corners of her lips turning upward. "Sorting and folding laundry are therapeutic—besides, it's sort of fun playing with little kids' clothing."

He chuckled at her. "I call it a pain in the neck—all those lace-trimmed ankle socks and other…frilly things."

"All a matter of perspective," she mused, contentedly folding one of Tammy's pastel rompers and adding it to a stack to her right. "Besides, it's hardly any trouble at all if I toss some of Jason's and Tammy's things in the washer with mine."

"I didn't intend for you to take on maid services—I told you that."

"I really don't mind. It gives me a chance to daydream about my own children."

"Your own," he repeated after her, the words catching in his throat.

A subliminal image forced itself on him. He imagined Carrie in the arms of a faceless man. A man who wasn't him. She would sleep with this man, letting him touch her as intimately as she'd allowed him, if only for those few unbridled moments before he'd regained his sanity. Inside her would grow a child who belonged to that other man. She'd love that child, not merely because she was enchanted with childhood. She'd cherish and care for their child because it was of her flesh and blood, and that of the man she loved and welcomed into her bed every night.

The image made him remarkably sad and angry at the same time. Perversely, he tormented himself by saying, "Tell me about the children you plan to have."

Carrie tilted her head to one side, which made her look more childlike than motherly. "They will have wonderfully huge and trusting eyes, maybe blue or a dark, smoky gray. And brown hair so soft it will be almost impossible to feel its texture. My children will love books and playing silly board games. But most of all, they'll love flying with me." She fell silent, watching her own hands fold one of Jason's T-shirts, as if it were the work of someone else.

"Why dark hair?" David asked abruptly.

"What?"

"Why did you say they'd have brown hair?"

She shrugged. "I don't know. I've always pictured my children having dark-brown hair, very glossy and soft."

"But you're blond," he said.

"So?"

He observed her as a telltale blush crept inward, across her cheeks from her hairline.

"My father had dark hair," she said. "That's probably why I envision them that way. I have my mother's coloring."

He nodded, but wasn't sure he believed her explanation. "So, you and your dark-haired, pixie-eyed little darlings...two is it?"

"Three, maybe four," she corrected him casually.

"My, what a brood—three or four cherubs and you...all flying off among the clouds to exciting destinations."

"Something like that." She tucked the legs of Jason's jeans at the knees and smoothed them with the flat of her hand.

"And what about Daddy?" he asked, moving a step closer to stand above her. The loose waves at her crown were mussed, and his fingers ached to disarray them more.

She looked up at him and scowled. "Why did you have to spoil such a pretty picture?"

Her comment shocked him. It seemed such a startling revelation of emotions she kept carefully hidden, hurts she'd never divulged, even when she'd confided to him about her family's past. "You don't like men very much, do you?"

"It isn't a matter of liking or disliking them. I enjoy being..." She nibbled her lower lip, obviously troubled by the sudden turn in the conversation. "I enjoy being with a man. I like companionship."

"Poodles give great companionship. A man who knows what he's doing can give a woman a great deal more."

"Well..." Then she mumbled something that sounded like, "I wouldn't know about that."

David stood ramrod still, not quite believing what he thought he'd just heard.

He watched her taking individual, deep breaths. Her rib cage expanded and contracted within her pajama top. The line of her long neck looked taut, like a bowstring pulled to release the arrow. She made small, settling motions with her hands over the piles of clothing, brushing off an imaginary speck of lint, dispelling a wrinkle that wasn't there.

"You've never made love," he stated, knowing it was true without her admission.

"*Virgin* is considered a dirty word by some people these days."

A unique and startling emotion welled up inside him. How many teenagers did he come across on the streets every day who had long ago given away what Carrie still cherished and protected within herself...what she had nearly entrusted to *him?*

"*Virginity* isn't a dirty word," he assured her, his voice barely above a whisper as he moved around in front of her. "It's a choice that makes you special."

She laughed, her voice sounding several notches tighter. "It makes me pretty hung up on something that seems to mean nothing to most people these days."

Slowly, he crouched, bringing himself down to her level. Waves of pure emotion emanated from her, rocking him. His hands found the tops of her shoulders and automatically started kneading them.

"You've been waiting for the man who's right for you. It's that simple."

"No," she said slowly, "I've just been setting a course around the turbulence."

"What does that mean?" He didn't dare laugh, didn't dare put any feeling, one way or another, into the question, for fear of offending her.

"I mean, I don't intend to become involved with a man if it means letting myself in for the kind of pain I know I can't survive."

"But the children you were speaking of..."

"There are such things as adoption and artificial insemination."

His hands lay motionless on the crisp fabric covering her shoulders. She was one surprise after another tonight. Something told him he should leave well enough alone and quit probing. He might learn more about her than he cared to.

But once he'd gotten her talking, she seemed to need to continue.

"I told you about my parents. And I see so many marriages turning sour all around me." She shot him a telling look. "You, as well as anyone, should know about that."

He nodded stiffly.

"I've wanted children for as long as I can remember. Whenever I see a child board my plane, I think to myself, if she were mine I'd bring her up front with me and teach her where to find the altimeter and the oil gauge and the airspeed indicator. We'd study her earth-science homework from the sky.

We'd practice her mathematics by adding and subtracting altitudes and distances between cities.''

"Like your dad used to do with you," David guessed.

"Yes," she said wistfully. "Lord, I miss him so much. He would have loved to have grandchildren, because he knew how much I wanted kids and he never got a chance to have the big family of his own that he'd planned."

"How would he have felt about the invisible husband?"

Carrie shook off David's hands as if irritated that he'd found a chink in the wall of logic she was trying to build. "My father was a pretty conservative man. I suppose he wouldn't have been thrilled with that part. He believed the traditional family was the backbone of our society."

"Maybe you should give his theory a try."

"No," she said quickly, glaring at him, her hazel eyes sparking with resistance. "I know a man who tried and had two great kids. Marriage didn't work for him. Why should it work for me?"

David shook his head bitterly. Leave it to her to use his own case as proof of her argument. "Maybe he chose the wrong woman," he heard himself say. Amazed with himself, he shifted from his baseball catcher's crouch and sat on the rug in front of Carrie. The words kept tumbling out. "Maybe he needed a woman who loved children, whose head was in the clouds...."

Carrie ran her tongue over her lips. "This is getting too...too personal," she rasped. "I don't think talking like this is good for either of us, David, under the circumstances."

"I'm upsetting you," he whispered, extending a finger to draw a line along the curve of her cheek and jaw. He'd wanted to touch her all day. Now he couldn't stop himself. "I don't want to make you unhappy. I just want to warn you that you shouldn't completely shut yourself off from the possibility of love."

"Why not? What are you going to tell me that I don't already know about it? That it's a kick while it's happening, then you pay in misery the rest of your life?"

"Not for the rest of your life. It's getting easier the longer Sheila is gone."

"Then you'll marry again?"

"No, I'll never marry." Why did the words come so awkwardly to him this time? He usually didn't skip a beat, because he meant what he said.

"But you'll take lovers. A string of short-term affairs, maybe even one-nighters, to satisfy your lust whenever it rears its ugly head."

"I wouldn't call my lust any uglier than the next man's." He started to laugh but stopped when she brushed aside his attempt at humor with an impatient wave of her hand. "Listen, I don't intend to become celibate, if that's what you mean. I *enjoy* making love to a woman, and I'll be the first to admit it. But since I don't seem capable of recognizing the right woman, one who can stay with me over the long haul, I think it's wise that I don't pretend I'm looking forward to another marriage. You and I have both made the same decision. We've just arrived at it from different directions."

"Then why encourage me to marry and have children?"

He sighed. Was that what he'd been doing? He was no longer sure. He tried to sort out his thoughts, but failed. "It's hard to explain."

"Try me."

He thought about her challenge. "When a man and a woman share in creating a baby, something special, something sacred, happens. Even if things go wrong between the two of you, later—"

"Like with you and Sheila?" she interrupted.

"Yes, exactly like me and Sheila. Even if all bloody hell breaks out, the fact that you've produced this tiny life is something that reaches beyond petty squabbles and even beyond major conflicts. I *liked* watching my babies grow inside a woman. I can't explain how it was.

"I stopped loving Sheila the day she made it clear that she agreed with her parents—that I was an inferior being to people of their class. But I never regretted creating those two children. And I think that my being here for them is very important to the kind of people they're becoming. I have to believe that they need me now just as much as when they were babies...and just as much as I need them.''

Carrie had listened to him in silence, overwhelmed by the tenderness and sincerity in his words. As he'd spoken, his hand had continued to stroke her cheek, her throat, her shoulders. Then it stopped, over her heart. Not touching, not moving, just waiting there. Waiting for her to push it away or press it to her breast...or just pretend it wasn't there so that he could touch her without either of them acknowledging what was happening. Again.

"You deserved to have a loving wife who could appreciate you for those sentiments," she murmured, not daring to breathe.

"I would like to see a baby grow inside you, Carrie. My baby."

She read the shock in his face, even as the words left his lips.

"I'm sorry. I don't know why I said that," he choked out. His eyes were filled with horror at what he'd just said. He looked as if he wanted to run from the room.

She couldn't help smiling dimly at the big, strong cop, who suddenly appeared so helpless. "Possibly because you meant it?"

"I—" David started to move his hand away, but she caught it and returned it to her chest. He continued speaking with obvious difficulty. "I just don't want you to think that your dream family is only possible if you go it alone. Give having children the old-fashioned way a chance, before you start working your way down the list of modern alternatives."

She could tell he was frantically backpedaling from words that had rocked both of them. Yet, she noticed, he wasn't denying anything, either.

"Well," she said softly, "my marrying or not marrying may not be up to me. I mean, if I can't trust a man to stay with me, don't you think I'd be better off, emotionally, to just accept that fact and have my children on my own?"

"That's playing safe. No one ever wins by playing safe. You can avoid some risks, but you can't hide from fate."

"Is fate the same as love?" she asked.

"Sometimes."

"Then you believe in fate?"

"Sometimes."

"Then you might, someday, believe in love again," she stated, feeling strangely sure of her ground.

He smiled tightly, his eyes darkening to the color of the Atlantic when seen from the air. They delved into hers. "You're playing word games, Carrie. I'm not sure I like that."

"But you like some kinds of games." What was she doing? Flirting with him? Why? To make him admit to something? Or *do* something?

His hand felt warm on her chest, comforting, reassuring…and terribly, terribly sensual.

"It depends upon the rules," he stated. "If they require deflowering a young woman who isn't sure she wants to be deflowered, I'm not your man."

"Then you don't want to make love to me?" she asked, holding her breath as she waited for his answer.

"I'd surrender my badge to make love to you, Carrie Monroe." He ground out the syllables, wearing a pained expression, as if glass shards were passing over his tongue. "But I don't think you're in love with me, and I'd like to believe that if we did *make* love, it would be because you were *in love* with me."

Carrie swallowed, then swallowed again, fighting to make sense of everything he was telling her. It all seemed so vital to her, although she still didn't understand why. "What about you? You're telling me you wouldn't make love to me because you're not *in love* with me. But that wouldn't stop you from doing it with another woman."

"If I did sleep with another woman," he said in a voice so low she had to concentrate on each word, "it wouldn't be making love, believe me."

A devastating shock wave of emotions shook Carrie to her core. So she'd been right—sex was just sex to David. It meant nothing more, nothing lasting. Carrie shoved David away and struggled to her feet, ignoring the stacks of laundry that toppled, desperately needing to escape from the room and from him.

David was too fast for her. His powerful hand shot up and wrapped around her forearm, easily pulling her back down onto the rug and into his arms.

"Why do I end up hurting you whenever I try to be kind to you?" he asked shakily.

A plaintive sob erupted from deep inside her. "I hurt because I want you to make love to me. I don't know why I do, or if it's smart or foolish, but I want you, David...if you want me. I want you to be my first." It would be better if he were her only, forever. But she couldn't say that, knowing how he felt. "Do you want me?"

The smoky glaze that fell over his eyes left her no doubt.

Chapter 10

David's touch conveyed as much constraint as passion. Behind his hooded sapphire gaze, Carrie deciphered male fantasies as ancient as humanity itself. He might have played each of them out, with her as his conduit to pleasure, and she knew she'd have little choice but to accept him for whatever kind of lover he elected to be. He could have forced her, if he chose. He was far stronger than she. He was accustomed to using his body in physical, sometimes even violent, ways.

But the initial shock she felt on realizing her vulnerability rapidly faded as David gently fingered a short curl of her hair between two fingers, sampling the texture, watching in fascination as pale golden strands glinted at his touch.

"I won't hurt you," he whispered.

She swallowed and nodded, unable to speak, barely capable of breathing. She sank into the braided rug, still seated, but feeling fathoms deeper.

David bent closer until their lips softly met, moist, but not parting. "If I touch you in a way you don't like or that frightens you—tell me."

Carrie nodded. "I want to touch you, too."

She could feel his lips ease into a laconic smile against hers. "You will, Carrie. I'll make sure of that."

The restrained lust in his voice sent ripples up her spine.

"Relax," he whispered, kissing her lightly, over and over, "you're as tense as a cat in a thunderstorm."

The musky, naturally masculine scent of him was headier than any cologne, far more erotic.

She tried to uncoil the muscles in her arms, her legs and stomach, but they remained taut. His palms moved up to frame her face, and his mouth lowered over hers again, this time to stay and delve deeper. She tasted his breath first, then his firm lips, lightly salty with nervous sweat, then the sweet honey of the inside of his mouth.

This much she knew she could handle. She'd had boyfriends before. She'd French-kissed, necked playfully. She'd allowed a few men the intimacy of caressing her breasts. She couldn't deny that the warmth of a man's hands excited her. Sometimes, she'd wanted more.

But Carrie realized what the problem had always been— she'd never gotten past the thinking point. She'd never been able to face the inevitable—that sooner or later, this man who wanted to claim her body would withdraw from her. He would no longer want to spend time with her, would no longer desire her. It was that fear of watching him change—grow cold and distant and uncaring, as she'd watched her father change from a loving husband to a bitter man who seemed more relieved than hurt when his wife left him—that fear of the ultimate rejection, that always gripped her. So that she never allowed a man entry into her heart.

Or her bed.

David's hands slid from her cheeks down the length of her throat to the soft, rising and falling mounds above her breasts. The anticipation of his touch turned her nipples hard; she went liquid inside.

"Am I moving too fast?" he whispered.

"No!" she gasped.

He grinned, feathering kisses across her mouth and cheek, letting his lips drift lazily from her throat, then lower as he laid her back on the floor of her bedroom. "I'm not frightening you, am I?"

"You're terrifying me."

He lifted his head and studied her solemnly, the heat of his own passion glowing in his eyes, like the blue flames of an acetylene torch. "Should I stop?"

Carrie shakily flicked her fingertips through the short, brown hairs in front of his ear, then let her hand sift upward into dark, neatly trimmed layers. "Please don't. A little terror is worth all the other feelings I'm having."

"You're sure?" he asked. "Pretty soon, it's going to be bloody agony for me if I have to—"

"You won't have to stop," she assured him. She was moved by his gallantry in the face of his own need. "I'd like you to do whatever you want."

He observed her doubtfully. "Let's settle for making love, long and slow, tonight. We can work our way up to my more exotic fantasies in time. I want you to remember this moment with only beautiful thoughts."

She smiled tremulously, her heart soaring. "I can't imagine it being any other way with you, David."

He slid his hands beneath her and, in one motion, enfolded her in his arms and lifted her from the floor. Gently he settled her on top of her bed, then stretched out beside her.

For what seemed a long time, they just lay together, soaking in each other's warmth, letting minds and hearts fill to overflowing with dreams that would soon be fulfilled.

Carrie had always wondered what her own climax would feel like, and now that it seemed imminent, she allowed herself the pleasure of imagining how David might take her there. Pleasing him was a scarier prospect. He'd been with many other women—women who were worldly and knew how to pleasure a man in dozens of ways.

Carrie suddenly felt at a loss. Of course she'd read books, seen movies. The choreographed gyrations of lithe, impossibly voluptuous actresses and brawny film heroes always left her mystified. Faked orgasms accompanied by generic groans of

"Oh, baby" seemed to have little in common with David and herself.

"I—I don't know what to do," she whispered, panicking.

"Let me show you," he said in a deep voice. "Will you?"

She understood that he was asking for her trust. She wanted nothing more than to give it to him.

Carrie relinquished the final threads of concern and timidity holding her back, but she couldn't make her mouth work to answer him. It didn't matter. David somehow knew.

His hands came to rest on her stomach. He took one button of her pajama top between thumb and forefinger and observed it solemnly, as if it held the secret of all life.

"If I'd known you were a virgin, I'd never have touched you that way—not so soon, anyway." He grimaced. "It must have been frightening…humiliating. I'm sorry."

She smiled softly at him, coaxing his eyes to rise to meet hers. Touching his face, as if to reassure herself that he was really here…with her…this way. "I didn't feel violated, if that's what you mean. But when you stopped, I was so aroused, I could have run a ten-minute mile carrying a pair of Frank's lug wrenches. I guess I'd already made up my mind that you were the man to make me a woman."

"You *are* a woman, a precious, perfect woman." He almost sounded angry. "You don't need a man to prove *that,* Carrie."

She loved him for saying what she'd most needed to hear. "I'd still prefer that you take part in the ritual, Detective. Just for the hell of it."

Amazing, she thought. At a moment like this, she'd found the courage to tease him. David flashed her a brief, dazzling grin. His eyes were the color of melting ice, the sheerest of blues. Then, abruptly, his playful expression was gone. He stared at her with renewed hunger.

Urgently his fingers worked the button through its hole, then moved on to the next one.

"I need to see you," he said tightly. "And I want you to see me."

"Yes." She choked out the word with considerable effort.

The word *see* spoke volumes. He intended not merely to look at her, but to absorb her very essence.

David parted the two halves of her pajama top, laying each alongside her body, to reveal her breasts and stomach. Trembling, Carrie drew an audible breath and closed her eyes.

"Look at me," he demanded. When she did as he asked, she witnessed in his expression a remarkable reflection of awe. He made her feel as special as if she were his first lover, ever. "I'm not going to hurt you. I'll never hurt you, Carrie. Understand? I'm going to give you as much pleasure as you're giving me, and *will* give me tonight."

He sounded so sure of himself she couldn't have questioned anything he told her then. "I'll try," she murmured, as she reached hesitantly to tug his jersey from the waist of his pants.

He chuckled, as if at a secret joke. Without knowing why, she laughed with him. For some reason she'd always thought of sex being serious business. All intense glares and indistinguishable animal grunts, never any talking or laughing. But David made her anticipate not only physical pleasure, but sharing fun.

Cupping her breasts, he caressed them gently, then turned her onto her side, facing him, so that they filled out for him. He took more time, drawing his palms over the nipples in erotic circles, urging them to arrogant pink peaks, while he tenderly kneaded the tingling flesh around them. Kissing her on the lips, he let his tongue ripple across her teeth and probe her mouth, tasting her and letting her sample him.

Carrie sighed, enjoying the end of one deep kiss, only to open her mouth again to encourage him to begin another. A wondrous sensation swelled within her. It was as if not only her body but her soul was accepting David Adams with all his best and worst qualities. As if something that had always been right—but she hadn't known was right—suddenly became as clear to her as the horizon on a cloudless day.

She lapped her arms around David's wide neck and welcomed his intoxicating kisses.

"I want to kiss you a little lower," he breathed between her lips.

She nodded.

His lips drifted down from hers, following the line of her throat, to the firm plateau above her breasts. He hesitated.

"Please, yes, please," she whispered.

Slipping down beside her on the white chenille bedspread until his head was level with her chest, he wrapped his right hand around her left breast and lifted its fullness toward his mouth. His eyes never left hers, as if he knew she needed the strength of his gaze to steady her. She touched his head, swept her fingers through his dark hair before curling them around the back of his neck.

The heat of his mouth reached her just before his lips closed over her breast. He drew the fullness between his lips and teeth, while teasing her nipple with the tip of his tongue. He sucked gently, then harder.

Carrie arched into him as she let out a thick moan of gratification that sounded as if it had come from somewhere other than her own throat. Waves of heat shot through her torso, centering low in her belly, intensifying with each subtle movement of his lips, tongue, teeth over her breast.

"Lower?" he whispered.

She was certain she would go mad. "Yes…oh, please, David. Yes."

His mouth trailed burning kisses down the center of her stomach, to her belly, where he paused to stroke the flat, feminine muscles directly over her womb. "Here," he murmured, catching her eyes with his, even as he kissed and stroked her there. "Here is where you will grow your beautiful babies when the time is right."

Her eyes widened with amazement, as he reverently kissed her again and again, sanctifying her dream. She had thought no man could ever understand the ageless, instinctive drive that urged a woman to create new life. David was releasing her from the need to explain or excuse herself.

But all rational thought abandoned her when his hand moved still lower, beneath the elastic of her pajama bottoms, to cover the pale blond triangle between her thighs. She sucked in a breath that reached down inside her and gripped her fiercely. "Oh, David—" She shuddered.

"I'll kiss you *there* someday," he promised. "It's too much for now. We have delicate work to do first."

She'd barely recovered a corner of her sanity before she felt him ease her pajama bottoms off her and skim them down her legs to toss them away. He moved his hand gently between her thighs.

At first, he seemed to touch her almost too softly, too slowly, for what her body needed from him. Then she realized he was testing her resistance, giving her as much time as possible to adjust to each step along the way. And in his eyes, she read something that more than amazed her. He was claiming her, inch by inch. He was leaving his mark with his hands and his lips, branding her as his own, even though he himself might not have realized his intent.

Slowly, he parted her moist femininity and slid one finger inside her. "Hug me tight, darling," he said. "It will be quick."

She wasn't so naive that she didn't understand what he meant. There would be pain, a tender membrane to rupture. But she'd never envisioned a man taking such intimate care of a woman her first time. Tears crested her lids as a sharp throb gave way to a dull, burning sensation. Almost immediately, the discomfort was replaced by a subtle warmth as he massaged her intimately.

He watched her eyes, gauging the level of her temporary pain, then lowered his mouth to her ear and whispered, "Good girl. The rest is a piece of cake."

She thought he was removing his hand, but he only withdrew it far enough to add another finger, then press into her higher, carefully stretching her, while flicking the callused pad of his thumb over the tiny, sensitive nub guarding her most intimate self.

The sensation ignited her as if she'd been a match.

Carrie drove her fingernails into the muscled flesh of David's shoulders and let out a cry of agonized delight, which she quickly muffled for fear of waking the children, on the floor above them.

When her shocked gaze locked with David's, fire blazed up in his eyes. "Let's try that again."

He brought her to a second quick climax so intense her body quaked. She pressed the back of her hand to her mouth to keep herself from crying out in ecstasy. She was rolling back down the other side of a fiery hill, when she became aware that David had shifted position and was unzipping his jeans, removing them along with his briefs. Her eyes automatically dropped to his arousal, and her body reacted in shallow, lush waves of heat.

From his wallet he pulled a foil-wrapped condom.

She couldn't help reaching out to touch him, full and rigid in his glorious need for her. She knew that he wanted her hand around him. As soon as he'd protected them, she instinctively curved her long fingers in a loving caress around him. He felt like a steel shaft wrapped in suede.

"You're magnificent," she whispered.

"The lady knows the right thing to say," he groaned, arching his back, supporting himself on one elbow as he leaned over her. "Carrie, I can't wait much longer."

She smiled at him softly, wishing he could read her thoughts, hoping he shared them. It felt to her as if David Adams and Carrie Monroe had always been meant to be together, in this way, at this time and throughout eternity. There was no doubt in her mind that he was the man she'd been waiting for, to be her first, to be her only.

And now she willingly opened herself to him as he eased his hips over hers. It was she who guided him inside her.

He drove deep.

The walls spun around her.

For the span of a dozen heartbeats, Carrie knew nothing but the black flecks in David's eyes...his rasping breath against her ear...throbbing crests of ecstasy that rocked her body...and altered forever the way she saw the world.

There was, at first, a terrifying sensation that he had literally perished in Carrie's arms. The best of his climaxes left him feeling spent, in dire need of a week's worth of sleep. But the lethargy usually wore off after an hour or so.

It wasn't at all like that with Carrie. How was it the French referred to the way a man felt after releasing himself? The "little death"? He had risen too high, fallen too hard, disintegrated into subatomic pieces. He was destroyed, not simply weakened. He was no longer of the same substance as the rest of mankind.

For what felt like the longest time, David floated through darkness created by his own closed eyes. Gradually, he became aware of a featherlight touch at the back of his head and neck, the soothing stroke of delicate fingers.

Carrie.

He let out a long breath and realized he was still inside her, as he lay heavily on top of her. He was afraid he must have crushed her by now.

"Are you all right?" he asked shakily. He didn't have the strength to lift his head from her silky shoulder and look directly at her.

"Just fine," she whispered contentedly. "Thank you, David."

Thank you? No woman had ever thanked him. He made himself stop that line of thought. He didn't want to compare Carrie with women from his past. Everything seemed new, pristine with her.

"I wasn't too rough?" he asked, pushing himself with effort to his elbows and cautiously lifting his hips away from her.

"Not at all," she whispered, smiling sweetly.

He saw questions in her eyes. "Yes?"

She blushed and turned her head to one side so that she wouldn't have to meet his eyes. "You felt...wonderful inside me."

He let out a chuckle, thrilled with her. "I'm glad. Very glad. Because I have to be honest with you, Carrie. I want to spend more time with you that way, a lot more time."

Her smile teetered, panic tightening her delicate features.

Idiot! he scolded himself. You're scaring her.

"I know what we said before, about not letting our living arrangement become sexual. But I don't believe either of us could have predicted the way we'd feel about each other," he blurted out defensively. "If you don't want to change the rules, I won't force you, Carrie. I swear I'll leave you alone. But I don't think I'll be able to keep my mind on work or anything else if you turn me away and—"

She pressed her hand over his lips. "Hush."

He couldn't recall a moment he'd been more afraid. She'd given him her body, and more. She'd given him her heart, and he had returned the gift. For whatever reasons existed, they had become one in ways that surpassed the physical dimension.

To tear himself apart from her now would be agonizing.

He stared at her pleadingly.

"Hush," she repeated, as if she were calming a young child. Carrie rolled over, easing him onto his back, leaning over him, her breasts pillowing against the furred ridges of his chest. She moved her hand away from his lips and kissed him firmly. "Detective David Adams, for an experienced cop, you certainly don't pick up on clues very well."

He blinked up at her, marveling at how chipper and full of energy she seemed, when he'd so recently given up the ghost. "What clues?"

"I think we need to renegotiate our sleeping arrangements," she said with a straight face.

He mulled over her words, his brain feeling sluggish for several seconds before the significance of what she'd said clicked. "You mean," he said slowly, feeling his way through a quagmire of emotions, "you want to sleep with me again?"

"I'm not sure how much actual sleeping we'll do," she admitted coyly. "But I'd like to make love again, yes."

"Then how does this affect...I mean, technically we're married, but we're not..."

"Committed to being man and wife? I think it's going to take some time to figure all this out," she said, her tone altering to a solemn one. "We shouldn't make any hasty decisions based on one night."

He gnawed his lip, then touched her forehead with his lips. "You're right. For a young woman who's new to certain sensations," he said, smiling at her, "you're operating with a remarkably clear head."

"I'm not sure how clear it is. I just want to make sure we don't do anything to hurt each other." She kissed him lightly on his chin, nose, his right and left cheek.

He couldn't believe his good fortune—that such a special woman should enter his life. His only regret was that she hadn't shown up seven or eight years earlier, before he'd hardened himself to trusting another person in love. It might have made all the difference in the world.

Maybe, he mused, his thoughts falling into shadows, she'd come along too late to do any good.

Maybe, a happier voice inside of him argued, she's just in time.

"We'll work on the not-hurting part," he promised. "Now—" he glanced at her pajama top and bottom, which lay on opposite sides of the room "—the children shouldn't come downstairs in the morning to find us sprawled naked on top of your bed."

"Not a good move," she agreed, watching him curiously as he retrieved her nightclothes for her.

"Your bed or mine, love?"

She beamed at him. "Yours."

Chapter 11

Carrie desperately fought the temptation to analyze what she and David had just done, or where their relationship was heading. As he reached down a wide hand and helped her to her feet, she wished only to live in the single, precious moment they'd created together.

She suspected she was losing herself to him, perhaps had already passed the point of turning back and holding on to that most fragile portion of herself, which should have remained untouched by any man.

It wasn't an anatomical part—had nothing to do with sex. It was a niche in her psyche she'd never relinquished to anyone. She'd guarded, cherished and protected it through a complex routine of hard work, long hours and time spent, literally, beyond any man's reach—somewhere above ten thousand feet.

The sky was a great place to hide, from so many things.

David had claimed her virginity, but he'd also claimed her soul. He now held her, so very precariously, cupped in his palm. She only prayed she'd survive the growing affection she felt for him. If he turned that hand over, she'd surely fall into an abyss so deep she could never hope to climb out. It would be as if she'd lost everything warm and bright and right in her life.

Trying to think no further, Carrie accepted David's hand and let him lead her upstairs, to his bedroom. He turned down the linens and watched her slide, naked, between the crisp, white sheets before lowering himself beside her. Then he pulled her body into the curve of his own and he made love to her again—leisurely, stroking her, whispering to her how beautiful her body was, riding with her a slowly rising tide of passion until her world swam with the colors of love.

David didn't have to report for his shift until 4 p.m. the next afternoon. He had hoped by then that his head would be clear and the spell Carrie had woven around him with her long, silky legs and sweet lips would have faded, allowing him to concentrate on his cases.

But by the time he'd worked seven hours and he and Pete were on the last stop of their shift, he felt as if he were still vibrating from Carrie's parting kiss. All night he'd felt distracted, unable to focus on the interviews they'd lined up. The D.A.'s office was pressing Lieutenant Rogers for more evidence against Rainey. They'd come up with little that night so far.

"Looks quiet," Pete commented, his eyes roaming the dark alleys on either side of Lexington where they'd parked the tac car. "Funny, ain't it? How a place like this can feel like it's holding its breath. Like it's human. Just waiting for you to—"

"Where did your pusher say he'd meet you?" David interrupted him. He was impatient to finish the night, even if they didn't have anything to show for their time. He wanted to get home to Carrie.

Pete pointed. "Down that second alley."

"Your wire still okay?"

Pete spoke into his shirtfront as David clamped earphones over his head. "Coming in clear, Commander?"

"Gotcha."

David slid down in the driver's seat, making himself all but invisible from outside the parked car. Pete climbed out and closed the car door soundlessly. He assumed his druggy walk and slunk off into the dark.

David watched for signs of movement in the shadows, listened for warning sounds. At this hour in good weather, there were usually small groups of people partying on the street corners. No one was in sight. From inside a nearby building rap music played.

Pete stumbled down the litter-strewn sidewalk, his head in constant, exaggerated motion, as he mimicked an addict on the prowl for his last fix for the night. His gait became even more erratic.

All David could hear over the miniature microphone taped to Pete's chest, inside his shirt, was his partner's wheezy breathing.

Pete had been working undercover for ten years, nearly a record for the department. His routines were perfect. He could imitate a guy high on coke, a PCP-strung-out wild man, a heroin addict on his fifteen-minute nod...or any combination of the sad possibilities of human degradation brought on by drug abuse. Pete was good at what he did. Some credit was due to his looking the part. With his stringy hair, unshaven face and collection of ill-fitting, dirtied-up clothing, he fitted right in with the lowest end of the city's drug culture.

David often watched with open admiration as his partner readied himself to go out on the street. Pete applied grease and soot like a veteran thespian donning his stage makeup. He used mortician's wax and cigarette ash to build up fake needle tracks on his arms if he was masquerading as a heroin addict, because most streetmen wanted to see tracks to make sure you weren't a cop, before they sold to you. He plucked out his nose hairs with tweezers if he was going under as a cokehead. Sniffing cocaine destroyed nose hairs. Pete knew the lingo: ask for a couple of *boys* for two little bags of cut heroin; *girls* meant coke. Like David, Pete knew the going rates, and most of the streetmen by sight and name.

All night they'd been chasing down Andrew Rainey's pushers. Only by bringing in at least one of them and threatening to throw him into prison for half his life would they get evidence against Rainey for a conviction.

So far, all Rainey's boys were keeping a low profile and their mouths shut. Sooner or later, though, they had to replenish their supplies from other sources and start selling again. Before long, they'd run out of money and wouldn't be able to support their own habits, which often ran to a thousand dollars a day in expensive Karachi cocaine.

David watched Pete reappear and veer down another alley. All night they'd been at this and had come up with nothing.

He let his eyes close for just a moment, to rest them. He wondered what Carrie was doing now. She had told him she'd be flying back from Ocean City by 5 p.m., then would finish up at the airport and be at the house by seven. One of her neighbors, a teenager who reminded him of Jennifer, was watching the kids until then. Carrie had planned to make the three of them a late supper, then play board games with Jason and Tammy until their bedtime.

He smiled, amused by a thought. Carrie could pilot a patched-together Beechcraft through a thunderstorm without blinking an eye, then cuddle up contentedly with two kids for a quiet night at home. She was indeed a complex and fascinating woman.

"Yo, someone's home after all," came a whispered voice over his earphones.

David pushed up in the seat, immediately alert, rubbing his eyes to focus them quickly in the dark. He could hear Pete sniffling, doing his cokehead bit. There was a rustling of clothing, footsteps—maybe two sets in addition to Pete's. Or maybe just one. Then—

"Lookin' for somethin', man?"

"Maybe," Pete said. "Need a gram."

"Girl or boy?"

"Boy."

"Don't got no gram, man. Stuff's thin tonight."

"Stuff's thin every night," Pete whined. "When you guys gonna stock the shelves?"

"Hey, ain't my fault. Cops pulled our man. No one's doin' much business these days."

More rustling. David could imagine Pete working himself into a frenzy. Looking around, shuffling his feet, craving his poison—showing the pusher he was ripe for a score.

"Listen, I can give you a quarter, nothin' more," the voice said at last. "All's I got for you. Rest is for my reg'lars—got to take care of my clients, you know?"

"How much?" Pete growled.

"For a quarter, seein's we got an emergency sitch-ee-a-tion? Have to make it five bills."

"Five hundred for a stinkin' quarter! You bastard—"

There was a flurry of activity…a grunt…curses swapped. Did Pete have the pusher on the ground, or was it the other way around? David couldn't take chances.

He tore off the earphones, flung open the car door, leaving it ajar so the slam wouldn't alert their prey. Looping the block, he ran full out until he hit the back end of the alley. Pete wouldn't thank him for interfering as long as his buy had a shot at going down. But David was pretty sure negotiations had broken off. Now all he wanted to do was guarantee his partner didn't end his shift courtesy of a blade between his ribs.

David flattened himself against the brick building and took three shallow breaths, listening hard, his heart booming in his chest like a kettledrum. The scuffling had stopped; steps were racing toward him. With any luck, Pete was herding the guy to him, just as they'd planned. In seconds they'd have him sandwiched between them.

David stepped into the middle of the alley, pulled his .38, gripped it between two hands and braced his feet wide. By now he could hear Pete bellowing, "Police! Freeze, damn it! Freeze!"

"Stop!" David shouted. "You're surrounded. Stop or I shoot." Adrenaline ripped through his veins. His muscles coiled within him, ready for action. He peered into dense, shifting shadows, waiting for the streetman to leap into sight.

A figure erupted out of the dark.

Pete nearly ran into him. "Where'd they go? Two of 'em...where the hell?" He gulped down air between words, his head swiveling right, left, right, tossing his ponytail crazily.

David blinked, trying to catch his own breath. "You had them in front of you. No one got past me. There's no other way out of the alley, except through the warehouse, and that should be locked."

"Should be!" Pete turned and ran back the way he'd come, pounding down the first concrete stairwell in sight.

David watched him tug at the door. "Don't go in there!" he shouted.

The door swung open in Pete's hand. He streaked inside, shouting behind him at David, "Call in a ten-one!"

No time, David muttered. He couldn't leave Pete alone long enough to radio for backup. Anything might happen in the five minutes he'd be gone. Two of them... He swore again.

David pressed himself against the outside of the building, listened for a moment, then ducked low and dove through the doorway. He could hear someone running. Only one set of footsteps. Pete's, he guessed. Maybe they'd already lost the two pushers. Maybe that would be the best thing that could happen that night—lose them.

Something feels wrong, David thought suddenly. Real wrong.

"Yo! You go high—I'll stay low." Pete's voice.

"Right," David responded, moving toward the iron-railed stairs he could barely make out through the gloom. Only the faint red glow from EXIT signs cut through the dark, making everything look as if it had been bathed in blood. He climbed the steps, pausing every third one to listen.

Nothing. No sounds. All clear, his brain signaled him.

But his gut refused to listen. Their prey had gotten away far too quickly and easily. It was almost as if they'd planned their escape route knowing there'd be a chase.

Had someone set up him and Pete? Why? Did Rainey have anything to do with it? Andrew didn't have much of an organization. He was a loner, liked to keep profits to himself. So who was running this show?

The answer struck him a split second before a burst of gunfire scattered his thoughts.

"Trap!" Pete shouted from somewhere below.

Ducking behind a row of steel cabinets, David swung around quickly, trying to see where the shots were coming from. The shooters seemed to be sheltering in a doorway to his right.

"Next stop," David growled, "down your throat!"

His gun drawn, but still unfired, he pushed off toward the doorway. He was halfway there, when a second round split the air. These shots from directly behind him.

Hot lead burned its way into his shoulder. He spun on the bullet's impact, and fell hard on the concrete floor. Intuitively, he stopped himself from crying out and giving away his position. He rolled under a table, then into the space between two file cabinets.

He heard a curse, running feet. Then a rush of activity as the darkness seemed to thin to a watery gray, making it difficult for him to see objects in the room.

"Dave! Dave!" came Pete's shout. "We lost them. Hey, where are you, man?"

"Here."

It took Pete only a minute to find him. Then he was on his knees beside him. "You all right?"

David thought about the question. "I—I'm not sure. I think I took a slug in the right shoulder." He tried to move, couldn't. "There were three of them. We figured two, but another one was watching all the time."

"Huh?"

David shook his head wearily. The grayness was filling his head. His shoulder hurt like hell.

"Hold on, partner." Pete stuffed something bulky inside David's right shirtfront, while pressing on his shoulder from behind. David could smell blood. His own, he was sure. "I'm gonna call for an ambulance. I'll only be gone a sec. I'm pretty sure they're gone. You just hold on. Hold on...hold..." His voice faded along with his running footsteps.

David wouldn't have been worried if Pete hadn't sounded so damn panicky. Pete never panicked. Pete is as cool as a narc gets. We narcs are always cool, David thought. We can handle anything. Bust down a door with a half-dozen armed runners behind it, waiting to blow off our heads? Hey, we can do that. No problem.

Closing his eyes, he thought of Tammy and Jason. His stomach suddenly clenched, and the pain in his shoulder felt worse. His kids. What would happen to them if he wasn't around?

They'd go to Sheila. Unless...

Carrie. Carrie with her gentle manner and sensible approach to life. Carrie with her brave, no-nonsense attitude toward problems. She'd make his kids a better mother than Sheila ever could.

Carrie's sweet face stayed with him as he felt himself being lifted. People worked quickly, shouting orders, maneuvering him as if he were a piece of furniture. Lift, cover, secure straps. Down steep stairs, the night air kissing his face. He was too weak to open his eyes and look up to see if there were any stars. But he could still see Carrie's face, and the half scared, half excited smile she'd given him the first time they'd made love.

"I don't want to die yet," he said.

"We'll do our best, Detective," a disembodied voice responded.

A siren shrieked. He thought of Carrie once more before oblivion took her away.

Carrie had put the children to bed at 8:30, then watched a B movie on TV. She brushed her teeth and changed into her nightdress. She didn't bother wearing a robe as she walked around the house, locking up. Unless David had to work overtime, he'd be home any minute.

Feeling relaxed and sleepy, she crawled into bed to wait for him.

She must have dozed off, because she woke up around 2 a.m. Rolling over in the comfortable double bed, she sought David's warmth. He wasn't there. She dozed for another hour, then awoke with a tight feeling in her chest and sat up in bed, listing rational excuses for his being so late. She got out of bed and checked on Tammy and Jason, pulling the sheets up beneath their chins and smoothing tendrils of hair from their plump, rosy cheeks. The gesture comforted her a little.

She was heating water for a cup of tea, when the doorbell rang. Her eyes shot to the clock over the oven: 4 a.m. Carrie's pulse quickened.

Her mouth suddenly dry, she ran to the door and peered through the peephole. A man in grimy blue jeans and torn sweatshirt, with dirt and what might have been blood smeared down the left side of his face, shifted from foot to foot impatiently. She glanced at the phone, prepared to dive for it and punch in 911.

"Carrie, it's me, Pete Turner. Open up!"

Stunned, she swiveled back to take another look. Even now, she barely recognized David's partner. "Pete!" she cried. Grabbing the key to the dead bolt from the table beside the door, she worked the locks and flung open the door.

The undercover cop stepped through and immediately closed the door behind him, locking it. He turned to face her, his expression grim. His eyes avoided hers. "Something's happened."

She heard the words but didn't absorb their implication for several seconds. Then it struck her that because Pete was here and David wasn't, the news was bad. Very bad. Her heart faltered.

"Oh, Lord," she gasped, feeling the floor drop away beneath her. "David! Is he...is he— I have to go to him!" She threw herself toward the door.

Pete stepped into her path, and she nearly plowed into him. "He's all right. I'm not sure they'll let you in to see him yet anyway. Might as well sit tight for now." Pete took her trembling arm and led her from the foyer, into the living room, pushing down gently to seat her on the couch. "He's going to make it, Carrie. He's okay."

"But *what happened?*" she choked out. Why wouldn't the room stop spinning? Her stomach spasmed twice; she was sure she was going to be sick. Carrie clenched her fists and wrapped her arms around her belly, holding on. "Tell me," she insisted.

"He was hit in the shoulder by a bullet. He was lucky. It went straight through—in the back, out the front. But he had me pretty damn scared, I have to tell you."

Pete ground the heels of his hands into his eye sockets, and she was struck by how truly awful he looked, even beneath the dirt.

"The water's hot," she blurted out. "I'll make you some tea."

"No. No, thanks," he muttered.

"Something stronger," she suggested. She wanted to run from the house—nightgown and all—jump into her car and drive straight to David. But the children were with her...and now that she knew David wasn't mortally wounded, she could force herself to wait. What she couldn't do was sit still. "Scotch," she mumbled. "I think there's some on the side-board."

Pete didn't object. She took his silence as a yes.

Carrie brought the bottle with her into the kitchen and poured some, neat, into a shot glass. She knocked it off in one quick swallow, then poured a more generous portion into an iced-tea glass and brought it to Pete in the living room. He looked up and accepted it with a grateful but vague smile.

"I stayed at the hospital while they worked on him. Didn't occur to me to call you. I'm sorry. Guess I should have. All I could think about was him, you know?"

She nodded numbly.

He took a long swallow of the liquor, holding it in his throat, his head tipped back and eyes closed, and at last swallowed. "The doc said he'd be good as new, as long as he took it easy and there wasn't any infection."

"It was serious enough for him to be admitted?" she asked.

"He lost a lot of blood. Damn," Pete said, shaking his head, "it was, like...all over the place. I thought he was gone for sure when I came back from radioing for help. Would have bled to death if the EMTs hadn't gotten there so fast. Thank God for those guys. They hear a cop's down and they're like Houdini—out of nowhere. Poof. Thank God." He took another drink. "Thank God."

Carrie kept her face composed, but inside she was falling apart. The man she'd married had nearly died. She might have become a widow. His children might have lost their father. No one had thought to call her.

"Pete," she whispered hoarsely, "you didn't just *forget*, did you?"

"Told you—was more concerned with him." He stared down into his glass, then drained it. "It was an ambush. Neither of us saw it coming until it was too late. I recognized the guy—it was Rainey. If I hadn't been there, that filthy scum would have strolled over to Dave after he was down and taken a head shot to finish him off."

Carrie stared at him, horrified. "I thought that was the man David put in jail."

"I'm talking about the guy's kid brother," he muttered darkly.

Then he looked around at her with such black intensity she cringed.

"You don't blame me, do you?" she asked softly.

"Dave sure hasn't been thinking straight since you glided into his life, lady. I guess I just don't know who you really are, or what you want from him." Pete put down his glass with a thump on the coffee table and stared at her as if waiting for an answer.

"I—I'm his wife," Carrie uttered.

"Are you?" he demanded in a low voice. "I don't remember hearing him talk about you at all until a few weeks ago. Then suddenly, here you are, Mrs. David Adams, taking care of his kids and sharing a house with him. What's this all about?"

"I—we're married," Carrie stammered. Her already queasy stomach flip-flopped again.

"Listen, Dave married Sheila because he thought he was in love. I saw what it did to him. He believed she was the best thing that ever happened to him. I hated her the minute I met her.

"She was a witch then, and she's a witch now. But he worshiped her, so what could I say? She gave him two kids, and I guess that's something."

He leaped up from the couch and started pacing the living room, his steps more desperate with each pass in front of the couch.

"He sure adores those two rug rats. But Sheila tore him to shreds when she started playing around and let him know she didn't love him. She's still out to destroy him, this time by taking Jason and Tammy away from him."

Carrie stared up into Pete's anger-flushed face. "So what you're trying to say is, you don't want him to be hurt again."

"You got it."

"I'm not going to hurt him. I want to help him," she stated.

"How? By marrying him even though you don't love him?"

"I never said I didn't love him."

"Listen, I know about your deal with him. He told me what his lawyer suggested, and I thought it was a bunch of hooey. I still do. If you're after money, let me tell you as a longtime friend, he doesn't have any to speak of, beyond what he might have promised you. He's not worth your effort. Go find some rich old geezer who can keep you for more than a year."

Rage blazed up inside Carrie, as hot and dangerous as an engine fire. Her first impulse was to slap the man silly for accusing her of marrying David for his money. In essence, though, that was what she'd done. Still, Pete made it sound like a totally one-sided arrangement, and it wasn't like that at all. David was benefiting from their deal as much as she was. Perhaps more.

Besides, a lot had happened between them that she hadn't had time to sort out in her own mind. And she certainly couldn't explain to Pete what she didn't herself understand.

"I care very much for David," she said softly from her seat on the couch. "I think he's a marvelous father, a dedicated police officer and a fascinating man."

Pete stopped in front of her to study her face from close quarters. After a moment he said, "You left something out. What about David the lover and husband? Still keeping separate bedrooms like at the apartment? I couldn't miss the living arrangements on moving day."

Carrie blinked at him, feeling the heat drain from her cheeks. "Our private life is none of your business," she said stiffly.

Pete's lips tightened for an instant, outlined by his unkempt beard. Then he took a step backward. "You're right. None of my business. I just don't want to see him ripped apart again. He's a good friend, the best." He sat down heavily on the couch and dropped his head onto one fist.

Carrie rested her hand on his arm. "I'm not going to hurt him, Pete," she promised. "David knows that. You can ask him."

He seemed not to have heard her.

"Pete?"

"I guess you'll want to get down to the hospital before too long. It's almost morning. Is Sheila supposed to take the kids today?"

"No. She called and asked us to keep them an extra day. Apparently she has to be out of town on business."

"Yeah, right." He snorted.

"I don't think I should take them to the hospital with me," Carrie thought out loud. "David might not want them to see him yet."

"I'll crash here until they wake up. Then they can make Uncle Pete breakfast while I shower. Dave won't mind if I borrow some of his clothes."

"*They'll* make breakfast? That should be interesting."

"Hey, you ain't lived till you've had Kool-Aid poured over a nice big bowl of Cheerios!"

Carrie chuckled, feeling a measure of relief in Pete's humor. Perhaps it was his way of signaling a truce. "I'll get dressed. Help yourself to anything in the kitchen. There are clean towels in the hallway closet, upstairs."

He lifted a hand in acknowledgment and stretched out on the couch, still in his battle uniform of torn jeans and blood-stained T-shirt. It didn't even bother her that she'd have to clean the couch after he left. She could face anything, as long as David was all right.

By the time Carrie let herself out the front door, Pete was snoring. Every nerve in her body prickled with the need to see David for herself. To see him and touch him and feel his breath moving in and out of his body—to assure herself that he was indeed alive.

Chapter 12

Carrie hesitated at the door only a moment before pushing it open and stepping through. She had no idea what to expect, but she was prepared for the worst.

David lay in a bed in Union Memorial Hospital, his head raised at a forty-five-degree angle, eyes closed. A sheet was draped across his lower body and pulled up to the middle of his chest over his hospital gown. She tiptoed in and closed the door behind her.

Slowly, she approached his bed, her eyes magnetized by the outline of the bandages wrapped up and over his right shoulder then around his bare chest, visible through the gown. He didn't move, except for the slow, reassuring rise and fall of his rib cage.

She moved closer, silently. Waited. And finally laid her hand over his.

"Feels nice," a voice rumbled, and it took her a moment to realize it was David's.

She started to pull away.

"Don't." His eyes were suddenly open, his fingers gripping her wrist.

Carrie was amazed to see his vivid blue eyes afire with sparks. They resembled those she'd witnessed when they'd made love. This time, she thought them less likely to be lust, more likely the result of sheer relief at being alive. "I thought I should come. Pete is with the children."

David gave an almost imperceptible nod. "He told you I was all right."

"Yes."

"Then why did you come at all?"

Carrie looked down at his wide fingers, locked around her wrist. "I had to see for myself that you were all right. Besides, a cop's wife would come to the hospital to see him, wouldn't she?"

His lips lifted in an appreciative smile, although she sensed the small motion cost him some effort. He was probably in more discomfort than he was letting on.

"Do Jason and Tammy know?"

"No," she said, "they were asleep when I left."

"Good, I want to explain this to them myself."

He shifted within the sheets, and the top one slid down. She looked away from his lap, where the hospital gown had pulled up, revealing a muscled thigh.

"Something wrong?" he asked.

"No. Nothing." Why was she feeling so flustered? It wasn't as if she hadn't already seen him naked. The thought summoned up intimate memories. She could suddenly feel his heart beating against her breasts, feel the rough texture of his skin. Smell him.

Her eyes gravitated to the bandaging. A shadow of reddish brown stain showed through the cotton gown from the underneath layers. She flinched.

He released her wrist, and she pulled it away.

"This little hole in me getting to you?"

She shook her head, not wanting to admit she was squeamish. "It's apparently your job to get shot at. Why should I—" Her voice cracked. She couldn't go on.

"It's okay to be frightened by violence," he said.

She'd heard him use that calming tone with his children.

"*I* was scared last night, Carrie. Real scared."

She turned back to face him. "Scared of dying? Who wouldn't be?"

"Not of dying. More of...of leaving behind the people I love."

"Jason and Tammy."

"Yes."

His eyes fixed on hers, holding them so that she found it impossible to look away.

"Others, too," he added.

Carrie's heart double-timed, until she willed it to calm down. He was talking about people he worked with, like Pete, she told herself. But the hope was there, alive and nudging her own feelings, making her want to take risks.

"David." She shook her head, cleared her throat, stalling for time while she searched for words that wouldn't be too painful to pronounce. "When Pete came to the house, before he could tell me what had happened, I knew that you'd been hurt. I prayed you were still alive. I didn't care what shape you were in...just as long as you were breathing and your mind was still functioning."

"It's functioning. So is the rest of me." His eyes twinkled mischievously.

"Good," she said, happy tears blurring her vision. "That's good."

"Come here." He reached for her with his uninjured arm and drew her down onto the bed beside him. "Really," he whispered, "I'm all right."

She gave him a weak smile, nodded, not able to trust her voice at all now.

"Say, since we're all feeling happy about things," he teased, blotting a tear from beneath her eye with his wide thumb, "I need you to go back to the house and bring me some clothes."

"Clothes?"

"Yes, I'm checking out of this place as soon as possible. I have work to do."

Carrie gingerly touched his bandaged shoulder. He winced. "Did the doctor say you could leave?"

"Doctors be damned. I'm all patched up, and time is wasting."

"But someone out there wants you *dead!*" Carrie cried. "Pete said it was an ambush. The man who did this to you is still free, right?"

"Right. Andrew Rainey, who may or may not be behind last night, is in jail, but his brother, Carl, is out. I expect Pete is right. Sounds like something Carl would pull. I doubt his brother has any idea what he's up to."

"Does it matter whether he has his brother's blessing?" Carrie demanded. "He apparently means to kill you to keep you from testifying against his brother!" Carrie was furious with David. Why didn't he take an attempt on his life seriously? "You need to at least give yourself time to heal so you'll be able to defend yourself—although I've been told you heal fast." She shot him a mocking grin.

"I do. As to Carl, he's probably far away from here by now. The police have all points bulletins out on him, covering the whole state. Carl may be dumb about some things, but he's a survivor. He'll run if things get too hot."

"Great," she said with conviction. "The farther away from you he gets, the better I like it."

David shook his head. "That's why I have to get out of here fast. Pete and I have to get to Carl Rainey before anyone else does."

Carrie narrowed her eyes. "Why? So you can beat a confession out of him?"

David laughed and picked up the fingers of her left hand in his. He played with their tips. "No, so we can get him talking about his brother. If we get him riled up enough, he'll blab his head off, even with his lawyer there advising him to shut up. Word on the street is, Carl's a hothead and likely to fly out of control when someone crosses him. I've crossed him. If he starts bragging about how powerful his big brother is, he might rattle off enough names and dates to nail Andrew for life."

Carrie eyed him grimly. "So you intend to simply walk out of here with a bullet wound that's less than six hours old."

"Yup."

"I don't suppose you even let them give you stitches."

"Wrong. Doc said he had to sew me up, fore and aft. I don't argue with the pros when we're talking holes in my body."

"Smart man," she said sweetly. Then her expression hardened. "But I don't think you're strong enough to be running all over Baltimore. I expect the floor nurse will have something to say about your leaving when I tell her your plans." Carrie extracted her hand from his and started to get up from the bed.

Leaning quickly over the edge, David reached for her and grabbed her wrist. "Get back here!" he growled.

Carrie pulled, trying to free herself, but he had a death grip on her with his good hand. "If I scream, I expect a pair of hefty orderlies will appear, whose duties include subduing AWOL patients."

He glared at her. "You don't think I'm strong enough to leave."

"That's what I said."

With a sudden tightening of the muscles in his hand, he yanked her back down onto the edge of the mattress. Carrie braced her hands on either side of his hips, aware of how close she was to scantily clothed, intimate portions of his anatomy.

"What if I were to *prove* I was strong enough for physical exertion?"

"Stop it, David!" she hissed as he looped her arm up over his shoulder, behind his neck. He clamped her wrist under his head, against the pillow, then smoothed his freed hand up her bare arm to the tender flesh in front of her shoulder. "What are you doing?" she was furious with him, but couldn't help giggling.

"I'm showing my wife how glad I am to see her...after I thought I might not." He beamed at her, as if proud of himself.

David's blue eyes danced with amusement as she tried to

extricate herself, pushing with her unrestrained hand against the mattress.

"Try shoving against this." He flipped aside the sheet to reveal his bare thigh. Muscled and hard, dusted with coarse hair.

"David! We can't have sex here in a hospital room!"

"This isn't sex—it's play," he argued.

She rolled her eyes at him. "Anyone could come in here and see us...playing."

"Then they can vouch for my full recovery."

Slowly, his left hand circled down her back, tracing fingertips through the fabric and over her flesh, exciting her even as she tried to remain immune to his touch. She was afraid he'd hurt himself, or she might hurt him if she resisted too fiercely.

"I like the way you feel, Carrie," he whispered. "All softness, but with strength underneath. I liked the way you felt the first time we touched. Do you know when that was?"

"N-no," she stammered.

He chuckled at her futile attempts to free herself. "It was on your plane, when I came forward to sit in the copilot's seat."

"We didn't touch."

"We did, for just a second. I reached over and rested my hand on your arm when I thanked you for saving my life. I knew then that I would find a way to make love to you."

"Liar." She laughed at him. "Now, let me go, or I'll claim police brutality."

"I don't intend to let you go. Not now. Not for a long, long time, Carrie. Stop fighting me. I'm not hurting you. You're safe. You're not going anywhere, and I'm not going anywhere. See, we're in a holding pattern."

She thought, He's right. Their hearts were circling, searching for a safe place to land. But in love there were even fewer guarantees of a safe landing than in aviation.

Her right arm was still wedged behind his neck but with less pressure on it. David's good arm was wrapped around her waist, gently holding her against his chest. Carrie breathed in, breathed out, in, out—aware that with every breath her breasts pressed against his chest, aware that as she leaned across his hips, she could feel his arousal.

That *he* found their playful wrestling match stimulating didn't surprise her. What shocked her was the exhilaration *she* felt.

Carrie swallowed. "Holding patterns can't last for long. You either have to come down for good, or you have to regain altitude."

"I'm not sure going up is physically possible, since I'm already about as high as I can go," he growled. "Kiss me, Carrie."

"What?"

"I'm asking you to kiss me."

Then he said the word she'd been sure wasn't in the tough cop's vocabulary.

"Please."

There was a poignant vulnerability in this man that she was only beginning to understand. She could read remaining traces of the fear he'd faced as he'd lain alone in the warehouse, his life's blood draining from his body. She could imagine Pete crouching over him, trying to stanch the bleeding, counting the minutes until the ambulance arrived, praying he hadn't lost his partner and best friend.

David had crossed death's dark chasm. He had survived a bullet intended to snuff him out of existence, and now she could see a hunger for life in him that needed to be fed. The love of his children was a miracle he'd always cherish. But they alone couldn't sustain him. He needed proof of his continuing life. And for a man—any man, she imagined—little else could better reassure him that he was functioning than the touch of a woman.

Her heart softened and the last traces of irritation with his pigheadedness seeped away. She wasn't sure what she was feeling. It was warm, tender, forgiving and generous. But she was also excited.

Carrie leaned forward until her breasts pressed against Da-

vid's chest and her breath mingled with his. His eyes widened
and grew dusky.

"Don't tease," he muttered from deep down in his throat.
"If you aren't going to—"

She blocked his next words, placing her lips over his, holding them there. Not kissing him yet, just touching lips to lips.
A holding pattern. She counted to ten, feeling David's warm
mouth open slowly beneath hers, coaxing her lips to part, also.

Gradually, their kiss deepened, until the intimacy of it sent
ripples of heat through her limbs, like tropical air currents
pressing against the undersides of the *Bay Lady*'s wings as she
flew south. Lifting. Lifting.

Through the pleasant haze of her arousal, Carrie felt David's
hand move with increased urgency over her back, hips, thighs,
through the material of her skirt. Then his fingers were sliding
beneath the hem of her skirt, inching up her bare thigh.

The realization fleetingly crossed her mind that she'd closed
the door to the hospital room on entering, but hadn't locked
it. Strangely, whether there was a door at all didn't seem to
matter. She only wanted to prolong this moment for as long
as possible. Wanted David's hands to investigate every cen-
timeter of her flesh, ached to feel him seek out the secret
places that responded to his caresses with liquid fire.

His breathing became uneven, rasping, deeper. Carrie felt
as if he'd thrown a switch inside her, increasing the sensitivity
of every nerve in her body.

"When I was lying there in the ambulance and they were
pumping plasma back into me," he gasped, "I thought of
you...and me...like this."

"Your life didn't flash before you?" she whispered
hoarsely, pressing her hips upward to meet his hand as he
cupped the soft mound of her womanhood between her thighs.

"No. Just you. I thought, I don't want to die without making
love to this woman again."

Carrie drew a sharp breath as his fingers found her moist
center. "David" was all she could manage. "Oh, David."

"I can't imagine my seeing you every morning, sleepy eyed
and warm from your bed, and not wanting to make love to

you. I can't watch you come out of the shower, all steamy and soft, wrapped in your frilly robe, and not want to rip it off you.'' His fingers moved in erotic rhythms to his words. ''I can't watch you sitting with my children on the couch, reading to them and playing all the characters' voices... without feeling you should be there always for all of us.''

She swallowed, unable to talk at all now. Emotions caught her up and hurled her in a dozen different directions. Was this what love felt like?

She couldn't say for sure. Whatever it was, she felt it pulling her into its grip, just as surely as an airplane is captured in a sudden downdraft, unable to escape despite the pilot's efforts.

Like a treacherous air current, David's effect on her could easily result in disaster. Yet knowing all this, understanding the dangers, she wanted him all the more.

Carrie lay tightly against David's chest, glorying in the sensations his fingers drew from the innermost regions of her body. With a shudder of pleasure, she raised herself up just enough to stroke his bare chest. She carefully avoided the bandaged area around his right shoulder, smoothing her hands over the muscled mounds and tight ridges of his belly, brushing the wiry hairs between her fingers, circling his flat, brown nipples with the pads of her fingers. She couldn't resist lowering her head to nibble one until it condensed into a hard nub. David stiffened with pleasure and let out a groan.

''Oh, woman, I can't...don't do that unless you want me to... Damn, that's good.'' His arm crushed her to him, as he squeezed his eyes shut in concentration.

Her hand moved downward until the center of her palm glided over a rich thatch of masculine fur. She wrapped her fingers around him.

It was as if someone had waved a magic wand, altering the atmosphere in the little room. Carrie felt the emotional leverage shift between them. She was suddenly the one in control.

The feeling was as powerful as when she sat in the pilot's seat the last seconds before she sped down the runway, pulled back on the yoke and zoomed off into a cloudless sky.

She lifted her eyes to David's, saw that he knew it, too. He was relinquishing the moment to her, letting her take charge. She felt his hand go still inside her. She slid her fingers slowly up to the tip of him, then down again.

"Carrie, you make a man feel helpless. I was only playing. What are you trying to do to me?"

"I want you to feel as alive as you've ever felt."

He closed his eyes and moaned with pleasure as she stroked him. His body pressed into the mattress—rigid, throbbing, hot. She fed off his reaction to her touch, her own passion soaring to match his. She felt a sudden, sharp, satisfying spasm.

As his hand slid from between her thighs, a honeylike dampness seeped from within her. Although she could have asked him for more, she wouldn't. All she was thinking of now was pleasuring *him.* Or rather, the many men he was— gentle father, avenging cop, ardent lover.

She leaned closer, brushing her breasts across his cheek. He turned his head and nuzzled his way beneath the cotton of her scoop-necked T-shirt. She hadn't bothered with a bra in her haste to come to him.

He drew her nipple into his mouth and sucked hungrily. Carrie arched into him as flames licked her from the inside. Then he was pulsing in her hand, stifling his groan of ecstasy against her breasts.

She could only cling to him, riding the wave with him until she lay trembling on top of him.

Barely a minute passed before a knock rattled the door of the hospital room. Carrie lifted her head and peered curiously at the mint-green panel as if it were a creature from another planet.

She felt David pulling down her skirt and lifting her away from him. She sat obligingly on the bed and watched him yank up the sheet.

"We've got company," he whispered, grinning at her.

She looked down at herself, feeling numb except for the pleasant full-body buzz following their lovemaking. Most of her right breast was still visible above her shirt. She tugged the fabric back into place, then smoothed the bottom edge of her shirt into the waistband of her skirt.

"Come in," David called out.

The door opened tentatively, and a portly man with silvering hair stepped through, a knowing smile on his lips, his eyes twinkling.

"Sorry to interrupt your reunion, Detective."

Carrie felt her cheeks flush with heat. She looked away from the two men and quickly combed her fingers through her hair.

When she turned back, David was smiling sheepishly at her. "I guess we weren't very discreet."

"No matter. Probably the best therapy there is."

The doctor waved off David's concern and held up the chart he'd evidently been studying in the hallway. Carrie wondered just how long he'd been standing out there.

"Let's talk about that shoulder now."

Carrie cleared her throat. "Is he...I mean, will David be all right?"

"Certainly looks as if he's feeling all right." The doctor chuckled.

She wished he'd stop doing that. *Men!* she thought

"He can leave?"

"Leave? Oh, it's a little early for that. The detective was in surgery only a few hours ago. Give us a day or two, to make sure everything is in working order."

"No way," David said. He moved his injured arm around. "See? Works just fine."

But Carrie didn't miss the way his face paled and tightened.

Neither did the doctor, apparently. "Yeah, right. You're a tough guy. Back on the street by tonight with the narcotics unit? I don't think so, Detective."

David tossed off the sheet and swung his feet off the bed. "You can't legally keep me here against my will. I'm checking out. If I have any problems, I'll be back to see you."

The doctor turned to Carrie. "Anything you can do to change Superman's mind?"

"I doubt it," she stated grimly. "He pretty much does what he wants, when he wants."

"I see." The doctor pulled a small pad of paper from his lab-coat pocket and scrawled something illegible on it as Carrie watched over his shoulder. "At least let your wife fill this prescription for you. It's just an analgesic laced with codeine. For the pain."

"I won't need it."

"You'll need it. Your veins are pumped full of painkillers now. When that wears off in a hour or two, you'll know it and thank me for this." He handed Carrie the slip of paper. "There may be some seepage from the wound for a day or two. That's a normal part of the healing process. But if it doesn't stop after that, you drag him in here fast."

"I will," she promised, and leveled a look at David that was as determined as he was stubborn.

Chapter 13

It was a beautiful summer day. The kind that tempted her to pack a tube of sunscreen and her bathing suit and file a flight plan for Ocean City, even if she didn't have passengers.

But that day, the *Bay Lady*'s passenger list was nearly full for a 10 a.m. flight to O.C., and the afternoon was totally free except for the 5 p.m. return flight. Which provided the best possible opportunity for about six hours of blissful goofing off.

Before David and the children had come along, Carrie would have zipped across the Eastern Shore of Maryland, unloaded her passengers at the little airport just west of the seaside resort, then taken the shuttle bus to the beach—to swim, sunbathe and gobble down crab cakes and famous Thrasher's fries smothered in ketchup.

But three days after the shooting, she was still worried about David. Somehow, it didn't feel right that she fly off to play at the beach while he was still nursing a wound. On the other hand, she argued with herself, she really shouldn't feel guilty. She'd offered to cancel her flights and stay home with him. He'd refused to take even one day off.

The children were another matter.

She sighed. Already Jason and Tammy had changed the way she looked at her carefree airborne excursions. She wanted the children to be with her whenever possible. She'd missed them during the two days they'd stayed with their mother. And, she reasoned, beaches and children did seem a natural match.

Why not? she thought.

The only difficulty was, she wasn't sure how David would react to Jason and Tammy flying with her. Or how open he was to her getting any closer to them than she already was.

Yes, she and David had become lovers, but neither had brought up the subject of their arrangement becoming permanent. In the three days since David had left the hospital, there had been no repeat of their intimate tryst in the hospital and there'd been no time to talk.

She wondered if he, too, was having second thoughts about their fragile relationship. She hoped his silence was merely a necessity, a need to concentrate on his work.

Sadly, their parting still seemed inevitable to Carrie. The more distance she kept between herself and David's children, the better off they all would be when the time came for them to leave.

Twelve months—that was the most she could count on. The truth drove a wedge of sorrow through her heart.

No longer enthusiastic about her trip to the ocean, Carrie tossed a few extras into her flight bag—bathing suit, sandals and a white, oversize shirt of her father's that she still wore as a beach wrap.

"After all," she muttered, "they're *his* kids, not mine. I shouldn't feel guilty for not taking them with me." Striding into the bathroom, she added a tube of coconut-scented sunscreen and a little jar of pink zinc-oxide cream for her nose. When she turned around, Tammy was standing behind her.

"Are you going away?" the little girl asked.

Carrie set her supplies on the sink and squatted in front of Tammy. She ran her hand over her soft curls, her heart melting despite her conviction to hold herself emotionally aloof from the child. "Not for long, Tams. I have to fly some people to the beach for their vacation. I'll be back before you and Jason go to bed tonight. Mary Beth, from next door, will stay with you.''

Jason stuck his head around the corner. ''Where you flying, Carrie-barrie?''

She laughed at him. ''To Ocean City, Jason-bason.'' They'd been working on rhyming words in his summer learning activities book, and it was just about driving David crazy. But Carrie loved the word games they played.

''To the beach?'' he squealed. ''You're going to the beach *today?*''

She could have lied. She *should* have lied. ''Yes, I'll spend a few hours on the beach before turning around and heading back home,'' she admitted.

''Can we come? Please, please, please...can we, Carrie?''

''The beach?'' Tammy echoed, belatedly catching on to the reason for Jason's excitement. ''Oh, I lo-o-o-o-ove swimming!''

Both kids ran at Carrie, knocking her off her precarious crouch, onto the bathroom tiles. They jumped up and down, squeezing her around the neck and squealing until her head rang and she was laughing so hard she lost her breath.

''Hey, remember this is flying in an airplane, gang. It's not like going for a drive in your dad's car. Have you ever flown before?''

Tammy looked at her older brother, as if she wasn't sure.

''No,'' Jason admitted. ''We never been on an airplane. Grandma and Grandpa fly down here, sometimes, to see us. Dad doesn't want us to fly up to see them.''

Carrie nodded. ''Well, then,'' she said, gently disentangling herself from four chubby arms, ''that may pose another problem. Your father may not want you to fly with me.''

''But you're our *new mother!*'' Jason protested. ''We should be able to go with you. You drive us in your car. Why's an airplane so different?''

Carrie's heart skipped two whole beats. *Our new mother.* Why did that sound so nice to her? Even though she knew it wasn't true. If Jason's words hadn't melted her heart, the look of disappointment in his soft, blue eyes, so like his father's, would have. At his age, she was sitting on her father's lap while he piloted the Cessna that had been the predecessor to the *Bay Lady*.

She sighed. "I'll see if I can reach your father and ask him if it's okay. But if he says no or I can't talk to him before flight time, we'll just have to wait for your first airplane ride."

Jason grinned, then spun around to his sister. "C'mon, let's go put on our bathing suits!"

"I want to take my pail and shovel!" Tammy called out as she scampered after him.

Carrie laughed at them. They were such a pair. Real little people.

The operator at Western District headquarters told her that Detective Adams was in the squad room, and he would ring there.

"Detective Turner, yo!" It was Pete.

Carrie automatically tensed at the sound of his voice. Their truce was no more than that. He still hadn't fully accepted her. Why should she blame him? By the time she won his trust, a year would have passed, and she'd walk away from David and his children, because that was what they'd agreed to do. No doubt Pete would see her as another Sheila, and feel justified in his opinion of her.

"Hi, Pete," she said softly, "this is Carrie. Is David around?"

"Yeah," he said gruffly. "Let me get him."

Drumming her fingers on the receiver, she waited for David to come to the phone.

"What's up?" a tense voice snapped.

He sounded wired, ready to snap. She felt sorry for him and wished she could do something to help make his job easier on him. "I'm flying to O.C. in a little over an hour. Jason and Tammy found out, and they want to come along."

"In your plane?"

"I wasn't planning on strapping a jet engine to my car," she teased.

"Anyone ever tell you you've got a smart mouth?"

"I try."

He let out a dry laugh. In the background she could hear voices calling his name. Things apparently weren't going well; they hadn't found Carl Rainey yet. Last night, David had told her that Andrew Rainey, still in jail without bail, steadfastly denied that Carl was even in town.

"Seriously, David, if you're worried about them flying with me or being so far away from you—"

"No, no, it's fine with me if they won't be in the way. I'm sure there's no safer pilot this side of the Mississippi."

Carrie felt a surge of pride with his confidence in her. "I don't think they'll be a problem. And they should enjoy a day at the beach."

"I know they will. I don't get them to the ocean often enough." He hesitated on the other end. "I appreciate your including them. They'll have fun, I'm sure...." His voice trailed off, leaving an uncomfortable tension singing along the line between them.

"But?"

"Nothing."

"There is something, David," she insisted.

He let out a long breath across the receiver. "I don't know how to let them enjoy being with you and at the same time warn them not to get too comfortable with you. There's a lot we haven't resolved."

"I know," she said softly. "I've just been thinking the same thing."

"It will be hard on them if you leave."

If! The word was brimming with hope. Did he want her to stay? But it didn't matter what he wanted or what she might feel at this moment. Emotions, people, dreams all changed so drastically. There are no guarantees, she reminded herself. "It will be hard on me, too...if I have to leave them...leave you," she added, feeling hollow at the thought.

"Yes," he agreed, before shouting at whoever had been trying to get him off the phone. He drew an audible breath and whispered, "I want you, Carrie."

She could picture him, standing in the middle of the bustling squad room, shielding the mouthpiece of the phone with his hand.

"Even now. Here, when I should be working. I don't know how to handle all these feelings."

There were more background noises. Even though David was whispering, she was certain he couldn't say all he wanted to.

"We need to talk," she murmured. "I don't know if I can trust your feelings or even my own. I'm afraid, David. Afraid of feeling too much, afraid of losing you in any of the hundreds of ways it could happen—and that includes your growing bored with me...or your getting blown away by some punk on a street corner."

There was a long silence—so long she feared he'd put down the phone and walked away from it. She could have kicked herself for coming right out and saying all she felt.

"David?" she murmured hoarsely. "Are you there?"

"I'm here. This is hard, Carrie, real hard on me. I'm used to taking risks, damn it. But I can't imagine a bigger one than this...or a scarier one. I can't imagine being without you. Then I tell myself, one day I'll come home and find you've gone."

"I wouldn't leave without telling you," she said weakly.

"Well, that's comforting," he grumbled. They were calling his name again. "I've got to go now. When will you be back with the kids?"

"Before dark," she promised. "And I'll take very good care of them for you."

"I know you will," he whispered. "I know that." And he hung up.

David stood looking down at the phone on the cluttered desk, frowning.

"Something wrong?" Pete asked.

"Carrie's taking the kids with her to the beach for the day. They're going to love it."

"So why do you look as if they've been whisked off the planet by an alien spaceship?"

David shook his head. How could he explain the tangle of

feelings inside him? Sometimes it seemed as if the issue was much larger than their trusting each other. He could almost feel fate working to bring them together, as if he and Carrie being together hadn't been up to them at all.

He wasn't a religious man, hadn't been much for church after his grandparents were gone. But he could believe that some power, some force greater than himself, intended Carrie to become a precious part of his life.

Then there was the other, opposing, force. It was sinister, intent upon destroying the beauty of what they shared. He feared that dark power, for even if he and Carrie learned to trust each other completely, this invisible thing lurking out there might find a way to keep them apart. It could destroy every chance they had of happiness. It was called death.

Life was incredibly fragile. If he hadn't realized that before the ambush in the warehouse, he knew it now.

"Hey," Pete said. "You've got to shake off this blue funk. That broad's doing a number on your head."

David swung around violently to face his partner, not bothering to disguise his irritation. "You mean, *my wife?* Don't talk about Carrie like that."

Pete observed him over the top of his soda can as he threw back his head and took a long drink. "Man, I hope she really does love you. I don't want to see you go through another freakin' divorce. First one was tough enough on me."

David shook his head. It was hard to stay mad at Pete for long, especially since the scraggly narc had saved his skin so recently. "Tough on you? Hey, what about me?"

"Just don't be thinkin' about her while we're out on the street. We've got to find our buddy Carl before he gets any more wild ideas about takin' you out." He drank the last swallow, then heaved the empty can at David. It ricocheted off the arm that reflexively shot up to ward off the missile and clanked across the floor. "You watch out for yourself, hear? I got no desire to hold your head again while you bleed all over me."

"Likewise," David assured him. He slung his left arm over his partner's shoulder and steered him toward the door. "Let's go get this creep."

Chapter 14

The unmarked police car pulled up beside the hangar as Carrie made her last trip from the plane, pushing a handcart loaded with light cargo. David's wide shoulders filled the open driver's door, then rose to dwarf the car.

"Hey, beautiful." He touched one finger to the tip of her nose as she wheeled past him, grinning. "Looks like you got a little sunburn."

"Forgot to use the sunblock. Your two darlings kept me running all day."

"I'll bet they did." He chuckled, following her for a dozen paces before impatiently tugging her free of the cart and pulling her into his arms to kiss her. "I've missed you."

She laid her head on his chest. "Me, too. Have they caught him yet?"

He didn't have to ask whom she meant. "No. Something will break soon, though."

Carrie wondered what he meant by "break." An anonymous tip pinpointing Carl Rainey's location? Or it might mean David's wanna-be killer would try to finish what he'd started.

Only when David was again in peril would the police have any chance of capturing the man.

She looked around, wondering how far away or how very close Carl Rainey was this very minute.

"Where's your shadow?" she asked.

"Pete? He's off duty until morning. Has to catch up on sleep sometime. So do I, in addition to some other things." David flashed her a wicked grin.

Carrie shivered in anticipation. "Then come on. The kids are in the office with Rose. Let's collect them and head for home."

David pushed the handcart, while Carrie walked at his side.

"Actually, there's something you should know," David said before they entered the hangar.

"Yes?"

"A couple of our sources indicate Carl may still be in the area."

"Someone has seen him?"

"We can't be sure. The stories conflict."

"Oh." A weight in the center of her body felt as if it were pulling her down. Her throat was suddenly so dry it hurt to speak. "So what happens now?"

"Routine stuff. I take you and the kids back to the house. Baltimore County has sprung for a twenty-four-hour watch on the place. Just a precaution."

Carrie focused on his words in the hope they would calm her, but she felt as if she were trying to breathe through layers of cotton. "It's not just you the police are worried about, is it?"

He looked away. "Everyone's just taking precautions. Rainey may figure he can't easily hit me again while I'm on duty, so he might try for a time when I'm off." David kept walking and she matched his stride.

"Then the children are in danger, too."

"I don't think so," he said slowly. "It's me he wants."

"But if he can't get *directly* to you—"

"Don't start me thinking like that!" Tension had etched deep lines across his forehead, and showed in the taut muscles ridging his neck. "How can I leave the three of you in the morning if I'm worried about— Listen, we've gotten just as many sightings of Rainey a hundred or more miles from here. Two of them from New York State, where he has a bunch of cousins who might risk hiding him. It's crazy to worry."

"I'm sorry," Carrie breathed. "It's hard."

He nodded. "Let's just get the kids home and in bed. I bet they're beat. They probably spent the entire day in the ocean."

"Just about," she admitted. "David?"

"What?"

"Don't get yourself shot again."

He grinned humorlessly at her. "Gee, what would I do without your sound advice?"

She cuffed him playfully on the jaw. "Fresh."

David drove around the knot of ramps and access roads through BWI Airport, west on Route 195 to the intersection of Rolling Road, then north through a beautifully landscaped residential neighborhood of older homes, to Frederick Road and from there into Catonsville. It was only a fifteen-minute ride to her elegant home. He could see why a commercial pilot set on raising a family would have thought the location ideal.

As he drove, Carrie curled up in the passenger seat beside him and closed her eyes. He watched her while keeping an eye on the light traffic. He tried not to think of the many marvelous things he'd discovered about her and about himself during the past weeks. Tried equally hard not to think about all he might lose at any moment.

He desperately wanted Carrie to stay in his life, couldn't imagine how desolate he'd be if she walked away from him. But how he could make it all work for them was still beyond him.

After helping Carrie get the kids inside with all their beach gear, he walked across the street and spoke to the patrolman in the olive-and-black squad car that was parked on the other side of the street. The county had just ordered spanking new squads in the quasi-military colors, and they were the ugliest things on wheels.

"Nothing happening here, Detective," the young officer inside reported.

David noted that his badge read Larson.

"Okay if I drive down the street for a burger? Only take me ten minutes or less with the drive-through."

"Sure. I'll be in for the night. When does your relief show up?"

"Depends on the calls we get. We're tight for personnel these days."

The county's budget, like the city's, had been cut to bare bones. Which meant response time to nonemergency citizens' calls was often hours instead of minutes. It was a small miracle the Wilkens District lieutenant had agreed to tying up a man on a house watch.

"If you have to leave tonight before your replacement shows up, just knock on the door and let me know," David said. "I'll stay up until another man shows."

Larson nodded. "Thanks. I'll be right back."

David watched him drive off, then jogged back across the street in the dark and down the driveway. Purple wisteria draped the porch railings and climbed overhead, casting snakelike shadows in the lavender light of the setting sun. Tea roses bloomed in tidy beds alongside the old-fashioned porch. Vibrant yellow-and-orange portulaca and dainty ice-white freesia burst through wood chips laid down to hold moisture beneath sunbaked soil. He had never paid much attention to flower names, but Carrie rattled off a bunch of them the other day as they'd strolled around the yard. His cop's mind for details had somehow filed them away as if they'd been crime-scene details. He walked around the outside of the house, checking windows and the inside of the detached garage.

David let himself in through the front vestibule, stepping under the stained-glass transom panel of grapes and vines that arched over the heavy mahogany door. Although there was no central AC in the house, the dim entryway was naturally cool day and night. He felt himself gearing down as if his body were a racing car, crossing the finish line.

No. He adjusted the image in his mind. He felt as if he'd come home. At last.

It was a wonderful sensation. With it came a wave of love and security he hadn't felt since his boyhood days in his grandfather's house.

He locked the dead bolt as well as the button lock in the doorknob. He listened for people sounds in the house.

"That you, David?" Carrie's voice drifted from the kitchen.

"Yeah. I'm relieving the uniform out front for a while. He should be back any minute."

She stepped through the hallway into the foyer, and smiled at him so sweetly it warmed his heart.

"How long is *a while?* I thought I was going to have you all to myself for the night."

"Are the kids in bed?"

She grinned naughtily at him. "Sound asleep."

Taking her hand, he led her toward the staircase, then stopped outside the kitchen door and sniffed. Delicious smells he couldn't quite identify wafted into the hall.

Laughing at his torn expression, she led him into the kitchen. He looked toward the stove. A skillet sizzled with bite-size pieces of chicken, broccoli, onions and red peppers. "Now you're making me choose—food or you."

"You may have both," she said, wrapping her arms around his neck and kissing him deeply. "Hungry?"

"In more ways than one," he admitted. "But I think I'll have to satisfy one appetite at a time."

"Good idea," she teased. "The food will get cold. I won't."

After they'd made love, David lay in the bed with Carrie, her head nestled in the dip between his shoulder and chest, her naked body draped lightly over his. He swept an errant blond curl from her cheek, tucking it behind her ear. He breathed in the scent of her—a mix of cooking spices, soap and natural woman-smells. Perhaps for the one time in his life, he felt perfectly at peace with himself and the world.

Before bringing her upstairs after supper, he'd walked out front to check on Larson. Another man, who looked even greener, was in his place. They'd talked for a few minutes.

"Every hour or so I'll walk around the outside of the house," the young cop said. "Just to make sure everything's tight."

"I'm glad you told me. I might have heard you and thought it was someone else."

"Don't go blasting away without giving me a warning."

The cop had laughed, but David knew he was serious.

Now he lay halfway between waking and sleeping—Carrie in his arms, his children slumbering peacefully in their rooms, his .38 under a magazine on the bedside table and a terrible fear nagging his heart that all that was good in his life could be snatched from him at any time.

Still, he wouldn't have traded places with any other man.

A part of his brain remained engaged, while the rest of his body sank into morphia. Outside, cicadas sang their screeching love songs, a dog barked in the distance, cars rumbled past the house, the occasional rise and fall of voices from late-night walkers faintly reached him.

Then everything seemed to go still, or maybe he allowed his brain to totally shut down for just a few minutes. He drifted in a sublime sleep, devoid of all that was cruel and dangerous. A child again, in Carrie's arms, he had no worries. Everything felt right and forever.

The sound that first roused him wasn't an alarming one. Just another car's engine, rumbling from a distance down Frederick Road, as so many others had during the night. Softly guttural at first, stopping at the light he'd noticed two blocks down, moving forward and picking up speed. The speed limit was only twenty-five miles an hour through the middle of Catonsville. At that speed, an engine settled into a contented hum and never rose above that.

But this engine didn't stop for the light, didn't hold to its relaxed, small-town hum. It picked up speed and roared through the night.

His eyes flew open.

Before he could move Carrie aside and throw himself out of bed, there was the squeal of brakes, the ominous creak of a car door...glass crashing somewhere downstairs.

"David!" Carrie cried, struggling to her elbows, blinking up at him even as he pulled on his jeans, grabbed his gun and raced barefoot for the bedroom door.

"Get the kids!" he shouted. He could smell gasoline, hear a dull crackling sound, knew instantly what had happened. "Take them out one of the dormer windows to the roof if you can."

From the second-floor landing he could see the evil glow of flames. It didn't take a genius to figure out what had happened. Carl Rainey, or someone paid by him, had heaved a Molotov cocktail, a homemade firebomb of rags stuffed into a bottle half full of gasoline, through one of the front windows. An old house like Carrie's would burn fast and hot.

He knew he'd seen a fire extinguisher in the kitchen, and ran for it. By the time he reached the living room, the carpet and draperies were in flames and thick, gray smoke was filling the room from the ceiling down. Someone was pounding on the front door, yelling.

David foamed each lick of flame that blazed up in one spot as soon as he'd quelled another. When he thought he might have smothered the last of the fire, he rushed to the door and let in the white-faced patrolman.

"Is everyone all right?" the man gasped, peering past David into the smoky interior of the house. "He came up fast...jammed on his brakes in front of the house. By the time I got out of my car and pulled my gun, he'd thrown the thing and was on his way."

"Why didn't you chase him?" David shouted. "For God's sake, you let that maniac get away!"

The cop looked baffled as he holstered his weapon. "And leave you with your wife and kids to barbecue?" He was shaking. "I didn't know if anyone was awake."

David heaved the extinguisher down on the singed carpet. He took three deep breaths and forced himself to release each one slowly. "You're right. Sorry." He raked a hand through his hair, thinking. Thinking hard and fast and randomly. Either the out-of-state sightings of Carl Rainey were false—by intent or accident—or one of the brothers had paid for tonight's dirty work.

"You radio for help yet?"

"They're on the way. And I reported the license number. At least I got that." The young cop smiled weakly.

"Good." David tuned in on a scraping sound from somewhere over their heads and looked up.

The cop drew his gun again.

"It's all right," David said. "By now my wife is sitting on the roof with two cranky kids. Let's go rescue them."

Carrie stood in the middle of her living room, surveying the damage through dry eyes. This was the room she'd played in with her friends as a child. The room where she'd sat on the floor and won at Monopoly over her father and been beaten repeatedly at Chutes and Ladders by the little girl next door who later became her best high-school friend.

The draperies were destroyed. The Oriental carpet, which was the only item of any great worth, was singed to black and probably beyond repair. The small, oak side table under the shattered window had been reduced to kindling, and the couch was peppered with black hollows where pools of gasoline had ignited and burned into the upholstery. It looked as if a giant had reached through the window to snuff out a monstrous cigar in the cushions. Broken glass lay everywhere.

Carrie reached out to steady herself on David's arm.

"We'll replace and repair," he said soothingly. "It will be all right."

"Thank God none of us was hurt," she said. "Thank God for that—none of this really matters."

He wrapped an arm around her. The cop in him yearned to be out in a car, chasing down the madman who'd done this. The man in him needed to be here, with Carrie.

He could almost forget the guy had tried to gun him down in the warehouse. He could convince himself that getting shot was part of his job. He, David Adams, was the cop; Carl was the bad guy. Classic enemies. Confrontation was inevitable.

But this—an attack on Carrie and his children—*this* he took personally.

"My squad leader will be here any minute," David said. "Then we'll figure out what happens next."

"What do you mean?"

"I'm not sure you and the kids will be safe here."

Carrie looked up at him, started to say something, then closed her mouth firmly and swallowed. "I'll put on a fresh pot of coffee." Between her, David, the patrolman and the firemen who'd spent almost an hour assuring no live sparks lingered in upholstery or carpet, they'd finished a pot.

Now the fire trucks had left. Only the chief remained, walking around the outside of the house, making notes for his report. Jason and Tammy were in the kitchen, sleepy eyed, eating pancakes and discussing the night's adventure.

As Carrie approached the kitchen, the little boy's excited voice reached out to her.

"I bet if Daddy didn't put out that fire, we would have had to jump into one of those trampoline things the firemen use on TV!"

"Would we bounce like on my bed?" Tammy asked, obviously relishing the idea.

At least they hadn't been traumatized by the incident. She'd taken care to make their escape to the roof sound like a game. Apparently it had worked. Later, when things calmed down, she'd go over emergency plans with them and explain the seriousness of a fire. For now, they were better off not knowing that someone had tried to kill them and their parents.

Parents.

Carrie mused over the word her brain had so easily supplied. They weren't her children, she reminded herself for the hundredth time. Yet they felt as dear to her as if she'd known them all their lives…as if they were her own. Whatever would she have done if she'd lost either of them in the blaze?

She made coffee, tossed out used paper cups from the first shift and wiped down the counters. She tried not to dwell on the answers to her own question.

David walked into the kitchen followed by a slim, gray-haired man wearing a serious expression. "Mrs. Adams," he said. "I'm Lieutenant Rogers, David's shift commander. Sorry about your house."

"Yes," she said. "Thank you." There seemed nothing more to say about what was already done.

"Hi, kids," the lieutenant said, lifting a hand toward the two seated at the kitchen table.

"Hi," Jason replied shyly.

Tammy slid down in her chair and hid behind her hands from the stranger.

Rogers smiled drolly. "I have a way with kids." He turned to David. "We've found the car he used—it was stolen. No surprise there. He ditched it less than a mile from here. Probably had another one parked nearby, waiting for him."

David nodded. "Right. He wouldn't take the chance that he'd happen on one. No word on where he might be?"

"Nope. Listen, David, after what happened tonight, I'm not sure we can protect your family." He glanced at Carrie. "Short of taking you all into protective custody." He turned back to David. "Since the Rainey boys aren't making any headway convincing you to back out of Andrew's case, they've apparently decided to settle for a payback. We knew Carl was unpredictable. Tonight proves he's not only that, he's ruthless. I don't think he'll quit until he's done what he set out to do, or until we stop him."

Carrie's stomach churned. She'd never felt so helpless. Pete walked in, and Carrie smiled tiredly at him.

"Heard you had an interesting night," he commented. "If you wanted to redecorate, Carrie, I'm sure Dave would have agreed to new furniture. Isn't this going over the top?"

Teasing, she was beginning to learn, was his way of making peace with her. She smiled gratefully at him. "When I change drapery styles, I go all the way."

"You hear anything this morning on the street about Rainey?" the lieutenant asked Pete.

He shook his head. "*Nada.* Not a peep. I made my rounds downtown before coming here. The street's quiet. No one's saying a thing. Either he's keeping this all to himself, or everyone's too scared to say anything." He turned to David and gave him a meaningful look. "Not even a whisper about the two guys who set you up at the warehouse. Maybe they were out-of-towners."

David shrugged, then turned to Rogers. "I don't want to leave Carrie and the children alone. We can't even be sure that he knew I was here. Maybe they were supposed to be his revenge. If I hadn't been here, there's no telling what would have happened. They might have all died in their sleep."

Carrie touched David on the arm. It wasn't a gesture of denial; it was a sign of support and a reminder. They'd made it. They were *alive*—and where there was life, there was hope.

Rogers stuck his thumbs in his belt and sucked in his already flat stomach as he observed David. "I know this is a lot to ask of you, Dave. But we need you if we're going to get this guy. You are the bait, and Pete knows him by sight. We've got photos, but they're old." He looked at Carrie, then back to David. "Is there somewhere your wife could take the kids for a few days, a week, until we grab this slimeball?"

"I'm not leaving David," Carrie said quickly.

The three men looked at her, then exchanged glances. David stepped closer to her and took her hands in his. "If you and the kids stay here, we'll have to pull more men off the search to protect the three of you. And as long as you're vulnerable, I won't be able to focus on what I'm supposed to be doing."

"Please," she begged, "don't ask me to leave you."

He wrapped his arms around her, while the other men looked tactfully away. "You took the kids to O.C. for the day, then came home and I was fine. This will be for just a little longer."

"But I—"

"Carrie, for God's sake, don't argue. Think about the children. This house obviously isn't a safe place for them or for you. Neither is the airport. Is there somewhere you can think of to fly them and stay for a little while?''

"Disney World!" Jason cried from the table.

The lieutenant let out a sharp laugh. "I think we've got the makings of an undercover cop over there."

David scowled. "Not if I can help it. Young man, eat your breakfast and mind your own business."

"David," Carrie whispered. "He doesn't understand...."

He nodded and closed his eyes for a moment. His face was distorted by strain. "Right. We're all tense. What about it, Carrie? Is there a safe place you can take the children?"

Carrie thought for a moment. "Rose has a beach cottage that belonged to one of her husbands. She doesn't use it often. I think it's in Rehoboth, just north of Ocean City, along the shore. It's very quiet, private."

"No one knows about it?" the lieutenant asked.

"Just Rose herself, and Frank, my mechanic. If I tell them to keep it to themselves, they will."

"Sounds perfect." He turned back to David. "Soon as you get your family off, come on downtown."

Carrie called the airport and left a message on the answering machine for Rose, instructing her to cancel the day's flights. It was only 7 a.m., not fully light out, by the time the fire chief and Lieutenant Rogers left. Pete stayed on, keeping an eye on the children while Carrie hurried upstairs to pack. David disappeared outside, and she suspected he was checking again for anything harmful outside the house. When she looked out the second-floor window, he was crawling around inside her car.

She'd held herself together while the men rushed through the house doing their jobs. But now, faced with an indefinite separation from David and the uncertainty of what a madman would do next, she was shaken. Her joints seemed weak, too loose to support her. Her heart's rhythm felt irregular, halting. Her head pounded.

She filled one suitcase with bathing suits, play clothes, underwear and pajamas from the children's bureaus, then returned downstairs to her room to toss together some of her own necessities.

David came in and sat on the edge of her bed.

She stood for a moment, swaying in front of the open drawer of her dresser, before dropping an armload of shorts and tops on the floor. Running to him, she fell to her knees and buried her face in his palms.

"I know," he said, pulling free one hand to rest it heavily on her head. He stroked her hair, then lifted her chin and bent low to kiss her softly on the lips. "I don't enjoy the thought of your leaving, but letting you stay would be selfish. I want you in my bed, in my arms."

She quivered at the emotion behind his kiss. For minutes that Carrie wished could stretch to eternity, they lost themselves in each other's arms. In some indefinable way, she sensed that this moment was a turning point for them.

This might be their last kiss. This might be the last time she touched David's whiskered cheek, heard his voice, felt his arms around her. For while she was gone, David would stop at nothing to find the man who'd tried to wipe out his family. He'd put himself at terrible risk.

A car horn sounded from in front of the house. David gently set her away from him, and their eyes locked for a second before he looked at the clock.

"For crying out loud, I forgot."

"Forgot what?" she asked.

"Sheila. She'd said she'd pick up the kids this morning."

"Oh, no." Carrie stood up, blotting tears she hadn't even realized she'd cried, with the backs of her hands. "What do we do?"

"I can't let her take them. There's no telling what sort of supervision they'd have while they're with her. If Rainey knows about her…" He shook his head, unwilling to put the nightmare in his head into words.

"Then I'll take them with me, as planned," Carrie said, moving with determination toward the closet. "You'll have to tell her what's happened."

He peered out the bedroom window. "I have a feeling she already has a pretty good idea."

Carrie looked over David's shoulder. Sheila had gotten out of her car and was standing on the sidewalk, staring at the front of the house.

"Go talk to her," she said. "I'll finish packing and be right down."

David took the stairs in threes and rushed out the front door just in time to see Tammy and Jason run from Pete to their mother, both children jabbering a mile a minute at her. Sheila's face was white, her lips pinched into a tight red line.

"What's been going on here?" she snapped, but didn't leave him time to answer. "They were supposed to be ready to leave at seven, on the dot. I'll be late for my first appointment."

Pete cast David a look of disbelief and turned to walk back toward the house.

David frowned at the woman he'd been convinced would make of his grim world a finer place. How could she be so self-centered? More to the point, how could he have seen anything special in her?

"There's been a change of plans," he said slowly. "I'm sending the kids out of town for a few days, until we find the person responsible for this." He waved a hand at the shattered window, rimmed with charred wood.

Sheila rolled her eyes. "You mean, this just happened? Someone intentionally...I thought you'd had a damn kitchen fire."

"No," he admitted with reluctance, knowing she'd find a way to use Rainey's attack to her advantage in court, "it has to do with a case. I won't go into the details, since I know you're in a hurry to get to work."

"I don't need explanations," she said, brushing away a feathery seed pod that had fallen from the mimosa tree above them onto the sleeve of her Eve Winslow designer suit. She tossed him a satisfied smile. "You were nearly roasted, the children with you. By the time we meet in court, dear David, there will be no question in the judge's mind who is the safer parent."

Tammy and Jason looked up at her, silent, absorbing her bitter words. He wondered how much they really understood of the arguments, or how drastically the outcome would affect their futures.

"That's why I'm taking precautions and getting them out of town," David said. "In this case, they wouldn't be any safer with you."

She lifted a plucked brow. "I don't suppose Rhode Island would be far enough away to ensure their safety?"

He shivered at her implication. That was exactly the point her lawyer would bring up. And he'd also point out that Detective Adams had refused to tell his wife where the children would be or how long he would hide them away, which was clearly against the divorce agreement.

Sheila made it easier on him. She didn't ask. She kissed Jason on the cheek, then Tammy, and sped away in her little sports car, looking quite cheerful. David felt sure she was relieved to be leaving without kids.

When he turned back toward the house, Pete was standing on the porch, watching her car go.

"Don't say it," David growled.

"If you kept track of all the times she showed her true colors and neglected those kids—"

"I know—I'd have an easy time in court."

He thought he saw a glimmer of a smile pull at Pete's lips, but it was gone a second later.

Chapter 15

Frank watched the *Bay Lady* pick up speed, collecting herself like a grand lady gathering her skirts at a ball to rise up an elegant staircase into the clouds. He lifted a hand in salute. Carrie and those two little ones—they made such a pretty picture. He hoped to hell those kids' father didn't break Carrie's heart.

Cops, he thought again, nothing but trouble.

Wiping the black grease from his hands on a rag, he turned away, still thinking about Carrie's hasty cancellation of her flights, and the terrible fire at the old house. "Maniacs," he muttered. "The world is full of maniacs these days."

He shook his head, watching the tarmac pass under his feet, all speckled with oil, grit and the occasional dried lump of chewing gum, so he didn't see the man until he nearly walked up onto the toes of his sparkling white-leather shoes.

Frank stopped with a jerk and drew his eyes up the height of the stranger. Fella wasn't much taller than his own five feet ten inches, but he looked tan and strong, like actors he'd seen who were no longer young but worked out with weights and could probably bench-press a light plane.

More than anything, it was his eyes that interested Frank. They looked as if they were two different colors—one a gray-green, the other a steel color, somewhere between black and charcoal. They had the look of evil in them.

He figured it was probably the way the sun was shining, a trick of the light.

"Help you?" Frank asked.

"We'll see," the man said. He gazed up into the clouds, shading his eyes from the brilliant July sun. "That plane that just took off—it's a charter, right?"

"Monroe Air, yup," Frank said, feeling a tingle of pride. He handled routine maintenance on a half-dozen other planes at BWI. But he'd never liked working for anyone more than the Monroes.

"I want to charter her," the man said. "When will the plane be back?"

Frank scratched his head. He didn't want to lose Carrie any business, much as she needed it. But he wasn't sure how much he was supposed to say about where she'd gone and why.

"I'm pretty sure the *Bay Lady* won't be available for a few days, but you can check with the receptionist. That's Rose. She's right in that building over there." He pointed at the low multiplane hangar.

The man knocked a cigarette out of a softpack, lit it, took a drag. "Gee, that's too bad. I wanted to arrange something real soon." He produced a twenty-dollar bill from his pants pocket and held it out to Frank. "I know it's short notice, but I'd be willing to pay extra if we could work something out. Where did you say she took the plane?"

She took the plane.

The words chilled him. Staring at the stranger's eyes, Frank fell back a step. "How did you know the pilot was a woman?"

"C'mon, pops. No games."

The twenty had disappeared, replaced by a short-bladed knife.

Rose nibbled on a donut hole, then gave up trying to talk herself out of still being hungry. She selected a whole jelly donut from the box she'd bought on the way to the airport that morning after the phone call from Carrie.

What with her flying off in such a hurry with the children and cops running all over the place, checking out the plane as though they thought maybe there was a bomb or something on it, she'd figured somebody would need a bite to eat. As it turned out, Jason and Tammy had already been fed, and the Emergency Response Team—that was what David, bless his heart, had called the young men who swarmed all over the *Bay Lady*—had been unsmiling and all business. Even his partner, Pete, whom she figured for the kind of stone-hearted cop you saw on those true-action police shows who could munch on fried chicken over a dead body...even he waved away her offer.

By the time Carrie started her engines, they were all piling hurriedly into vans, leaving her with a sack of fresh donut holes and the better part of a dozen sugary donuts.

She sighed. Maybe Frank would make an exception to his rigid breakfast diet of coffee, one egg and dry toast. Maybe, even if he wouldn't eat any now, he'd take them home and put them in his freezer for desserts. He really didn't eat enough. If she'd been around to cook for him...

But that was an old issue, one she'd already dealt with, she thought sadly.

Rearranging the remaining donuts in an attractive display within the box, Rose crossed the hangar and started through the open doors into the sunlight. She looked across the black tarmac, rippling with early-morning heat devils. Frank was nowhere around.

But his big, steel toolbox lay on the ground, near the tether lines of a little single-prop tail-dragger he'd been overhauling. The gray-metal trays were out of the box, a few tools scattered about the pavement. She thought how odd it was that he'd left his things like that, even for a few minutes. He was always so fussy about them.

Turning, Rose walked back into the hangar. She took the donuts with her for safekeeping. They'd melt in the sun, and Frank didn't like lemon anyways.

She bit into dough oozing yellow filling.

* * *

The phone rang almost steadily for the next two hours, so Rose didn't think about Frank and the donuts for that long. When she remembered, she picked up the box with what was left of its contents and went out to look for him.

The first thing that caught her eye was the toolbox. Not one screwdriver had been moved. The trays still baked on the tarmac.

An intuitive shiver ascended Rose's limbs and centered in her chest like a puddle of icy water on its way to freezing. She dropped the donut box and ran out onto the paved apron, shading her eyes from the sun's glare, looking up and down, up and down, but could see no sign of Frank. On a weekday at midmorning, there was little going on. Two mechanics were standing and smoking, down the line of planes. Neither one was Frank.

She was about to go ask them if they'd seen him, when she heard a muffled groan. Spinning around, she scanned the weed-bordered fence line behind her. Nothing moved. The only sound was the rumble of another monster jet taking off from the far side of the field, leaving the ground trembling.

Rose took a step toward the patch of tall grass hugging the chain-link fence. It was sprinkled with poppies and black-eyed Susans. In the middle of the stretch right in front of her was a hollow spot. She waded through the waist-high blades, and found Frank.

"Oh!" she cried, dropping to her fleshy knees. "Oh, Lord Almighty, Frank, what happened?"

She tried to get an arm under him to help him to his feet, then saw the blood when his hand dropped away from his stomach.

"No!" she cried.

She heard herself screaming for help, although she couldn't feel her mouth moving; saw the two mechanics spin around, looking for the source of the screams. She couldn't make her legs lift her, grabbed a fistful of grass and waved it above her head.

One shouted at the other, "Over there! It's coming from there!"

"Frank!" she sobbed.

He opened his eyes, stared at her as if trying to recognize her. "Carrie," he wheezed.

"No, it's Rose."

"Carrie," he repeated. "Man…man had knife. Gone after her."

Rose stopped breathing. "You *told* him where—"

"He was going into the…the hangar after you," Frank whispered. "Couldn't let him hurt you, Rosie. Thought I could stop him before… Thought if I got the knife away—"

Rose cradled him as he lost consciousness.

Most of the flight had been smooth, under clear summer skies. The children were so excited they hadn't stopped talking the whole way across the Eastern Shore. Their exuberance helped lift the black cloud that had hovered menacingly over Carrie as she'd taken off from BWI a few minutes earlier.

Everything will be all right, she told herself.

The police would pick up the man responsible for shooting David and firebombing her house. David had told her on the way to the airport that the FBI had been called in. They didn't take kindly to people who attacked law enforcement officials, especially in their homes with their families.

It will be okay, she repeated, a desperate mantra. *It will. It has to be.*

Before she passed over Salisbury, not far from Ocean City, clouds of a different sort started rolling in from the southwest, dark, dangerous swells that spit threatening flashes of lightning. She knew she'd beat the storm. But they might not have much of a beach day.

Carrie decided she'd have to find some way to occupy the children, at least until afternoon, when the weather might improve. Maybe she'd rent a car at the airport and they'd stop at the boardwalk on the way to Rose's cottage. With all the arcades and rides and beach-food stands, she could keep them happy for hours and out of the rain.

* * *

When the call came in, David was sitting at his desk with Pete, combing through every speck of information they had on Carl Rainey. They were trying to find anything that might help the rapidly thrown-together task force of feds, state cops and local police locate him.

He listened to Rose's desperate pleas, and his blood ran cold. With every word she choked out, his heart rammed harder and harder against his ribs.

"What is it?" Pete asked when David slammed down the receiver and leaped from his chair in one motion.

David raced across the squad room, his mind grasping at the horrible details, as Pete tore after him.

"Carl Rainey. Two hours ago, maybe more, he forced Carrie's mechanic to tell him where she was."

"Jeez," Pete said. "Driving, he's only two and a half hours away. If he flew—"

"Rose couldn't get her on the plane's radio because Carrie had already left the local airport. She tried to call the beach house to warn her. There's a recording on the line—the phone's out of order. Which means he could have already cut the line." David let out a string of curses as he ran, heading for Dispatch, down the end of the long, mint-green corridor that seemed miles long. "He's going to kill all three of them!"

"He might be playing mind games with you, trying to throw us off his track. He might think he can still buy his brother's freedom—you know, use them as hostages. He hasn't actually killed anyone yet."

"He knifed the mechanic. The old man's critical at St. Agnes. They don't give him much of a chance."

"Jeez."

David alternately dodged around and crashed into uniformed police officers, lawyers and their clients, and a mail cart—blind to all of them. The only faces he saw were Carrie's, Jason's and Tammy's.

What sort of match would they be for a cold-blooded killer?

Veering around the corner at the end of the hall, he burst through a door marked Dispatcher and shouted at the woman wearing headphones, "Margie, get me a goddamn helicopter!"

After nearly three hours of Ski-Ball, Whop the Froggy, Crash-Devil bumper cars and assorted other arcade games and rides, Carrie had had enough.

"I think we should go find the beach house and make some lunch," she told her two giggling charges.

Jason groaned. "I was just starting to have fun. Look—" he pointed outside to the boardwalk "—it's still raining. It's yucky out there."

"It won't be yucky in the beach house," Carrie assured him. "We'll have a nice lunch. By then, maybe the sun will have come out and we can go for a swim."

"Is the beach house pink?" Tammy asked.

"Will you quit with the pink!" Jason grumbled.

Carrie tousled his hair and held out her hand to him. "Come on. Rose said there's an old-fashioned country store on the way to the house. You can pick out what you want for meals today."

As she drove, Carrie had to admit that swimming didn't appear to be a likely option for the afternoon. One sooty bank of clouds after another followed her up the shoreline. By the time they'd picked up their groceries and reached the driftwood-gray cottage overlooking the Atlantic, the sky had turned a malevolent greenish black and the radio was forecasting violent storm warnings, with winds gusting to thirty miles an hour and high tides.

The cottage was set in a hollow between grassy sand dunes, which made it feel well protected. But the only side that actually needed protection was the one facing the ocean, and that had been cleared to offer a pretty view. An unfortunate arrangement, with a storm approaching.

Other summer homes scattered the shoreline, some on the same side of the narrow highway, more on the bay side. All were well spaced. In the rising wind, Carrie could see or hear nothing that would indicate her neighbors' houses were occupied.

She rushed the children from the rental car onto the sandy porch, pulled Rose's key from her purse and stuck it into the lock.

The door eased open before she had a chance to turn the key.

Carrie froze, staring at her hand...the key...the unlocked door. Rose had said no one had used the house in nearly two years. She'd also told her a local real estate firm that doubled as a management agency checked it every week to make sure nothing had been disturbed.

The door stood open, waiting.

"Is anyone here?" Carrie called out.

"Why don't we go in?" Jason asked.

"I'm all wet." Tammy sniffled. "The rain's blowing on me."

The wind howled. The sky thickened into a swirling black soup. From nearby, the surf crashed and surged up the beach.

There was no sound from inside the house.

"We'd better get you dried off," Carrie said, deciding she was in danger of becoming paranoid.

As soon as she'd unloaded the car and gotten the children settled in, she would telephone David. He would tell her that everything was under control. Maybe the FBI had already picked up that awful man, or at least sent him running to Mexico or wherever criminals on the lam went these days.

She herded the two youngsters into the front room. The shades were pulled; sheets lay over furnishings she could only faintly make out. A salty mustiness pervaded everything.

Jason closed the door behind them, blocking out the wind's roar.

"Thought you'd never get here," a low voice said.

Carrie whipped around, instinctively putting herself between the children and whoever was in the room with them.

She gasped. "Who—"

"Oh, you should really be able to guess. Didn't care for my early wake-up call this morning?"

A figure stepped out of the corner. Just enough light seeped between the slats of the miniblinds to reveal a man in dark shirt and pants. And white shoes. He looked like someone playing a bit part in an old gangster movie. She might have laughed at him if not for the present circumstances.

She was certain she'd never seen him before. Then she remembered the old photograph and the police sketch David had shown her on the way to the airport that morning. The squarish shape of the face, the deeply socketed eyes, the leer that mocked the camera...now mocked her.

Carl Rainey, the man who'd shot David.

Her stomach twisted into a tight wad. The sound of her own blood rushing through her ears nearly drowned out his next words.

"Families are important."

She thought she'd heard him wrong. "What?"

"I said—" he stepped toward her "—families are important."

"Y-yes, they are," she agreed, concentrating on keeping her voice as steady as possible. *Talk to him. Reason with him. If he means what he says, maybe he won't hurt the children.* "Families are very important."

He nodded once, his eyes chillingly fixed on her. "My brother is my only family."

"Oh," she said.

"He always looked out for me when I was a kid. Always."

"That's nice." She was aware of Tammy clutching the hem of her shorts, her damp little face pressed against the back of her thigh.

Jason stepped to her side and glared at the man. "You're a stranger," he said accusingly. "Get out of this house."

Carrie quickly seized the boy's shirt collar before he could move again. "Hush, Jase."

Carl chuckled. "Just like his old man. Feisty little brat."

Carrie could feel Jason tighten. "No," she whispered hoarsely.

"I don't like this place," Tammy whimpered. "I wanna go home."

"Kids. Don't know a good thing when they got it." Carl stuck his hands in his pockets and studied Tammy. "When I was her age, didn't appreciate my big brother. No way. But now I understand what he did for me. Did you know he's in jail now?''

Carrie nodded. There seemed no point in lying.

''Yeah. In jail, because of the brats' daddy.'' Carl's face altered frighteningly in the dim light. ''Ain't like he hasn't been there before. But they never had nothing on him that stuck. He's slick, Andy is.''

''Now it's different. The police have plenty of proof he's been trafficking in drugs,'' Carrie stated.

Carl glared at her. ''No, they don't! They don't have squat—only one lousy cop with too much balls for his own good.''

Carrie had no idea what the police had collected for evidence, but she guessed it would rattle the man if he thought their case no longer depended upon David's testimony alone. ''No,'' she said firmly. ''Even if you keep Detective Adams out of court, the D.A. has plenty of other witnesses, as well as hard evidence.''

''You're lying!'' Carl lurched toward her, his face a mask of rage.

Carrie fell backward, dragging the two trembling kids with her. ''No,'' she said. ''No, I'm not. The only thing you can do to help your brother now is admit that shooting Detective Adams and torching my house were your ideas. At least then your brother won't be blamed for planning either incident. They were all your doing, weren't they, Carl?''

She saw his eyes flicker with uncertainty, then meet hers again.

''Yeah. Andy didn't want me doing nothin'. I hung for a while to see if his lawyer could get him out on his own. But the bastard wasn't doing crap for him. So I had to take care of Andy. *I* had to help him! Me!''

''You're a good brother,'' she whispered hoarsely.

He smiled. ''Yeah, I guess I am.''

''But holding me or the detective's children hostage won't keep your brother from going to court.''

Carl brought his hands out of his pockets. Something made a sharp click. "I figured."

Carrie looked down. His right fingertips balanced a thin, short blade.

"The detective's a stubborn man. A stupid man," Carl growled. "Andy always taught me—if some guy screws you, you make him pay for it. Make him pay enough, you don't get screwed again. Can't think of no better way to make the detective pay than this," he hissed.

"No!" Carrie screamed. She shot a look behind her; the door was closed, would take time to swing open. Then what? Run for the car? They'd never make it. Her eyes automatically swept the room.

"If you're lookin' for a telephone, forget it, Mrs. Detective. Line's already been cut. Besides—" Carl chuckled throatily "—do you really think you'd have time to dial?"

He held the blade up between them. And stepped confidently forward.

"Run!" Carrie screamed, shoving Jason and Tammy toward the door. "Run, now!"

Tammy scrambled away from her, tugged the door open. Carrie could hear her crying as she darted into a gust of sand. Jason stood his ground.

Out of the corner of her eye, she saw a fierce look flash across his dark eyes. His father's bulldog stubbornness showed in the set of his jaw. She remembered the boy's words: *I want to be just like him.*

A superhero.

"Jason no!" she screamed, at the same moment he broke around her and dove at Carl Rainey.

His speed took her by surprise. The little boy threw his entire body at the man's leg, knocking it out from under him before he could brace himself or move out of the way. Carl went down with a crash on the wooden floor. But held on to the knife.

Carrie flew at him with the instinctive ferocity of a mother animal protecting her young. She didn't think. She acted out of pure passion.

Seizing the nearest object, a ladder-back chair, she swung it up over her head and brought it down on Rainey's right arm just as the knife began a slicing arc toward the child gripping his leg.

The chair splintered on impact, pieces of it flying across the room.

With a wail of pain, Carl grabbed for his own arm. The knife skittered out of his limp fingers, under a sofa.

Carrie recognized her own voice…shouting, screaming, railing at him so loudly her ears rang. Her body vibrated with unleashed primitive hormones.

She pulled Jason off Rainey and tossed the boy, as if he were no heavier than a fluff of dust, toward the safety of the open door. Spinning back, she snatched up a jagged length of chair leg and brandished it in Rainey's face. A loud whirring sound filled her ears.

"You stay away from my children! *My children!* You hear me, you bastard. I will kill you if you touch them. I'll kill you!"

She would have bashed him again if a strong arm hadn't closed around her waist and pulled her away. Through the crimson haze of her fury, she was vaguely aware of people, lots of people, rushing into the room.

Chapter 16

The days passed. Each one came closer to something Carrie could call normal.

For the first three nights after the beach-house incident, she hardly slept at all. So much adrenaline had pumped into her body, it took that long to drain it out. Carrie felt as if she were operating in overdrive twenty-four hours a day. She scrubbed walls, floors, windows. When she started talking about stripping the woodwork and refinishing it, David called a halt to the chores.

Fortunately, he was given day duty so he could be with her and the children at night. He spent a lot of time reading to Jason and Tammy in his deep, reassuring voice. For himself and Carrie, he rented movies—always light comedies and sweet romances. He pulled Carrie down on the couch with him, wrapping his long, muscular arms around her protectively, pressing her back against his chest. They ate popcorn and drank root beer and discovered they could laugh again.

He told her, when she finally asked, what had happened in the last few minutes before Rainey had been read his rights and escorted in handcuffs from the beach house. How he and

Pete and a state police sharpshooter had set down in the sand, only twenty-five feet from the house.

Tammy had been hiding under the porch—terrified, crying hysterically. When she saw her father, she immediately ran to him. The pilot kept her with him while the other three men, weapons drawn, followed what sounded like the battle cries of a legion of Amazons.

David had been nearly paralyzed with fear. He dreaded seeing what they'd find in the house. He was certain that two of the three people he most loved in the world would be dead.

Instead, what he found was his uninjured son, seated in the open doorway...staring in amazement at a wild woman who loomed over a man with a shattered arm, cowering on the floor.

"If we'd arrived five minutes later, I'm not sure in how many pieces we would have found Carl," he finished solemnly.

Carrie shuddered at the memory, burying her face in the crook of David's arm as she leaned back against him for support. "For five minutes, I think I truly must have been insane. I'll never forget that feeling of being totally out of control."

"I'll never forget pulling you away from that man," David said, nuzzling the back of her neck. "You were like a she-tiger, defending your litter. I thought I was going to have to call Pete for help. I swear, you had the strength of two line-backers."

"Violence is never something to be proud of." Carrie sighed. She was thinking about Frank—how he'd tried to protect Rose and all of them. It had earned him a long stay in the hospital and a slow, painful recovery. But he was alive. Both she and Rose were thankful for that. Rose had shown it by telling Frank she was reconsidering another marriage, but only to the right man.

"Since you survived a knife in the belly, Frank Dixon," she announced, "I figure you can survive me."

Carrie was overjoyed for them.

She realized David was still talking as he nudged her chin to one side with his knuckles so that he could reach her lips.

He kissed her softly between sentences. "And I'll never forget what you said that day at the beach house."

"What?"

"The words that you shouted at Rainey. They keep replaying in my head." He paused and gazed down at her, his deep-blue eyes shading over with emotion. "You said they were your children. *Yours.*"

"I know," she whispered. "It just came out, although I sometimes wonder if the thought wasn't there all along, somewhere down deep in my mind...or my heart. Does it bother you that I feel that way?"

He held her closer, touched his lips to her temple. "No. It sounds right. They're as much your children as mine. You may not have given birth to them in the usual way, years ago, but then...you are an unusual woman. In that beach house, you gave them their lives. To me, that's just another way of saying you gave birth."

Carrie melted in his arms. It seemed as if nothing could exceed her happiness at that moment.

But she was wrong.

When the day came for the court hearing, she stood at David's side with Jason and Tammy between them, waiting with the two attorneys for Sheila to arrive.

Thirty minutes later, Sheila still hadn't shown up. Her lawyer asked for a slight additional delay, left to make telephone calls, then came back to request a new hearing date. After speaking briefly with David, the children and Carrie, the judge told the attorneys he saw no grounds for any change in the custody, unless it was to be in Detective Adams's favor, as he had at least taken the children's future seriously enough to appear in court.

Carrie felt a little sorry for Sheila. The woman must have realized her scheme to take away the children was doomed; she would never be able to please her parents.

It was a little over two months after Carl Rainey's capture that the *Baltimore Sun* ran a story about Andrew Rainey changing his plea to guilty, for thirteen counts of illegal drug trafficking. As predicted, Carl had shot off his mouth in front of six witnesses—including his own lawyer—and a tape recorder, bragging about his big brother's power and influence in the drug world. The names he'd rattled off led to more arrests and more confessions. And fewer drugs up and down the East Coast.

One day not long after, David met Carrie at the airport with roses.

"What are these for?" she asked, grinning at him as she sniffed the heady perfume of the scarlet buds.

"For my bride. It's our three-month anniversary."

Carrie looked at him, then away. The days had slipped by, and neither of them had brought up the question of the future. Her heart climbed into her throat. "I like anniversaries."

"Me, too."

"Do you suppose there will be a six-month one?"

David made a thoughtful face before answering. "I expect there will be a six-year one. If I make it that long, I predict we'll have a sixty-year celebration, too."

She stared up at him, feeling suddenly dizzy, and deliriously giddy. "What about your vow to never marry again?"

"It's a little too late for that."

"I know we're technically married, but we'd agreed—"

"We'd agreed to twelve months in exchange for a sum of money. I've changed my mind. You can have the money to bail out your business, but I want more than a year with you."

She looked at him through narrowed eyes.

"What about you?" he asked, his voice sounding tighter. "If I can trust you to stay married to me, can you trust me to stay in love with you?"

"You're in love with me?" she asked.

"I think that's fairly evident, although I may not have said it. Listen to me," he said quickly when she opened her mouth to respond. "I think I finally understand something. It isn't marriage you have to learn to trust—it's the person. I trusted you with my children's lives, and you didn't let me down. How can I not trust you with my heart?"

Carrie dropped the roses on the tarmac and clasped her arms around his neck. "Oh, David, I could never love any man more. You were my first love. You'll be my last. If you ever leave me—''

His mouth closed over hers, cutting off her words as well as her doubts.

When he pulled away, his eyes carried a message she couldn't argue.

"I love you, Carrie. And I will as long as the sky is blue and the Earth spins under your wings. Always."

Carrie gave herself totally up to him then. She figured, it's only when you keep looking back that you can't see the future. And their future, she knew, would be full of joy and love, and children to cherish, and very, very blue skies.

* * * * *

Bestselling author

JOAN JOHNSTON

continues her wildly popular miniseries with an
all-new, longer-length novel

The Virgin Groom

HAWK'S WAY

One minute, Mac Macready was a living legend in
Texas—every kid's idol, every man's envy, every
woman's fantasy. The next, his fiancée dumped him,
his career was hanging in the balance and his future
was looking mighty uncertain. Then there was the
matter of his scandalous secret, which didn't stand a
chance of staying a secret. So would he succumb to
Jewel Whitelaw's shocking proposal—or take cold
showers for the rest of the long, hot summer...?

Available August 1997
wherever Silhouette books are sold.

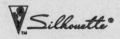

Look us up on-line at: http://www.romance.net   HAWK

Intimate Moments is proud to bring you an unforgettable miniseries.

BEVERLY BIRD

The Wedding Ring

Wrapped in the warmth of family tradition, three couples say "I do!"

LOVING MARIAH
(Intimate Moments #790, June 1997)
Adam Wallace searches for his kidnapped
son...which leads him to the Amish heartland
and lovely schoolteacher Mariah Fisher.

MARRYING JAKE
(Intimate Moments #802, August 1997)
Commitment-shy Jake Wallace unravels the
ongoing mystery of stolen babies and helps
Katya Essler learn to believe in love again.

SAVING SUSANNAH
(Intimate Moments #814, October1997)
Kimberly Wallace needs a bone marrow donor
to save her daughter's life. Will the temporary
nanny position to Joe Lapp's children be the
answer to her prayers?

INTIMATE MOMENTS®
™ *Silhouette®*

Look us up on-line at: http://www.romance.net   WEDR

Share in the joy of yuletide romance with brand-new
stories by two of the genre's most beloved writers

DIANA PALMER
and
JOAN JOHNSTON
in

LONE STAR
CHRISTMAS

Diana Palmer and Joan Johnston share their favorite
Christmas anecdotes and personal stories in this
special hardbound edition.

Diana Palmer delivers an irresistible spin-off of her
LONG, TALL TEXANS series and Joan Johnston crafts an
unforgettable new chapter to **HAWK'S WAY** in this wonderful
keepsake edition celebrating the holiday season. So
perfect for gift giving, you'll want one for yourself…and
one to give to a special friend!

Available in November at your favorite retail outlet!

Only from

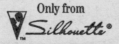

Look us up on-line at: http://www.romance.net   JJDPXMAS

New York Times Bestselling Authors

JENNIFER BLAKE
JANET DAILEY
ELIZABETH GAGE

Three *New York Times* bestselling authors bring you three very sensuous, contemporary love stories—all centered around one magical night!

It is a warm, spring night and masquerading as legendary lovers, the elite of New Orleans society have come to celebrate the twenty-fifth anniversary of the Duchaise masquerade ball. But amidst the beauty, music and revelry, some of the world's most legendary lovers are in trouble....

Come midnight at this year's Duchaise ball, passion and scandal will be...

Unmasked

Revealed at your favorite retail outlet in July 1997.

MIRA The brightest star in women's fiction

Look us up on-line at: http://www.romance.net

MANTHOL

COMING NEXT MONTH

#799 I'M HAVING YOUR BABY?!—Linda Turner
The Lone Star Social Club
Workaholic Joe Taylor was thrilled when his wayward wife returned to him—and pregnant, no less! Then he realized that Annie had no idea how she got that way, at which point joy quickly turned to shock. What a way to find out he was about to become a father—or was he?

#800 NEVER TRUST A LADY—Kathleen Creighton
Small-town single mom Jane Carlysle had been known to complain that nothing exciting ever happened to her. Then Interpol agent Tom Hawkins swept into her life and, amidst a whirlwind of danger, swept her off her feet! But was it just part of his job to seduce the prime suspect?

#801 HER IDEAL MAN—Ruth Wind
The Last Roundup
A one-night *fling* turned into a lifetime *thing* for Anna and Tyler when she wound up pregnant after a night of passion. And now that she was married, this big-city woman was determined to see that Tyler behaved like the perfect Western hubby—but that involved the one emotion he had vowed never to feel again: love.

#802 MARRYING JAKE—Beverly Bird
The Wedding Ring
As a single mother of four, Katya yearned for Jake Wallace's heated touch, for a future spent in his protective embrace. But the jaded cop had come to Amish country with a mission, and falling in love with an innocent woman was not part of the plan.

#803 HEAVEN IN HIS ARMS—Maura Seger
Tad Jenkins was a wealthy, world-famous hell-raiser and heartbreaker, and Lisa Preston wasn't about to let her simple but organized life be uprooted and rocked by his passionate advances. But Tad already had everything mapped out. All Lisa had to do was succumb...and how could she ever resist?

#804 A MARRIAGE TO FIGHT FOR—Raina Lynn
Garrett Hughes' undercover DEA work had torn their marriage apart. But now, after four lonely years, Maggie had Garrett back in her arms. Injured and emotionally empty, he pushed her away, but Maggie was determined. This time she would fight for her marriage—and her husband—with all she had.